THE PORT WINE STAIN

THE PORT WINE STAIN
is part of the
Classic Irish Fiction Series
edited by Peter Fallon
and published by
The O'Brien Press Dublin
and
Allison & Busby London

Also by Patrick Boyle

Like Any Other Man
At Night All Cats Are Grey
All Looks Yellow to the Jaundiced Eye
A View from Calvary

Patrick Boyle

THE PORT WINE STAIN

Patrick Boyle's Best Stories

Introduced by Benedict Kiely

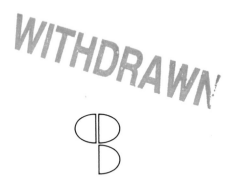

The O'Brien Press Dublin
Allison & Busby London

FIRST PUBLISHED 1983 BY THE O'BRIEN PRESS
20 VICTORIA ROAD DUBLIN 6 IRELAND
AND ALLISON & BUSBY LTD
6A NOEL STREET, LONDON W1V 3RB

British Library Cataloguing in Publication Data

Boyle, Patrick

The Port Wine Stain. – (Classic Irish fiction, ISSN 0332-1347; 3)

I. Title   II. Series

823'.914 [F]   PR6052.0/

ISBN 0-86278-010-1   The O'Brien Press
ISBN 0-85031-497-6   Allison & Busby

PUBLISHED WITH THE ASSISTANCE OF
THE ARTS COUNCIL (AN CHOMHAIRLE EALAÍON)
BOOK DESIGN: MICHAEL O'BRIEN
TYPESETTING: DESIGN & ART FACILITIES
BINDING: JOHN F. NEWMAN
PRINTED IN THE REPUBLIC OF IRELAND

CONTENTS

The publishers would also like
to thank Mrs 'Teddy' Boyle
for her kindness and help
in the preparation of this book
for publication.

Introduction

Pat Boyle I knew a lot about before I knew Pat Boyle, if you know what I mean. As a young bank-official he had been stationed, or garrisoned, in my own native town of Omagh in the County Tyrone, in the North of Ireland: and some of his stories reflect the mood of that place, and the name is mentioned when in the story called simply, *Sally*, Aunt Mary threatens to send her holidaying nephew back to Omagh if he can't settle down and enjoy himself in the village of Drumkeel.

It was interesting that a man who had worked for so long in a bank should come, somewhat late, to the writing of good fiction: interesting, but too much has been made of it, for the first stories of his that I read did not reveal an amateur taking time off from granting or withholding overdrafts. It was obvious that this man had a gift for the short story, that he knew how to select his material from what, over a pretty rich experience, he had seen and heard and felt. It was clear, too, that he was not content just with his gift. Any raconteur in a pub might, hit or miss, have that: but this writer had been working hard at the techniques of the trade. Those brusque, offhand openings that, in a few sentences, drag the reader deep into the story were by no means simply the gift of the gods to the gifted writer. They were well-planned and worked over.

Yet it wasn't until I read *The Betrayers* that I stopped in my stride, and raised the hat or touched the forelock with something in the nature of awe. 'No other writer,' I said then, 'except Turgenev could have written this.' That's the sort of

9

remark that a frustrated reviewer might, and frequently does, make: but what I was thinking of then was the Turgenev who wrote *First Love* and I could think of no higher praise to give a writer of the story, short or long. That was some years ago and I have had no cause to alter my opinion.

What were the things that got me about *The Betrayers?* The confrontation between youth and age, once again a nephew and an aunt, in an old house by Macgilligan Strand to the east of Lough Foyle; the primal innocence in which the simple farmer buys the circus pony to train her, he hopes, for domestic uses, and in which he falls in love with the maid in the house of the young boy's aunt and tries to woo her, symbolically, through the training of the pony; the shattering intrusion into that idyllic world of the brute-beast in the shape of the lecherous constable; the destruction and degradation of innocence and of a young boy's dream; and, above all, the unending regret that is a prelude to death.

There may be in every writer a poem or a story or a novel that's a sort of root at the centre of things, and out of it tendrils may grow in all directions. In the case of Pat Boyle that root could, perhaps, be found in *The Betrayers*. It could be recommended as an introduction to his novel and his three collections, so far, of short stories: and there's another novel on the way.

The sea has a lot to say in the stories of Pat Boyle: the sea by the flatness of Macgilligan Strand in *The Betrayers*, the sea by the rocks of Donegal in the most ironic love-story called *Three is Company*, the eastern sea in another ironic love-story, *The Rule of Three*. Like Flann O'Brien he seems to be fascinated by triads and trinities. With the two stories just mentioned I had to struggle for the granting of the right, which both had, to appear in this selection. *Three is Company* won, rather by pinprick or blind choice than by the strength of my judgement: a story that shows Boyle at home with the sea and at his descriptive best. At this moment in the story a young married woman and her husband's friend who is half in love with her are wandering on the Donegal coast: 'The sun was low over Hawk Head. Already the lengthening shadows of the cliffs reached out, turning the sea to a pool of molten moss. On the horizon, the island was still steeped in sunshine, the heat haze lingering over it so that to Frank it looked like a reptile drowsing in the steaming muck of some tropical swamp. Hawk Head and Glen Head on either side of him, dozed too, their massive muzzles tucked between outstretched paws. Sounds had become muted to the whisper of the surf and the distant wailing of the gulls.

'The sea stretched around them in an oily calm with shifting whorls of colour – green, red, purple, grey – moving over its surface. It had a curious soothing effect as though the swimming colours were cast upon eyelids closed against the glare of the sun. At the same time there was a nagging compulsion to seek out and clothe in words – perhaps in a single line of poetry – the exact descriptions of those coloured spirals, dappling the surface of the sea like huge, myopic, staring eyes...

'He was dressed and waiting for her before the cormorant at last surfaced with a fish. Pushing its back up, it juggled deftly with its struggling prey until it was gripped by the tail. With a quick flip the fish was swallowed back in one gulp. The cormorant then reared itself up in the water and commenced to fan its wings vigorously across its breast as though beating warmth into its body. At length it took off, running on the surface of the water, sustained by fast flapping wings until it gained height and flew, low and swift and with craning neck, out to the open sea where, with wings outstretched in heraldic attitude, it perched on the peak of a massive rock guarding the entrance of the cove.'

The sea may be a sunshot idyllic bathing-pool for a couple who are half in love, but its very beauty afflicts the writer with the nagging feeling that he should find words with which to describe it. The sea may be beautiful but in it, unceasingly, life preys upon life. That heraldic cormorant, perched on the rock, digesting his catch, is also a relation of the guillemot, befouled by an oil-slick, washed up helpless on Portmarnock Strand in the story, *The Rule of Three*. When the narrator in that story tries to rescue the doomed bird it turns on him savagely. Destroyed by the activities of man it cannot, in its blind savage heart, accept the approach of the man who would aid it.

For in Pat Boyle's work idyllicism gets short shrift. Life survives, some of the time, but the struggle for survival is never easy. The threat to life begins, as most of us should know and as Pat Boyle reminds us, with disillusion and the destruction of youthful dreams. He deals, delicately and comically, with that matter in the story called *Sally*, in which, as you will see, a young fellow called Jim, from the select Campsie Avenue in Omagh, is holidaying in the village of Drumkeel with his Aunt Mary. There he meets Sally McGahan, a shopkeeper's daughter, home on holiday from her convent school. They get to play tennis together and Sally is very good and, although he is very very good he finds it as much as he can do to assert his male mastery. She invites him to the home of her parents who are prim and proper and object to dancehalls and pop music and the like. Jim and Sally get to playing the piano upstairs while her parents sit downstairs. Sally is very good at the proper sort of music, and in the proper sort of style she has been taught at school. Jim and Sally get to playing duets in that proper sort of music. The incongruities in the set-up show Boyle at his best as a comic writer and, as you will see, he has a great gift for provoking laughter. Take a look at the sequence in *Sally* that commences: 'The curtains were still half-drawn in the sitting room, giving it an air of snug seclusion . . .'

After that secretive, hilarious, musical wooing they conspire to get together to a dance in Bundoran. But on the dancefloor he discovers the full oddity in Sally's character: that being a domineering sort of girl, and never having danced except in the convent school, she has always been accustomed to play the part of the male dancer. For a genuine two-fisted male to take the floor with her reduces the whole business to the level of a wrestling match. So he flies from her: and practically wills her into the arms of a randy and disreputable friend, only enviously to watch them afterwards as they glide around the floor like happy skaters:

12

and to hear his friend whisper to him as they circle past that Sally is, in the liveliest sense of the word, deadly. It's great comedy, but the sense of loss and disillusion are complete: and there are depths below the simplicities of disillusion. There is never anything mean about his irony which can be, now and again, as genial as a May morning. But he is a master of the sort of contrast that makes for effective irony and, at times, he can be brutal about it.

One of the appallingly memorable details about the policeman in *The Betrayers* is that he has a hairy back like a badger: and the badger himself makes a ceremonial appearance, under his Latin name, in the story, *Meles Vulgaris*. A man, abed with his wife, cannot wipe out of his mind the day in his boyhood when he saw a badger done to death by the dogs, a bloody end for the badger, a bloody victory for the dogs. He lies on his bed and remembers and reads a book about the life and nature of the badger: about the cry of the badger which some naturalists hold may have sexual origins, or may have some connection with the funeral rites of that strange animal. But that cry is still in his ears, 'the wild defiant shout of an animal ringed about with enemies'. He knows that his own life has been one retreat after another by comparison with such bayed-about, desperate bravery. As he takes his wife in his arms, love and betrayal and loneliness are all one and the same thing, and he sees only, 'a mangled body, mired and misshaped, bloodied muzzle grinning senselessly at a senseless sky,' hears only, 'the scream of agony that death alone could arrest'.

For another husband, cowering with a hangover under the blankets, in the story, *At Night All Cats are Grey* (not here included), the domestic cat, clawing on the crinkling eiderdown, is the denial of everything the brave, doomed badger stood for. The cat is second-rate contentment which is to be avoided by all means, and 'soapy good health and sanity and main drainage, and all the other Christian virtues.' Wondering who in hell's wife he had made a pass at the night before, the errant husband experiences a comic desire for the lawless, for a world of tip-and-run delight. For the old farmer in the story, *Go Away, Old Man, Go Away*, the ironic contrast is everything but comic. His young wife despises him and he suspects that she has interests elsewhere: a folk theme as old as the rocks. Once, on a hot day in the farmyard, he feels that she is relenting towards him, but he is rejected again and with an obscene remark: and in the final passage of that story, land and sea and the white bird of the air join with her rank youth in mocking his arid aged passion.

Death only can arrest the ultimate agony but is also the ultimate disillusion, the ultimate betrayal. He has written in *Rise up, My Love, and Come Away* a sad, lyrical story in which the spirit of a distracted woman who has committed suicide contemplates her gravestone, and her life and death. Death can be sad, awkward, ordinary. Death can be a gulpin of a card-player as in the story, *Oh Death Where is Thy Sting-aling-aling*. That story is not in this selection nor is *All Looks Yellow to the Jaundiced Eye* in which Death is totally and utterly destructive, can take over the whole scheme of things. In that story another man on the land in the heat of summer goes crazy, slaughters a few rabbits and the domestic fowl and his own dog, murders his wife and before he destroys himself hears: 'the intolerable cry – the howl of a wild beast, harried and starving, whom only the hunter can release from its torments'. Death is the hunter.

It is a vision from which one turns away with a certain relief to realise that humanity, even if with difficulty, still survives, and that the pages of Pat Boyle are crowded with comic, loveable, hopeful and hopeless, but still striving, human beings. There is the drunken bank-manager kicking at the ledgers in the strongroom, in a morning frenzy in the novel, *Like Any Other Man*. (It was jocosely said to me in a Dublin pub that to write such a novel about an Irish parish priest would be bad enough: but to write it about a bank-manager showed there was no religion left in the bloody country.) Then there is Shaybo, the keeper of a public lavatory, who has acquired philosophy of a sort from observing men, not quite at their noblest. He gives his name to another story, not included herein.

14

Pat Boyle once said to me that he had thought for a long time that there must be some class of a man about whom nobody had yet written a story: and Pat, quite rightly, as far as I know, came up with Shaybo. The first paragraph of that story is a fair and comic judgment on a fair amount of human life: 'You'd be right in thinking that an underground jakes is a poor place for a smoke and a chat. The more so when the sun is knocking the sparks off the glass roof and stirring up a stink that would bloody near talk to you. But when you haven't the price of a packet of fags and when Shaybo Gallagher, the Corporation attendant, is a county-man of your own, a bit of hardship is neither here nor there.'

A bit of hardship is neither here nor there? A profound acceptance of life.

Benedict Kiely

Go Away, Old Man, Go Away

A sting of heat was beginning to creep into the morning sun. Like a warm hand, it clamped down on the old man's scrawny neck as if it meant to push him down into the mounds of cut turf he was so busily spreading. It wormed its way through the layers of cardigans and undershirts, it scorched his meagre shrunken buttocks, it soaked through his boots so that his scalded feet chafed against the damp wrinkled socks. Sweat trickled down his face, smarting his eyes and salting his mouth, but he worked on steadily, rolling the heaped-up sods back through his straddled legs like a terrier rooting frantically at a burrow.

Stretched ahead of him to the bog-hole were rows of cut turf, lying in close-packed heaps just as they were heeled up by the barrowmen. The skin had barely formed on the spongy wet sods and often he had to ease them apart as though they were slabs of toffee. As he scrabbled and plucked and clawed, he kept up a continuous muttering grumble, punctuated by grunts of exertion.

His irritation was increased by the growling insistence of an empty stomach. Each time he stooped his guts would plunge madly around, whinnying like a horse fresh from the grass. Soon all minor grievances, his aching back, the heavy woollen drawers lacerating his fork, his scalded feet – all became blended into and seemed to increase the clamour of his empty belly. More and more frequently he paused, squatted down on his hunkers, glaring across the bog at the cottage on the roadside a few fields away. Once he saw someone come to the door and he straightened up, wiping his hands on his trousers while he waited for her to call him but she only took a look up the road and went in again.

The fowlman, he thought. I'll gamble a bob that's who she's keeping an eye out for. Damn the hait she cares if I die in my tracks with the hunger as long as she's there for the egg money. So help me God, I'd get more attention if I was a clocking hen. Dancing and jack-acting is all that one cares for. Oh, a nice stumer of a wife I let myself in for!

He started in, half-heartedly, to work again but soon gave it up.

'I'll not put up with it a day more,' he muttered.

He picked up his coat and started off up the deeply rutted track leading out of the bog.

By the time he reached the main road his temper had cooled and he began, as usual, looking for excuses for her. Maybe the fire had gone against her. Or she had to go for water. She was terrible sore on water, that one. Scrubbing at herself night, noon and morning. The smell of the soap trailing after her round the house till you'd nearly trip over it, it's that strong. He wrinkled his nose and sniffed. That time he had come on her, washing herself in the room. Standing there in her pelt with the pride and sleekness and grandeur shining out of her white skin like you'd see it in a blood mare. Admiring herself in the glass, no less. Posing and stroking and smirking at herself as if she were some class of a cat. My God, she could have been struck dead for less. And then rushing at him like a mad thing, spitting and cursing and slamming the door in his face. It had been that way from the start. Never letting him as much as put a hand next or near her. Cringing away from him in the bed as though he was a black stranger. He sighed. Well, it wouldn't last that way for ever. She would come round some time. He would just have to take her easy and thole a while longer.

He hesitated for a second on the porch, then cleared his throat and pushed in the door briskly.

'Are you aiming to starve me, girl?' he asked.

There was no one there.

The kitchen floor was unswept; the table still littered with yesterday's dishes; the fire burned down to a few coals of turf. He unhooked the kettle swinging from the crane and shook it.

'Are you within there, woman?' he roared.

He heard the bed creak and the slow reluctant steps dragging along the floor. He shook the kettle again savagely.

'Motherajaysus, are ye still in yer bed?'

She came out of the room and stopped in the doorway, yawning and scratching her head – a fine strapping piece, bubbed and bottomed like a tinker woman, with oily jet-black hair, thick sensual lips and dark eyes, blurred and heavy with sleep. The dirty woollen-jumper, sweat-stained at the armpits, barely reached the rumpled partly-fastened skirt. Her bare legs were brown-blotched with the heat of the fire.

She yawned again and knuckled her eyes.

'I just threw myself on the bed a minute,' she said. 'Til the kettle would come to the boil.'

Speechless, he swung aloft the steaming kettle, as if he were exorcising her with a smoking thurible.

She stared at him, open-mouthed.

'What are you aiming to do with that thing?' she demanded.

She darted across the room.

'Give it here, man,' she said, trying to snatch the kettle from him.

He pushed her away roughly.

'Lookat here,' he said dramatically, tilting up the kettle over the hearth so that the few remaining drops went sizzling into the fire. 'Boiled to nothing.'

The sleep had gone out of her eyes: the listlessness from her body. Her sallow face was flushed and her thick lips pouted aggressively. But though her features were distorted with rage, there was about her a curious air of satisfaction as though the very volume of her emotion brought with it some measure of bodily fulfilment.

'Is it trying to quench the fire you are?' she asked.

'Quench be damned. Wouldn't a good spit smother it?'

'Maybe if you had the trouble of lighting it, you wouldn't

19

be so quick –'

She broke off and, stooping, commenced heaping up the glowing embers with the tongs.

'Listen here, me young tit,' he said, addressing the swaying rump-filled skirt. 'It would fit you better if you stopped home at nights instead of roaming the country. You'll have the priest naming you yet from the altar.'

The strip of white flesh below her rucked-up jumper, winking at every movement, kept ogling him slyly.

'A man at my time of life slaving and sweating like a Turk while his wife goes trapeezing around the country to every bit of a dance or a card game that's held in the parish. Sure I must be the laughing stock of half Europe.'

His gaze travelled down to the creased hollows behind her knees.

'Letting a man off to his work without a bite to eat. Have you no shame in you?'

He moistened his flabby craving lips.

'The women . . . they're a terror . . . the same the world over . . . rising a mutiny wherever they be . . . '

He pushed out a tentative hand, but at once let it fall to his side and remained staring at her dumbly, his eyes sick and glazed with desire.

Across her shoulder she looked – taunting him with bold mocking eyes.

'Give over,' she said. 'It's the same ould tune – day in, day out. It's a wonder you took me at all, the way you go on.'

The old man struggled for speech.

'Ye- Ye- Ye- Ye're damned smart, aren't ye.'

Failing to think of any more crushing remark, he spat viciously into the heart of the fire and turned away. At the door he shouted back:

'And don't be the whole day getting me me bloody bit of breakfast.'

Outside, he squatted on the low window-sill – tired, hungry, emotionally deflated.

You common idiot, he told himself. Letting that one get the better of you with a few flirts of her backside and her stooping over the fire to give you a right view of her wherewithal. As if it wasn't sticking out like the side of a church at the best of times. Up half the night jack-acting and then basking the day long in her bed, snoring and grunting like a sow at the pigging. And across in the bog making slaughter of himself is no less a person than the boss of the house – the boss; how are you! – hugging his grinding puddings with sheer starvation. The impudent trollop, slooching around half-dressed, the bare ones scalded off her with the heat of the fire and the two elders swinging out of her like she was six months gone. God above, man, I don't know what you see in her.

The sun beat down on him, soaking him with listless warmth so that he sagged forward, his chin knuckle-propped, staring with drowsy cat-blinking eyes at the sweeping expanse of dun-coloured bog.

His eyes closed and the scraggy dewlap settled its folds deeper round his knuckled hands. From one nostril a green dangle of snot rattled out and in with each wheezing breath like the flickering tongue of a snake.

Her voice roused him.

'Did the fowl cart go by?'

He looked at her stupidly. Blobs of colour swayed and danced before his eyes. His legs and the back of his neck were stiff and sore.

'Henh?' he said, rinsing the foulness from his mouth with fresh-sucked spittle.

'I suppose you fell asleep and let him pass unbeknownst. Didn't you know I had three fat pullets ready waiting for him? He'll not be here again till next week.'

He noticed she had changed her clothes, put on stockings and brushed her hair.

'Aye, so,' he said.

'Well, can't you answer me anyway? Did you see e'er a sign of the fowlman?'

'Would that be why you were toveying yerself up instead of getting me me breakfast?'

'You'll get your breakfast time enough, never fret.'

'It's borne in on me that it's only when there's callers coming round the house that you take time to tidy yourself. Other times you're not so particular.'

She glowered down at him in sulky silence.

'If it's the fowlman or the post-boy or even a stinking ould tramp itself, you're into the room pulling and hauling at yourself. Wasting the day blethering to the likes of them but never a civil word for your own husband. Though God knows it's little enough to expect from you for the wheen of minutes you spend at home every day.'

'Is it staying at home at the fire I'd be? Listening to you nagging and backbiting? You'd scald the heart off of a saint with that bitter ould viper's tongue of yours. I'll go out of my mind if I have to listen to much more of it.'

He rasped his hand across his stubbly chin and gazed up at her with an air of patient resignation.

'That's right. That's right. I'm to blame for everything. It was me let the fire down. It was me kept you in your bed all morning. It's me hunts you out at night to the dances.'

He struck his knee with his fist.

'So-help-me-Jaysus, there was peace in this house till you come into it. I'd a right to leave you stewing in misery where you were. A bit of a tin shanty with all the winds of the world whistling through the chinks and that so-called father of yours pasted to the bed, dragging his guts up and spitting them round the floor till you could bloody near skate on it. That's what I took you from. And let you never forget it, me girl.'

He knew as he finished that he had said too much.

Two quick steps brought her standing over him, her face mottled with rage.

'Throwing the like of that up in my teeth,' she said. 'I'm as well got as the most of them, if the truth were known. There was none of this talk when you were plastering over me to have you. Oh, you made promises then to no end! Telling me the fine easy life I'd have with all the money you'd saved. Well, it's easy to count what I've seen of it. If it weren't for the few ha'pence I get for the eggs I'd be in rags.'

22

She looked down contemptuously at him hunched up in misery on the window-sill.

'That your dirty money may choke you, you hungry old scaldcrow. I've a mind to pack my duds and clear out of here this minute.'

He heard her go inside and then the angry clatter of roughly handled dishes. After that – silence.

His heart missed a beat. Surely to God she was never in earnest. An awful desolation swept over him, leaving him sick and trembling.

He started to rise but stopped when he heard her voice, deep and husky, singing very low as if to herself:

> *For an old man he is old*
> *And an old man he is grey.*

He could picture her leaning across the table, head tilted back, eyes half-closed, a cool impudent smile on her face.

> *And an old man's nose is damp and cold*
> *Go away, old man, go away!*

Furtively he wiped the drop off his nose with the back of his hand. The venomous targe, he thought. There's no length she'll not go to bait me.

She was singing again. Louder and with a kind of a glad lilt to her voice.

> *But a young man he is young*
> *And a young man he is gay*
> *And a young man's kiss will bruise your lips*
> *Come away, young man, come away!*

So that was it, by the Lord. That was how she spent her nights. Lurking in outhouses or sprawled her length at the back of a ditch or maybe under the dry arch of a bridge. With any one of a hundred young rams from the four quarters of the universe. Giving them what *he* should have been getting.

The nights she'd slip out without a word and come back hours later with two glowing coals for eyes. Her cheeks flushed, her hair tossed. 'It's a grand windy night,' she'd maybe say and sit gazing into the fire with a queer twisted smile at the corner of her lips. Thinking back on the night's doings. Feeling the moist seeking lips and the groping hands roving her body. Hearing wild, whispered words and harsh breathing and maybe the sudden step on the road to put them cowering down with their hearts pounding. Seeing the whiteness of a face looming over her, strained and vicious.

And across the fire from her is sitting . . . himself. Blind to it all.

He closed his eyes to shut out the torturing vision but his relentless imagination kept on insinuating new and ever more humiliating possibilities.

How many? In God's name how many in the parish had had her? Was there one at all he could look straight in the face and not be left wondering? Why, even that little brat she'd been on the look-out for all morning could have been . . .

He tried to thrust the thought away from him but it had taken root. Wasn't he nearly always out working when the cart called? Wouldn't he be down in the bog this minute only for she sleeping in? And wouldn't that little whelp be inside bargaining for the fowl with the whole house to himself?

The bitterness rose in his throat like a ball of puke.

It's too much, he thought. It's more than mortal man can stand.

He got to his feet and looked aimlessly about him. Something would have to be done. Things could not go on this way. Suddenly he started off towards the hen-house, muttering to himself:

'There'll be an end put to his capers.'

Unbarring the door he flung it open.

'Chook! Chook! Chook!' he called in a loud aggressive voice.

There was a flutter of startled wings and a raucous babble

24

of excited cluckings.

He glanced over his shoulder apprehensively, then tried again, sinking his voice to a seductive whisper.

'Chooooook, chook, chook. Come on the little chookies.'

He rasped his fingers together enticingly.

They came scampering out, heads craned forward, wings tucked tight against bodies, as if they were skaters racing to reach him.

Grabbing the nearest bird by the neck, he squeezed tight with finger and thumb on its gullet. A few frantic wing flaps and he had hold of its legs, hauling on its neck like an archer bending a bow.

He flung the quivering body aside and called again.

'Chook, chook, chook. Oh, the poor wee chook-chooks.'

They stood around, eyeing him with a cagey stare, never budging an inch. Picking up a handful of gravel he shook it out on the ground.

Pushing, scrambling, they surged round him, pecking at the bare ground. This time he chose carefully – a fine fat pullet, larded with meat. He stooped down cautiously and picked it up, one hand pinioning the wings to the body, the other nipping the squawk rising in its thrapple. Holding it up before him, he watched the gaping beak and the frantic scampering legs.

'What hurry is on you, girl?' he said. 'You'll get to the pot soon enough.'

Its neck was hard to stretch and by the time he had finished the fowl had scattered. Only one remained, picking half-heartedly at a bedded stone.

It sidled away from him, neatly avoiding his clutch. Stooping, he followed it up, his hands outspread as if to impart a blessing but it slid from under them in little mincing spurts. At the gable end of the house he caught up with it and grabbed it by the legs. The accumulation of rage that had been festering in him all morning broke out at last.

'Ye little blirt,' he roared. 'I'll put manners on ye.'

He swung it up, flapping wings and squawing beak, and made pulp of it against the wall. He kept flailing away,

25

although the bird's head was almost torn off. His face and hands were spattered with blood: the lime-washed wall red wealed. A fluffy nimbus floated over his head. In time with each welt, he ground out:

'I'll teach ye . . . to turn my house . . . into a bloody knocking shop.'

He heard her footsteps running around the house but paid no heed. It was the rough grip on his shoulder that brought him back to reality.

'What d'you think you're doing, man?' she demanded. 'Are you gone mad?'

He shook himself free and glared at her, the dead bird swinging from his hand, its head scraping the ground.

'Have you lost the use of your tongue?' she asked.

His lips moved noiselessly, seeking the right words – the bitter lacerating words. He held the limp body up, shaking it before her face.

'That'll be one less for your fancy man when he calls,' he said, throwing it down at her feet. 'And if you look beyond you'll see two more he'll be at the loss of.'

His hand was still up, thumbing over his shoulder, when she slapped his face.

The shock of the sudden blow left him dazed for a moment. He rubbed his tingling cheek, gazing at her stupidly. Then he let a roar out of him.

'Sowbitch!' he shouted and flogged the back of his fist across her mouth, feeling the rasp of his knuckles on her clenched teeth.

He stood over her, his arm drawn back threateningly.

'Ye low trollop,' he said. 'I've a right to hammer the living daylights out of ye.'

At the sight of the blood trickling from the corner of her mouth the anger died in him. They stood facing each other, so close that he could see a tiny reflected sun glittering at him from each of her eyes. There was a kind of blindness about her eyes, he thought, as though the sight in them was turned inwards. And her face too, with a queer unmindful look to it, like you'd see in the face of someone you're talking

26

to and him listening all the time to the sound of music or great talk going on behind him.

The curious expression of her face and eyes, the glossy sheen of her freshly combed hair, the smell of scent and sweat and warm flesh sent a tepid ripple of desire through him.

'There's no rhyme or reason for a doggery the like of this,' he said. 'It's a fret to man . . . the way people gut other . . . for nothing.'

'Or next to nothing,' he added.

He put an awkward hand on her shoulder.

At once she swung in towards him, gripping him with savage arms, grinding her tensed body against him, clawing and tearing at his coat with frantic urgent fingers.

The intensity of her passion appalled him. This is awful, he thought. Outside my own house in the broad light of day.

I'm a done man if anyone sees me.

He made to push her off but his hands buried themselves in the softness of her breasts. The ache that had been coiling and twisting around inside him came back worse than ever. Crab-like his hands began exploring, finger after cautious clumsy finger, ready to shrink back at the slightest rebuff. As though calmed by his touch the convulsive shudderings died away and she lay against him inertly, breathing heavily with small pathetic gulps like a child sobbing itself to sleep. He felt the urge to comfort her – to dry her eyes and stroke her hair and say the crazy foolish things that had been shamelocked in his heart for all these years. His lacerated dignity, the turmoil of his thoughts, the pent-up torrent of his love that could be breached by the smallest, the most casual gesture of affection – all these things he pleaded through the pressure of his rough unskilful hands.

She sprang away from him, her eyes blazing, her blood-smeared face torn with hate and revulsion.

'Take your filthy hands offa me,' she screamed. 'At this age of your life to be pawing and groping at a woman! 'Tis of the grave you should be thinking, you doting old fool.'

She turned away and walked with a contemptuous swagger

towards the house. Leaning against the doorjamb she watched him, her eyes spiteful: pitiless. Deliberately, in a low mocking voice, she commenced to sing:

For an old man he is old
And an old man he is grey
And an old man's love is a thing of shame
Go away, old man, go away!

For a few moments she stayed, her eyes fixed on his grimly squared shoulders and rigid stubborn back, expecting an answering jibe. When he did not rise to the bait, she turned and went in.

He stood as she had left him – stiffly erect, hands locked behind his back, his lined face expressionless but for the twitching lips.

From far across the bog a lone gull called. And called again; a tiny fretful wail as if mourning something irretrievably lost – the twinkling silver of breaking mackerel, a calm sea frosted with moonlight, the tall waves bowing their grizzled arrogant heads to the land.

The old man turned his head towards the sound, staring miserably, hopelessly, blindly ahead; the tears coursing unheeded down his ravaged face.

He heard her come to the door.

'Your breakfast's ready,' she called. And back over her shoulder as she wheeled round, 'Or maybe you've something more important to do.'

Her jibing laugh was merged in the tinkling of delf.

Again the gull mewled, a harsh discordant cackle, then rose on lazy sun-bleached wings. High overhead it flew, piping shrilly, its swaying, searching neck outstretched, settling down at last in a freshly ploughed field to gorge its empty craw.

The Port Wine Stain

'Six weeks to half-sole a pair of shoes! It's a disgrace. But what can you expect? Half the day reading the Bible and the other half playing cards, little wonder he has no time for work.'

That was how my mother sized up Andy Foster, the cobbler. Though she had the grace to add:

'Of course there's no harm in an odd game of patience, Jim. When the housework's done. And a body should read a chapter of the Bible every night. But there's no sense going to extremes.'

She held up the shoes, examining them critically.

'You must hand it to him, though. He does a nice neat job. It's a pity the poor man's face is raddled with the port wine stain.'

She put the shoes away in the cupboard and turned to face me.

'You should thank God every morning, Jim, with the first breath you draw that you can travel the roads by daylight instead of creeping out after dark like that poor disfigured creature.'

At school I learned that the port wine stain was either a curse-mark laid by God on the cobbler as a punishment for his drunken dissolute past or else some awful disease he had contracted before coming to the village. Like leprosy, it was highly contagious and any contact with it might prove fatal. It was dangerous even to shout 'Scar-face' at the cobbler as he had once thrown a paring-knife at one of the older boys before the nick-name was properly out of his mouth.

Mother was indignant when I told her this. She said the curse-mark was nothing but an affliction from God and that those who provoked the cobbler would do well to remember the two and forty children torn to pieces by wild animals for jeering at Elisha's bald head.

When I was eventually entrusted with the job of collecting from the cobbler a pair of shoes left in weeks back to be soled and heeled, my mother, after warning me not to come back without them, said:

'Now don't be gaping at him, Jim. You'll only hurt the poor man's feelings. And remember, no mocking or jeering. God's hand will be swift and sore if you do.'

All the way to the village I could think of nothing but that final warning and the need to avert my eyes from the cobbler's gorgon gaze. By the time I reached the dark little shop I was in such a state of funk that I would hardly have dared venture in but for the reassuring figure of a policeman standing at the door of the nearby barracks.

Keeping my eyes firmly downcast. I stood at the counter and blurted out my message:

'Me-mother-wants-the-shoes-she-left-in-a-month-back.'

'Go away, boy. Can't you see I'm busy?' a deep voice growled.

I would have been contented enough to accept the dismissal but I knew a further effort was demanded.

'She-said-to-wait-till-they're-ready,' I muttered, still addressing my boots.

'You're welcome,' the gruff voice replied. '*The patient man is better than the valiant.* Proverbs 16.'

I stuffed my hands in my pockets and prepared to wait.

The only sound was a steady rustling, so familiar and yet so out of place that at last I was forced to look up.

Mother was right. The big, grey-haired man seated at the work-bench was playing cards – seven-up patience.

At once I forgot my fears. Elbows on the counter I leant across, watching the fall of the cards. When the rustling ceased and the silence began to drag, I could contain myself no longer.

'Mr Foster,' I said. 'You want to shift that red Queen. It's blocking up the play.'

The cobbler faced round to glare at me and I saw the port wine stain for the first time.

It was dark red, almost plum-coloured, entirely covering the right side of his face. It started under his coarse grey hair and oozed down over his forehead till it engulfed one eye, closing the eyelid in a drowsy leer: it welled down the side of his nose, leaving the nostril puffed out almost to the corner of the mouth: it flowed over his ear, gorging it with thick dark blood so that it hung bloated and shapeless: it spread across his jaw to the centre of his chin, dragging down the heavy thickened lower lip in a grotesque pout that exposed the broken and discoloured teeth to the gums: it seemed to seep into the open mouth, perhaps as flecks of bloodied foam to be swallowed back in disgust – how else account for the restless flickering tongue that kept making tiny petulant noises as it clicked against his palate. The stain even invaded the unblemished side of his face, forming on his forehead and chin a ragged purple fringe like the indented coastline pictured on a school atlas.

Like molten lava, the stain had scorched all before it, leaving not a trace of beard, eyebrow or eyelashes – only a smooth expanse of taut glistening skin that must surely have the tacky feeling of raw liver. Appalled though I was at the thought of a face partly constructed of raw meat, I could not help thinking of the glory to be gained if I could boast in school of having discovered, through my courageous finger-prodding of the cobbler's cheek, that the curse-mark did not bounce back as ordinary skin should, but filled up again slowly like uncooked liver.

We stayed staring at each other while you could count ten, the cobbler making no concession to the fear and disgust that must have shown on my face.

At last he spoke, 'I suppose your mother taught you how to play patience as well as give ould lip?'

'She did indeed, sir,' I replied. 'Three different kinds.'

The cobbler commenced to laugh. It was like a locomotive starting off – a succession of explosive puffs from the funnel, loud, startling, steam-laden: a burst of throaty coughing as the driving wheels skid in a false start; then the rhythmic wheezing chuckle from the steel belly as the engine gets under way.

At length he gathered himself together sufficiently to say, 'You're a prime boy, all right. Who would think a wee scaldy like you would be a master-man at the cards?'

He started chuckling again. I tried hard to keep a straight face but against the cobbler's laughter there was no defence. I broke into a fit of giggling that rapidly turned into hysteria. My shrill hoots and screeches so scourged the cobbler that he could do nothing but wheeze and splutter and cough. If the funeral bell had not started to ring we would have laughed ourselves sick.

When the funeral had passed the cobbler said, 'Come round here and show me these new-fangled versions you're bragging about.'

After that I called each day on my way home from school.

Andy was always glad to see me, putting away at once whatever he was doing, clearing a space on the workbench and producing with a flourish the pack of cards from the window-sill. My seat was on the cobbler's left, allowing him to conceal the port wine stain but exposing me to the angry gaze of irritable customers complaining about the delay.

The cobbler had one answer for them all. A long look over his shoulder at the frightening pile of unmended footwear heaped up in a corner of the room. A slow regretful shake of the head, signifying that the wanted shoes had still to work their way up from the very core of the mound. The few words of advice and comfort flung as casually as meal to chickens, 'The impatient man shall work folly. Come in again next week.'

Before the customer was well clear of the door he would be into the cards again.

Cassino we played, the only card-game – barring patience – that the cobbler knew. It was a rowdy brawling affair. Cries of protest and shouts of triumph were continuous. Cards were thumped on the work-bench or flourished derisively under an opponent's nose. Nagging or bullying were legitimate weapons for sapping morale.

If the cobbler was studying his hand, trying to work out a plan of campaign, I tried to distract him by a flow of grumbles and jeers.

'Get a move on, Andy, you're holding up the play. It'll be nightfall before we're through. What's holding you anyway? Are you thinking of passing off that nine of diamonds as Big Cassino when it gets too dark to see what we're doing? Or are you just trying to hatch out a clutch of aces?'

Let him start easing out a card from his hand and I forestalled him, waving one of my own high in the air and shouting truculently, 'Play it if you dare, Andy. I've the beat of it here.'

He would commence fumbling around, plucking at one card after another in an agony of indecision, until at last he slammed one down on the bench, saying, 'Make what you like of that, me young cock-sparrow.'

When, with shouts of glee, I swept his card up and maybe along with it a couple of aces and Little Cassino he would chuckle delightedly as if he got more fun out of losing than winning.

I was constantly devising new pin-pricks to put the cobbler off his game. On one occasion, impatient at the hold-up in the play, I laid down my cards, hooked my forefingers into the corners of my mouth and called softly, 'Hey, Andy!'

As the cobbler turned his head, I pulled at my mouth till it was slotted like a pillar box, thrust out my tongue and rolled my eyes madly round in their sockets.

Andy did not laugh. He gazed at me, mouth agape, tongue clicking furiously as it always did in moments of embarrassment.

I stared back at him aghast. So familiar had I become with the cobbler that the port wine stain no longer registered on my consciousness. Now I discovered that the ugly bloated flesh of nose, lip and ear still filled me with disgust and repulsion. Yet in spite of the prospect of dire and instant punishment for trifling with a curse from God – a punishment maybe leaving on my face the angry print of a divine Hand – I felt the urge to discover, once and for all, the nature of the plum-coloured skin of the cobbler's cheek, so glossy, so unwrinkled, so utterly alien and inhuman. I was even toying with the thought of reaching out to put the matter to the final test when the cobbler's laugh broke out.

'Dear but you're the right villain,' he spluttered. 'Trying to put me off my play with your jack-acting.'

The laughter was so patently forced that, stricken with shame, I turned away muttering, 'Sorry, Andy,' as I gathered up my cards.

The cobbler's only other interest, as Mother had proclaimed, was the Bible. It was the mine from which he quarried the quotations that clinched an argument or pointed up an absurdity, that clarified, instructed, reproved. My eagerness to win – and win quickly – gave the cobbler many opportunities for criticism. He would clear his throat and growl, '*Substance got in haste shall be diminished*,' or: '*He that is greedy of gain troubleth his own house.*'

There was no sting in these reproofs and I had a sneaking suspicion they were learned off by heart so that they could be produced at the appropriate time, like rabbits from a hat, as proof of a deep knowledge of Biblical lore.

But once when I repeated an item of scandal picked up in school, the cobbler rounded on me with chapter and verse, '*The words of a talebearer are as wounds and they go down into the innermost part of the belly*. Proverbs 26, verse 22.'

His voice, harsh and full of anger, had me cringing in terror as if it was the growling voice of God himself.

Each day, at the end of the card session, the Bible was taken down from the shelf and the cobbler read from it a chapter picked out the previous night, explaining the illusions and obscurities that might mislead the unwary. Head flung back like a preacher, his glance barely grazing the page, he declaimed the passage, his deep rumbling voice moulding and polishing the words until meaning and glittering sound were one.

34

I listened enthralled to the tales of prophets, kings, soldiers, peasants: to deeds of splendour and treachery: to the epic of palaces, temples and monuments, doomed to destruction before ever a stone was laid. I shuddered cheerfully at the tally of death and disaster – death by famine, pestilence or the visitation of God: murder by stealth in the darkness of the night or in the broad light of day by the command of tyrants: the slaughter of a kinsman, the implacable butchery of an enemy tribe, the decimation of a peaceful city. I learned that the ant is wiser than the wise: that the lizard lodges in the palaces of kings: that foxes, little foxes, can spoil a vineyard: that the golden calf was the symbol of a people's subjection to the ox – a people too stiff-necked and lazy to till the soil. This biblical lore, some of it as familiar as the toothache, the cobbler set forth in his rich velvety voice, savouring every syllable, so that the word was made flesh – vivid, exciting, immediate.

There was no knowing how our friendship might have turned out had I not one day, after fetching over the Bible, had the sudden notion of scrambling up on the work-bench and sitting there, knees dangling, my breath fanning the disfigured cheek.

Poor Andy was mortified. He made a move to rise from his seat, changed his mind and sat on, shuffling his feet and shifting about uneasily. At length, to cover his embarrassment, he opened the Bible at random and commenced to read the first passage that met his eye, *'I am a man that hath seen affliction by the rod of his wrath:*

'He hath led me and brought me into darkness but not the light . . . '

I paid no attention to this meaningless incantation. I was too preoccupied with the sudden chance of impressing those at school who expected more from my vaunted friendship with the cobbler than footling tales of card-playing and Bible-thumping. No use describing the drooping, lashless eyelid: the sagging lower lip, moist with spittle like an over-ripe mushroom; these disfigurements were known to all and sundry. Something more was required.

35

The cobbler read on, '*My flesh and my skin hath made me old: he hath broken my bones . . .* '

This was my opportunity to boast of being granted, like Thomas the unbeliever, the privilege of touching the ravaged flesh of my friend. There was nothing to hinder me. The fear of divine vengeance, instant and appropriate, had lost its dreadful immediacy. No punishment awaited me except the remote possibility that my friendship with Andy might be endangered.

The cobbler's sombre voice rolled over me, '*He hath set me in dark places, as they that be dead of old . . .* '

Perhaps if the blemished skin was really dead and sodden, as I suspected, Andy would not even feel the touch of a finger. Tentatively I pursed my lips, leaned over and blew smartly on the flawed cheek, half-expecting the answering twitch, like the twitching flanks of a fly-tormented beast. Unheedingly the cobbler continued to read but at last the growing bitterness in the deep rumbling voice forced me to listen to the words.

'*He hath enclosed my ways with hewn stone, he hath made my path crooked:*

'*He hath turned aside my ways and broken me to pieces: he hath made me desolate . . .* '

I had a vision of a ruined temple set in the midst of an arid desolate plain. Huge blocks of tumbled masonry and a ring of pillar stumps like worn-down fangs encircled a sunken courtyard, choking off all exit down the maze of crooked paths reeling senselessly into the distance – the tracks beaten down by drunken curse-marked pilgrims. In the centre of the courtyard a shrivelled figure lay stretched in the burning sun, its arms and legs broken and twisted by torture – lonely and terror-stricken, too weakened by hunger and thirst to make the effort needed to escape.

The cobbler's voice, hoarse with anguish, brought me back to reality, '*I am made a derision to all my people and their song all the day –* '

He made an effort to continue, but gave up and remained with head bent, staring down at the open page, his lips moving soundlessly, his eyes moist with tears.

He was actually crying. It was grown-up, undignified grief, but it would serve my purpose. For this was indeed my chance. At long last I had the pretext for satisfying my curiosity. I reached over and stroked his cheek.

'Poor Andy!' I murmured. 'Poor old Andy!'

Retribution came swift and startling. Before I could draw back, I found myself grabbed, dragged off the work-bench and held imprisoned, my head crushed against the cobbler's shoulder.

In the hope that my punishment might be mitigated by submission, I did not shout or struggle. Docilely I waited the inevitable outburst of fury, prepared to recognise at last that surely God is not mocked.

Suddenly, to my shocked surprise, the cobbler commenced to shudder and moan like a sick animal. His breathing became harsh and stertorous. There was a sound of grating teeth. It seemed to be an onset of convulsions or epilepsy. Perhaps something even more serious. Cautiously I tried to worm myself free so that I could run for the doctor. But the more I squirmed and wriggled the tighter became the cobbler's grip.

More alarming still, he was now muttering wildly to himself in rushing disconnected snatches of speech. Like a funeral bell, I could hear the constant tolling of my name: 'Jim! Oh Jim!' the only sound I could identify in the unintelligible gabble. Death at the hands of a raving madman seemed the price that an offended God meant to exact for my transgression.

This thought started me struggling in earnest, tugging and pulling at the clamping hands. Just when I had nearly freed myself, the cobbler swung round and trapped me between constricting knees.

Dourly and in silence I fought on, flinging myself wildly from side to side, trying desperately to escape, whilst the cobbler with his free hands stroked my hair, patted my back and made soft soothing noises like you would to a frightened colt.

I felt there was something sinister about this attempt to quieten me. Just in time I looked up. The cobbler was bending over me, eyes closed, lips twitching rapidly in mute frantic appeal and I knew with a dreadful certainty that the hideous curse-marked face was about to be thrust against my own, seeking God knows what of pity and sympathy. He started to wheeze and whine like a brute beast. It was too much.

'Let go of me, Andy! Let me go!' I shouted.

The cobbler clapped one hand over my mouth.

'Hush, Jim,' he whispered, in a queer, hoarse, excited voice, leaning down till his warm breath fouled my cheek with spittle.

Frantic with fear and disgust, I tore away the stifling hand.

'Let me go, Heel-ball,' I screamed. 'Don't come near me with your rotten stinking poxy face.'

I felt the cobbler flinch and jerked myself free of his slackening grasp. At the door I stopped and looked back.

He was slumped in the chair, arms and legs sagging like a cheap worn-out cloth doll, saliva dribbling out of his mouth instead of sawdust. He stared back at me, slack-jawed, his tongue clacking the time of day like an eight-day clock. The hurt bewildered look on his face only served to goad me to further insults, 'It's in the mad-house you should be. Carrying on like that. Don't you know that thing is catching? Like the leprosy.'

I looked down at my rumpled clothes and my indignation grew.

'You have my shirt tore,' I said. 'And there's a button off my jacket.'

The cobbler's misery was piteous to watch.

'I . . . I . . . I'm sorry, Jim,' he mumbled. 'I thought because you . . . '

His voice trailed into silence, although his mouth continued to open and close as if he were swallowing back a bitter unspoken cud of grief.

'Well, you thought wrong, whatever it was,' I said. I was sick with loathing and hatred, as much for myself as for him, and I meant to make him pay for his share in my humiliation.

'And what's more,' I went on, 'my stomach's turned looking at you chewing and slobbering over the cards. And I'm fed up with your silly old Cassino, wherever you picked it up. And I'm sick to death listening to your ould Bible blather – it's worse than Sunday school, and that's no picnic. And I'm never coming in here again the longest day I live.'

The words were choking me but I got them out somehow.

I turned to go but Andy's voice halted me.

'Jim,' he said. 'Would you have it in you to forgive the presumption of a lonely foolish old man?'

I stayed silent.

He went on:

'Will you listen before you go to one last passage from the Book? I promise you it's the last one I'll ever trouble you with.'

I refused to answer, fearing the treachery of speech.

He closed the Bible slowly, with a gesture of finality.

'He that despiseth his friend is mean of heart,' he said, speaking the words very slowly and without trace of emotion. 'It was Solomon said that, Jim. And he was the wisest man in all Israel.'

As I made off, with the tears spurting from my eyes, I heard him call after me, 'You'll be in the morrow on your way past.'

But I did not call in the next day. Nor the day after. Nor ever again. Coming back from school I kept to the far side of the street with my face averted. Before very long I had joined a group of boys, more daring than the rest, and was shouting 'Scar-face, Heel-ball, Poxy-puss' with the best of them. I was mean of heart, as Andy had foreseen. Mean and cowardly and bitter. But how else could I exorcise the limping miserable ghosts that haunted my memory – the sound of Andy, snuffling and whining like a terrier bitch that my mother, for some reason or other, locked into an outhouse and the stealthy conniving note in his voice when he whispered: 'Hush, Jim.'

Meles Vulgaris

'What are you reading, darling?'

Her voice was muffled by the turtle-necked sweater out of which she was struggling.

He pulled the bedclothes further up his chest, adjusted the pillow and turned a page.

'Come again?'

'There wasn't a cheep –' her chin emerged – 'out of you –' the sweater was peeled from her rolled back ears – 'all evening. It must be –' a last effort and she was free – 'a powerful book.'

'Uh-huh.'

She pitched the sweater on to a chair seat, shook out her wiry black hair and examined herself critically in the mirror.

'Sitting hunched up over an old book since tea-time,' she told the frowning sun-tanned reflection, 'without a word to say for yourself.' Eyes – sloe-black, deep set, heavy lidded – gazed back at her appraisingly. 'You know, darling, it's lonely all day in the house by yourself.' With tentative fingertips, she smoothed out the crow's feet. 'No one to talk to till you're home for the weekends.' Her gaze slid over the tiny frightening folds and wrinkles of the neck and sought comfort in the firm brown flesh of arms and shoulders. The mirrored face smiled ruefully. 'It's a wonder I don't start talking to myself.'

'Uh-huh.' With finger and thumb, he rasped gently the lifted ready-to-be-turned leaf.

She swung round.

'I believe you weren't listening to a word I said.'

'Sorry, honey. I wasn't paying attention.'

She reached out a hand. Curious.

'What's it about, anyway?'

He handed her the book.

'*The Badger*'. She leafed the pages rapidly. 'It looks like some sort of a text book.'

'So it is.'

Frowning, she studied the stylised animal on the jacket.

'Why the sudden interest in badgers?' she asked.

'I saw it –' he nodded towards the book 'displayed in a book shop window.'

'But what on earth induced you to buy it?'

'A sudden impulse. It reminded me of that holiday we had in the Blue Stack mountains. When we saw the badger fight.'

Her face lit up.

'But that was years ago.'

He rolled over on his side, tucked the bedclothes in round his shoulders and burrowed into the pillow.

'Oh,' he mumbled, 'I remember it – remember it right well.'

He yawned.

'The book tells you how the little fellows tick.'

The common badger – meles vulgaris – a genus of burrowing carnivores, is found in hilly or wooded districts in almost every part of the country. More common in the West than in the East.

Sunday morning after Mass. Around the church gate the usual crowd of men standing about in groups, talking football, greyhounds, hangovers, weather. From the outskirts Micky Hogan beckoning. Moving away from the crowd before he spoke.

'Are you for the match the day?'

'I don't know. Why?'

'They're drawing a badger up at Johnny John's.'

'D'you tell me! What dogs have they got? Mind you, it's not everyone will chance getting his dog mauled or maybe killed by a brock.'

'Hawker Downey is bringing along that treacherous whelp of a Kerry Blue of his. A right mauling might put manners on it.'

'Any others?'

'They have another Kerry Blue lined up. A good one.'

'Whose?'

'The curate's. The boys are going to whip it when he's gone to the match.'

'Och, go to God. There'll be the queer rumpus when he finds out.'

'The dog'll be at the gate to meet him when he gets back from the game. It might be a wee scratch or two the worse for the trip but sure the silly brute is always in trouble. You should take the car and we'll head into the Blue Stacks. It'll be right gas.'

'How did they catch the badger?'

'D'you mind the Johnny Johns complaining about the fox slaughtering their fowl?'

'Aye.'

'Well, they found pad marks yesterday morning outside the hen house. The tracks led to a badger's earth not a stone's throw from the house. The nest was dug up, the sow and the three cubs killed and Mister Brock himself is for the high jump this afternoon.'

The badger is a member of the order Carnivora and has large canine teeth but, contrary to popular belief, it does not prey on poultry or young lambs. It feeds on insects, small mammals, molluscs and earthworms, supplemented by vegetable material such as fruit, nuts and grass.

Still riffling the pages of the book, she stared blindly at the unfamiliar photographs. Tenderness welled up inside her, tearing at throat and eyes. Perhaps he too was thinking of their first holiday together after they were married. When he had taken the firm's car and they had driven into the foothills of Croaghgorm to his Aunt Ellen's tiny farm-house. There was no money to go any place else. But who cared? They had spent three weeks there, coddled and fussed over by Aunt Ellen.

They had moved round together in a daze. Drunk with love. Shouting their crazy enchantment at the echoing hills. Bound together with such hunger for each other that the warmth left the blazing summer sun if they moved apart.

For those three weeks they had only one body between them – a parched thirsty body that soaked up happiness like a sponge. It was on the last day of that unforgettable holiday that they brought Micky with them to the badger fight in the Blue Stacks.

The baiting had already started when the car bumped and slithered up the last stretch of track and into Johnny John's yard. A crowd of mountainy men stood around watching Hawker Downey – a fussy, wee, know-all – trying to coax, drag, push his stupid gulpin of a dog into an overturned barrel. Each time he got the Kerry Blue's forequarters inside the barrel, the dog would wriggle free dashing around among the onlookers, wagging its stumpy tail.

The crowd hooted and jeered.

'Put your shoulder to him, Downey.'

'Take away the cowardly cur.'

'Give the curate's dog a trial.'

'Crawl into the barrel yourself, Hawker.'

Downey was nettled. He got the dog by the scruff of the neck and the skin of the rump and fairly hurled it into the barrel.

'Sic him, Garry!' he urged. 'Sic the brock!'

Never did dog react quicker. It bounced back out of the barrel, shot between Downey's splayed legs and never cried halt till it reached the safety of the dunghill, where it ploutered about in the soggy muck, wagging a doubtful, disillusioned tail. Whistles, threats, curses, wouldn't shift it.

There was nothing for it but to try out the curate's dog. Much against his will Micky Hogan, who sometimes exercised the dog for Father Bradley, was prevailed on to handle it.

'I'll gamble the curate will blame me for this day's work, if he gets to hear of it. So keep your traps shut. All of you,' he said.

The Kerry Blue trotted at his heels to the barrel mouth. He patted its flank.

'In you go, champ,' he said.

The dog moved in willingly enough. For as long as it took Micky to straighten up, take a cigarette butt from behind his ear and light it, the dog stayed stiff-legged, tail quivering, before it backed out slowly. Once clear of the barrel it stopped, shaking its head violently.

Micky grabbed it. Examined the muzzle.

'Not a scratch,' he announced. 'There's only one remedy for this disease. The toe of me boot.'

'You may give over, Hogan,' a querulous voice called. It was the old fellow himself. Johnny John. He was standing at the kitchen door, watching the proceedings with a sardonic smile. 'I told the young fellows to get fox-terriers. But of course they knew better. Those dogs you've got aren't worth a curse. They'll never face the barrel.'

'For why?'

'The smell of the brock has them stomached.'

One of the characteristics of the badger is the possession of musk- or stink-glands. These anal glands are used as a result of fear or excitement. The recognition of danger will stimulate secretion and trigger off the defence mechanism.

A hand ruffled his hair.

'Unhook me, will you, honey.'

Reaching up a hand towards the voice, he pawed the air blindly.

'Come on, lazy-bones,' she urged. 'I can't get this wretched thing off.'

His eyes opened to black bra straps biting into sun-browned skin. As he fumbled with the hooks, buried deep in flesh, she chattered on:

44

'How's that for a tan? I was the whole week stretched out on the lawn. Sun-bathing. We get so little sun it would be a shame not to make the most of this hot spell. God knows, it's hard enough to get a decent tan up. Olive oil helps, of course. But then you must be careful not to fall asleep or you'll get fried. Properly fried.'

The loosened bra fell away. With outstretched arms she spun around.

'Becoming, isn't it?'

The brown body appeared to be encompassed by a monstrous pair of white plastic goggles out of which glared two angry bulging bloodshot eyes.

His flesh crept with embarrassment.

'Most exotic,' he said.

She flushed with pleasure.

'You really think so?'

He yawned wide and loud.

'Sure.'

His head dropped back on the pillow.

It was decided to let the dogs attack in the open where the rank smell would be dispersed. The crowd scattered back from the barrel. The two dogs were leashed.

One of the young Johnny Johns gripped the bottom of the barrel. Tilted it. Slowly. To knee level. Scrabbling noises. Higher still. More scrabbling noises. Up to hip level. Silence.

'He's lodged, boy,' called Johnny John. 'You may shake him out of it.'

The young fellow shook the barrel. Cautiously. Nothing happened. Harder this time. Still no result.

'You'll get no windfalls that way,' someone shouted.

'Slew the barrel round, Peter,' the old man ordered.

A murmur of appreciation went round.

'Sound man.'

'The old dog for the hard road.'

'It takes yourself Johnny.'

Slowly Peter swung the barrel on its base. The crowd began to close in. The old man moved out from the porch. One of the dogs whimpered.

At the quarter turn the badger came slithering out, still clawing wildly for purchase.

It crouched, facing its tormentors, the grey-black hair on its body bristling like a hedgehog, its black and white head flat to the ground. Although it remained motionless, its whole body, from snout to stumpy tail seethed with controlled energy.

This fierce smothered tension dominated the crowd with a threatening fist. No one moved. Peter still held up the tilted barrel. Hogan's smoked down butt scorched the palm of his hand unheeded. Halted in mid-stride Johnny John waited, ash-plant poised.

Again a dog whimpered.

The crouching badger leaped forward. It picked no gap in the ranks of its enemies. It hurled itself at them and they broke before it. Shouting and cursing: shouldering, elbowing, pushing each other, in their anxiety to get out of the path of this savage creature running amuck; they backed away.

Through this opening dashed the badger. Ahead lay freedom. A length of laneway, a thick hedge, a familiar track reeking with the smell of its kind, the safety – somewhere – of an unravaged sett.

There was one enemy left. Johnny John.

Wily and tough as the brock itself, he had moved out towards the yard gate and now, with stamping feet and flailing ash-plant, he headed the badger back towards the closed and bolted outhouses.

Baffled, uncertain, the badger slowed down, scuttling along with a lurching, waddling gait. The length of the outhouses it ran, seeking shelter – scurrying, hesitating, scurrying again – like a businessman hunting for a seat in a crowded train.

> The feet of the badger are plantigrade: the animal walks on the flat of its feet, including the heel, in contrast to the Ungulates, which walk on their toes.

He clung doggedly to his share of the bedclothes as she

46

plunged into bed, wriggling and threshing around, till she was coiled up under the glow of the bed light, an open magazine held between pillow and bedclothes.

The glossy leaves crackled imposingly as she flicked them over, seeing not mink-coated figures, luscious dishes of food, enormous luxury automobiles, but grim, hungry, plush-covered hills.

'Why don't we go back there again?' she said. 'Sometime.'

'Where?' His voice was muffled by the pillow.

'Croaghgorm.'

The bed springs creaked as he shifted peevishly.

'What would we be going there for? Aunt Ellen's dead.'

'We could stay some place else. A farm-house in the hills.'

Again he shifted. Rolling over on his back. To the ceiling he spoke – patiently, reasonably, wearily.

'Look, Sheila. In a cottage in Croaghgorm you would last exactly one night. No hot water. No foam rubber mattress. No thick pile carpets. No radiogram. Above all nothing to do. Except you tramp the mountains, helping them to herd sheep.'

Her heart contracted as she felt the spring of the moss under her bare feet, the cool squelch of mud oozing between her toes.

'Or sit in the house all day blinded by a smoking turf fire.'

She drew in her breath, sniffing the acrid, heady, wholly delicious, fragrance of burning turf: watched with sleepy eyes the flames die down as the brown ash formed: heard the tired sigh as the burnt out sods collapsed.

'Not forgetting the peaceful night's rest you'll have with sheep dogs barking, cattle bawling and roosters crowing their heads off at day-break.'

She rolled over facing him.

'We must go, dear. Sometime. If it's only for the day.'

'All right. All right.'

He pulled the bedclothes over his head.

The badger disappeared into the opening between two outhouses.

'He's got away.'

'Why didn't you mill him, Johnny?'

'Loose the dogs.'

The old man pranced about in the gap, waving the stick.

'He picked the baiting-pitch himself,' he said, as the crowd gathered in the opening. 'And a better choice he couldn't have made if he'd searched all Ireland.'

.It was a cul-de-sac. The gable ends of two outhouses – one of concrete, the other galvanised iron – a few yards apart, linked by a man-high stone wall.

Around these confines the badger sniffed, scratching the ground here and there with a tentative forepaw. Where the zinc shed met the wall, it started digging.

By the time the decision had been reached to send in Hawker's dog first, the badger had rooted out a hole large enough to warrant the use of its hind paws. With these it scattered back the uprooted clay into an ever-rising parapet. When the Kerry Blue came charging in, the badger wheeled around, keeping to the shelter of its burrow, to face its assailant, teeth bared in a silent snarl.

It crouched motionless but for the grinning muzzle that swung from side to side parrying the probing onslaughts of the dog. This swaying exotically-striped head, slender, graceful, compact with fierce vigilance seemed to repudiate the huddled body, craven, lumpish, dingy, belonging surely to a different and inferior species.

The dog pounced. It grabbed the badger at the back of the head where the long grey body-hairs begin. Secure from the snapping jaws by this shrewd grip, it whipped up the striped head, shook it violently and slammed it back to the ground. It pinned down the badger's head, pressing it into the loose clay whilst it gnawed and grunted, grunted and gnawed, shifting its grip deeper and deeper through the thick hair, as if it sought to sink its teeth into solid flesh.

Always it was thwarted. Choked by the mass of coarse wiry hair, it was forced to loosen its hold, gulping in a quick mouthful of air before it pounced again.

The badger crouched supine, muzzle buried in the clay. Waiting.

At last the gasping dog released its hold. For one vulnerable second it loomed over its enemy, its slavering jaws content to threaten. In that second the badger struck.

The striped head reared up. Snapping jaws closed on a dangling ear. A yelp. Frenzied scuffling as the growling dog sought to free itself. A wild howl. The badger, still gripping the torn ear, had lashed out with one of its fore-feet, raking the dog's muzzle – once, twice – with its long gouging claws before the poor brute broke free. Bleeding from lacerated ear and jowl, it backed away yapping.

Johnny John struck the ground with his stick.

'You may take the cowardly brute to hell out of that,' he said. 'A Kerry Blue's no use to fight once it starts giving tongue.'

Downey grabbed his dog and lugged it away. The badger went back to its burrowing. Micky Hogan started to unleash the second dog, now trembling and straining at the lead.

'You mightn't bother your barney, Hogan,' said Johnny John. 'That dog'll never best a brock. Didn't I tell you it was a soople, snapping animal you wanted. Not a big lazy get the like of thon, that'll fall asleep on the grip.'

Micky looked up.

'I'm surprised at you, Johnny,' he said. 'Have you no respect for the cloth?' He stooped over the dog. 'Go in there, Father Fergus, and show this anti-clerical gentleman how you handle a heretic.' He released the dog. 'Off you go, chum.'

The dog advanced cautiously. Every few paces it paused, straddle-legged, watchful, snarling muzzle out-thrust, its gaze fastened on the badger, now faced round awaiting its attacker. It advanced to within arm's length of the striped muzzle before it came to a halt, crouched on stiffened forefeet. It growled softly, continuously – a growl so far back in its throat that it sounded like a harmless gentle purr.

The badger held its ground, beady eyes bright, alert, muzzle cocked, lips drawn back in its soundless snarl.

The two animals crouched, locked into stasis by the hate and fear that glared back at them from alien eyes. So long did they remain poised that a shout went up when the tension was broken at last by the pouncing dog.

'He's nailed him!'

'Good on you, Fergus!'

'Hold tight to him!'

Johnny John said quietly:

'There'll be trouble when he loosens yon grip.'

The dog had gripped the badger by the snout and was tugging it from its burrow into open ground. The badger with splayed feet, resisted. It was of no avail. Heaving and jerking, the Kerry Blue drew the badger inch by struggling inch over the clay parapet until it had the thirty pound carcase out on level ground. At this moment the dog's hindfeet lost their purchase on the moiled ground.

The sudden skid loosened the hold of the dog's jaws. It was the badger's chance. Teeth crunched. A yelp of pain from the dog. The badger's clumsy body came to life – squirming, wriggling, jerking. At last it was free. Snout torn and bleeding. One eye damaged. Dragged from its sheltering burrow. But free.

It began to sidle towards the uprooted trench. The dog blocked its path, menacing the badger with bared and bloody teeth.

'The brock has relieved the poor bugger of half his bucking tongue,' someone said in an awe-stricken voice.

'What did I tell you?' said Johnny John.

This time there was no preliminary sparring. The dog closed in at once, only manoeuvring so that his attack came from the badger's rear, safe from the deadly teeth and claws. Like a boxer using his reach, the dog took advantage of longer legs and greater agility. It leapt around the badger, darting out and in, feinting to charge until it lured its enemy into position. Then it pounced.

Sometimes it succeeded in straddling the badger, flattening it on the ground, where it could tear and maul the defenceless animal's head. But not for long. The badger would break free, roll over on its back and rip with lethal claws the dog's unprotected belly.

Slow, ungainly, its heavy, stumpy-legged body unsuited to swift exchanges, the badger was content to remain on the defensive. But always it was dangerous. Let the Kerry Blue fail to duck away quick enough after releasing its grip and another gash was added to its scored and bleeding body.

Except for the scuffle of paws on the trampled clay, the panting of the dog as it sparred for an opening, an occasional grunt from either animal, the struggle was fought out with quiet decorum. Indeed for long stretches there was complete silence as the two animals lay locked together, jerking spasmodically as the dog strove to deepen its grip or the badger to free itself.

If both had not been so mired and bloodied – the badger's slender elegant head being so plastered with blood and clay that the parti-coloured striping could no longer be discerned – they could have been tricking together harmlessly. Or dozing in the sun. Or even coupling.

It was evident that the strain of continual attack was wearying the dog. Its movements were now clumsy, sluggish: its lithe evasions slowing down. At last the inevitable happened.

The Kerry Blue came charging in obliquely. Swerved to escape the grinning expectant muzzle. Halted. A moment of teetering indecision. A shout from the crowd.

'The brock has got him!'

'It'll tear the throat out of him!'

'Maybe we should separate them, lads?'

'Throw Downey's craven cur in on top of them.'

Hawker called:

'Will I let Garry have another go at him, Johnny?'

The old man squirted a jet of tobacco-juice towards the straining dog. Said he:

'Damn the differ it'll make. The brock is the boss. He'll beat the two of them.'

Hawker loosed the dog.

'Sic him!' he said. 'Sic the bastard!'

The dog went in, running low to the ground, watching its comrade back away, dragging after it the badger, in a frantic effort to break the throttling hold. Ignoring threats, jeers and pleadings, it waited its opportunity. An unexpected jerk put the badger's legs sprawling. The wary dog pounced, grabbing the badger by a hind leg. Tugging at its hold, it swung the badger off the ground till it dangled belly up, its teeth still sunk in its enemy's throat.

Before the badger could right itself, the dog slammed the helpless body down on its back and, shifting its hold, bit deep into the tender flesh of the groin.

So swiftly did the badger release its grip and lash out with scourging claws at the already lacerated muzzle of its new assailant that the agonised yapping of both dogs – the throttled and the mauled – broke out simultaneously. Still yapping, they fled to either side of the enclosure where they wheeled round, barking and growling. They were in poor shape. Bloody. Mangled. Shivering with fright.

'That burrowing bastard has made a slaughter-house job of them,' said Micky Hogan.

Johnny John spat, a quick explosive spurt. He said:

'Didn't I warn you the brock would master the pair of them? Better if you call in your wretched curs before he drives them ahead of him into the village.'

The badger had limped back into the scooped out trench. It commenced digging again. With its forepaws only. Soon its claws could be heard rasping on the cement foundation of the shed. It stopped. Changed position and burrowed again till once more it was stopped by the cement. Twice more it tried, before it started on the galvanised iron. Inserting a paw under the bottom of the sheeting it commenced to tear at it, tearing and tugging until at last it managed to secure a purchase for its jaws.

'In the name of God,' someone said, with a nervous laugh, 'does it mean to pull down the building over its head like Samson?'

The badger was worrying at the metal sheeting – tugging, snapping, gnawing – its body coiling and uncoiling, as it strove to chew or tear its way to freedom.

'You'd think it was crunching biscuits,' one of the young

Johnny Johns said. 'With jaws the like of yon, it'd chaw itself out of Sing Sing.'

The badger has extremely powerful jaws. A peculiar feature of the lower jaw is that it locks in a transverse elongated socket in such a complete manner that it will not dislocate: if it comes away at all the skull will be fractured.

An elbow jogged him.

'Are you asleep?'

'Eugh! . . . Eh? . . . Aye!' A long sighing breath. Part moan, part fretful wail.

'Come off it, Brer Fox. You're codding nobody. Lying awake there brooding on the silly old badgers you were reading about all evening.'

She ran a teasing finger down the bones of his spine.

'Wha's-a-matter? Wha-dja-want?'

'Oh, nothing. I thought you were asleep.'

'Darling. I've had a long, hard day. I'm jaded out. Beat to the ropes. Let's go to sleep, what d'you say?'

He clutched the bedclothes. Huddled down lower in the bed. Breathed loudly, steadily through his nose.

The men were debating the fate of the badger.

'Destroy the brute. That's the only thing left to be done.'

'Look at the shape it's left the dogs.'

'What'll the curate say when he sees the cut of Fergus?'

'Small odds about those whining hoors,' said Johnny John. 'Didn't the brock lather the daylights out of the pair of them? We'd be poor sports to slaughter it after that.'

'Let it go,' he urged.

'So that it can raid more hen-houses?'

'Or spread ruin round the district with its burrowing?'

'Aye! Or maybe start attacking the young lambs?'

Johnny John was overborne.

'All right,' he said, 'Fetch out a mattock.'

It was decided that Clarke, the village butcher, would dispatch the badger. Mattock at the ready, he moved in

53

towards the gnawing animal. A few paces from the burrow he halted as the badger swung round to face him. Three cautious steps brought him within striking distance of the snarling muzzle. He hefted the mattock. Balanced it carefully, judging his target. Brought the blade smashing down square on the badger's poll, driving its head deep into the clay. A neat professional stroke.

The butcher stood over the motionless body, leaning on the shaft of the mattock. He was about to turn away, satisfied with a job well done, when the badger stirred. Raised its bloodied muzzle from the clay. Struggled erect.

Again Clarke chopped the heavy-bladed weapon down on the badger's skull, crushing the mangled head to the ground. Slowly, painfully, the snarling muzzle was raised in defiance.

Twice more the butcher swung down the mattock before Johnny John's shouts penetrated his shocked bewilderment.

'In God's name, give over, Butcher. You'll never do away with the brute that way.'

The old man rushed into the enclosure.

'Gimme that tool, man,' he said, grabbing the mattock. 'You'll take the edge off the blade. D'you not know that a brock's skull will stand up to a charge of buckshot?'

A feature of the badger is the extraordinary growth of the interparietal ridge of bone on the dorsal surface of the skull in the mid line. This ridge is half an inch deep in places and serves to protect the main surface of the skull from blows delivered directly from above, though its prime purpose is for the attachment of the powerful jaw muscles.

'Tell me,' she murmured, her breath fanning his ear, 'what attraction a badger has got that the rest of us lack?'

She had rolled over, cuddling herself against his back.

'Can't you let a fellow sleep?' He edged away unobtrusively.

'What has it got?' she insisted, snuggling closer.

'It's got courage. Courage. Tenacity. Fortitude.'

'Where do the rest of us come in?' Her hand burrowed into the jacket of his pyjamas. 'Wouldn't we all act the same way with our back to the wall? Courage and ferocity!' She sniffed. 'There's more to it than that. Surely?' Her fingers drummed an urgent message on his chest. 'You'd never ask someone to take second place to a stupid old badger.' A warm leg slid over his own. 'Would you, darling?'

'Sheila . . . please!'

He shook himself free. Reached up and switched off the light. Fists clenched, eyes squeezed shut – he lay, trying to ignore the reproach in her rigid, outstretched body. When at last her breathing had steadied to the rhythm of sleep, he tugged the bedclothes back over himself, relaxed and opened his eyes to the dark.

Queer, he thought, how she had got to the core of things. Unwittingly. For surely, without tenacity, courage and ferocity were futile.

The courage of the badger is legendary. A shy, inoffensive animal, with no natural enemies, it will yet, if cornered, exhibit a ferocity noteworthy in a creature of such small dimensions. It is utterly fearless. Whether bird, beast or reptile: the forces of nature or the savagery of man – nothing can daunt it.

Johnny John was standing an arm's length from the badger.

'There's only one way to kill a brock,' he said, over his shoulder.

He raised the mattock. 'A clout on the muzzle.'

He swung down the blade.

At the same instant the badger charged. The squelch of the blade on the animal's back and the cry of dismay from the old man came together.

'So help me God,' he wailed, 'I didn't mean to do it.'

He dropped the mattock. With horror-stricken gaze he watched the badger. Hindquarters flattened to the ground, girning muzzle still lifted in challenge, it continued towards him, dragging its helpless body forward on stubborn forepaws.

'A wee tap on the nose. As God is my judge, that's what I tried to do,' Johnny John pleaded.

'Come away out of that, Da, or it'll maybe maul you,' one of the boys called out.

The mattock lay across the badger's path. An insurmountable barrier to the crippled beast. Feebly it pawed at the heavy implement striving to push or pull it aside. Without success. At last, the infuriated animal sank its teeth in the wooden shaft, lifting the handle clear of the ground. Unable to drag itself further forward, it lay stretched out, eyes glaring madly ahead, clenched jaws holding aloft the murderous weapon. The matted, filthy, blood-stained animal had already the ugly anonymous appearance of death.

The old man was near to tears. In his distress he shuffled a few steps to either side, beating the fist of one hand into the palm of the other.

'Where's my stick?' he muttered. 'Where hell's my stick?'

He shook his fist at the watching crowd.

'It's all your fault, you ignorant pack of hallions. Didn't I pray and plead with you to let the brock go? Now look what you've done.'

He moved back towards them, changing direction aimlessly, his gaze scanning the ground.

'Where did I drop my stick? It must be someplace hereabouts.'

He looked up.

'Let none of you ever boast of this day's work. It was pure butchery, that's what it was. A cowardly bit of blackguardism. There's more spunk in the brock than in the whole bloody issue of you.'

He halted.

'Will some of you find me stick . . . or some other implement . . . He looked back over his shoulder, as though fearful of being overheard. 'Till I put an end to its . . . Oh, Mother of God!'

The badger had released its grip on the mattock. It rolled over on its back. Screaming.

It kept screaming – a loud sustained yell of defiance that not even the onslaught of death could subdue to a whimper: that ceased abruptly only with the slack-jaw and the glazing eye.

There are many conflicting theories regarding the significance of the badger's peculiar yell. Some naturalists believe it to have sexual origins: others that it has some connection with the death or funeral rites of this strange animal. All are agreed on the blood-curdling quality of the cry.

Lying wide-eyed and sleepless, he tried to close his ears to the appalling sound. It was no use. The voice of the dying badger refused to be silenced.

For all these years it had resounded in his memory with the urgency of a trumpet call – the wild defiant shout of an animal ringed about with enemies. He had thought to cast himself in this heroic mould. To be a maverick. Forever in the ranks of the embattled minority. Instead there had been a slow erosion of ideals, a cowardly retreat from one decent belief after another until at last he found himself in the ranks of the majority. The ring of the craven curs that hemmed in and crushed the unruly, those few who dared cry: '*Non serviam!*'

The badger cry was now a pitiful sound. A shrill squeal of protest. The rage tinged with terror: the defiance with despair. The cry of something crushed, defeated, abandoned.

Desolation – a grey waste of futility and failure – engulfed him. His skin crawled. His limbs cringed in revulsion at the extent of his betrayal. Shivering, he eased over towards the warmth beside him. At once the rhythm of her breathing changed. She was awake. Had been all along. Lying there. Listening. Waiting to smother him with forgiveness. To hell with that for a caper. There was no absolution needed in this case.

The springs creaked as he shifted back, dragging the bedclothes with him. It would be the price of her if she got her death of cold. The answer to her prayer. He coiled himself up, tucking in round his neck the bedclothes stretched between them.

Hardly was he settled down for sleep than the tranquil breathing became intolerable. He could envisage the patient, anguished, uncomplaining eyes of a holy picture staring into the darkness. Nursing its bitter wounds. God knows, you'd find it hard not to pity her.

He turned towards her.

'Sheila,' he whispered.

Once more the tiny catch in her breathing.

Gently he stroked the tense stubborn body, feeling it yield to his touch. She rolled over. Facing him.

'What's wrong?' she murmured.

Disconcerted, he stammered:

'Are . . . are . . . are you awake?'

She snuggled closer.

Feebly he grappled with her questing hand, warm and sticky with sweat. Lips fastened on his. Murmured:

'You *do* . . . want me . . . don't you?'

She buried her face in his neck.

'Grrr!' she growled happily. 'It's good to know I'm still on the wanted list.'

Acting out the familiar prologue, he held her in his arms, seeing only a mangled body, mired and misshapen, bloodied muzzle grinning senselessly at a senseless sky: hearing only the scream of agony that death alone could arrest.

A feeling of loneliness swept over him. A bitter, hopeless loneliness that he knew to be surrender. The sin of Judas. The ultimate and unforgivable catastrophe.

He shivered.

'Darling!' Hoarse, breathless, she clutched at him with avid, furious hands. 'Oh, darling! Darling!'

The Betrayers

'She's lying down.'

I never grasped the true significance of this statement until the summer I was packed off to spend the entire school holidays with my Aunt Mary at Benowen Strand, near the narrows of Lough Foyle, where you could stand on the shore and see, due North, the coastline of Southern Ireland. You got the impression that a good spit with the wind behind it, would carry across the narrow neck of sea and river to that poor priest-ridden country.

Aunt Mary's big old stone-built house and Willie Nesbitt's thatched cottage were the only dwellings in this tiny settlement, perched in the middle of a bleak stretch of windswept dunes. It was here I first learned that 'lying down' did not mean merely the assumption of a prone or horizontal position. It meant also a closed door past which one must always tiptoe. It meant drawn blinds at mid-day in an airless bedroom. It meant my aunt's voice resolutely uncomplaining:

'Leave the tray down beside the bed, Jim. And darling, *do* try to close the door quietly behind you.'

She suffered from attacks of migraine, especially during hot weather and the continuous spell of sweltering sunshine that characterised that summer kept her confined to her room most days with splitting headaches. 'She's lying down' had become part of the normal routine of the house. I had long since ceased to question her prolonged absences. One of the by-products of her ill-health was that I was forced, through sheer boredom, to spend most of my evenings in the kitchen with the only other occupant of the house – the maid.

This was all very well when Jane, Willie Nesbitt's sister, was the maid. But then she was a long string of pump-water, with clinker-built teeth, sallow skin and an ironed out chest. When she went to work in England and the new girl from the County Donegal came, it was a different kettle of fish. Her name was Cassie, Cassie Moran. She arrived the same day as the piebald mare, a drunken purchase of Willie Nesbitt's.

Cassie seemed to materialise in the kitchen, without ever having gone through the process of arrival. I came on her sitting straddle-legged before the kitchen range, reading a women's magazine. She looked up, said: 'Hi!' and went back to her reading.

As for the piebald, I saw her first by torchlight as Willie, blethering away like a ha'penny book and near smothering me with the smell of porter, opened the half-door of the stable.

'I hear tell your new girl arrived the day,' he said, flashing his torch on the mare.

'What d'you think of her?' he asked.

I looked at the sleek exotic creature, sidling away from the beam of light, ears flattened, nostrils flared, her whole body shivering with nervous tension.

'She's a proper beaut!' I said, not rightly knowing if I meant Cassie or the mare.

Next morning, in the broad light of day you could have faulted neither of them.

The mare was a lovely creature, a skewbald actually, patched brown and white with a narrow strip of black separating the two colours. With her air of dainty elegance she had the appearance of a circus pony – a beast that no farmer in his right senses and with a proper regard for the dignity of his craft, would allow into his yard.

Cassie too looked a thoroughbred. Small, dainty, raven-haired, she had the kind of complexion seen only on the covers of the glossier women's magazines. Willie Nesbitt gave his verdict as we watched her carrrying water back from the well:

'She's a well set up wee cuddy, all right. As neat a pair of hocks as you'd wish to see. They're two of a kind, herself and the pony!'

And indeed it was true. Cassie never moved from place to place like an orthodox biped. She plunged. With the frisky abandon of a colt she would dart across a room or fly up the stairs, taking them two at a time. Prowling among the sandhills, she progressed in little scuttling rushes, as though chasing a barking terrier. She had an animal wariness that showed in the sudden tilt of the head as she listened to some sound that only the cocked ear of a horse could discern.

For the first couple of weeks I was too busy to investigate Cassie. Every spare minute was devoted to watching Willie working on the pony. Up till now she had been treated as a pet, never broken to saddle or harness. But Willie was confident he could master her.

'I'll have her drawing gravel and sea-weed before the summer's out,' he said.

There was every chance of it. Willie – a squat, baldy, chinless forty – who lived with his widowed mother, ran a few score of sheep and three scrawny bullocks on the surrounding warren of sand-dunes. He milked one cow and each spring he went to the moss to cut and rear his turf. He laboured a rood or so of garden which he set in main-crop potatoes, savoy cabbage and swedes. That was the extent of his farming. But he had other gifts. He could set snares, lobster pots or a long line better than anyone in the locality. He could lift a salmon out of the water under the nose of the water-bailiff. He had an old-fashioned single-barrelled shotgun that, in his hands, was every bit as accurate as the most expensive Purdey. Above all he had an understanding of animals, especially horses, that was uncanny.

Willie felt there was one thing needed altering before he started to break the pony to harness. To keep calling her Sally, a name that called up her pampered past, would only be a handicap. A new name was required. As usual, Willie consulted the Bible.

'Sheba!' he announced at last. 'That's what we'll call her. After Solomon's woman that brought him the apes and the peacocks and the Arabian horses. Yon wee pony has Arab blood in her, I'd stake my solemn oath.'

So Sheba she became. But if Willie thought a change of name would effect a change of nature, he was soon proved wrong. For once the pony got used to her new owner and surroundings, she became temperamental and capricious. If thwarted she would paw the ground, shaking her head violently till her mane rose in a crest of foam. It was the behaviour of a spoiled brat and, as an only child, I could not but admire her performance.

Each morning she was released into the wire-fenced paddock beside the cottage where, after kicking up her heels and whinnying with delight, she would settle down contentedly enough to graze.

She took to the bridle with the minimum of trouble, allowing the bit to be forced between her jaws with little more than token resistance. Willie led her round and round the paddock at walking pace, the mare occasionally breaking into little jigging sidesteps, through sheer high spirits. Once when he stooped to tie up a trailing bootlace, she butted him playfully on the rump. Moving a pace or two away he tried once more to knot the lace. Again Sheba butted the tempting target. He flung the reins over her head and moved away. The pony kept at his heels, her mincing gait a contrast to Willie's flat-footed slouch. When he stopped, Sheba sidled up to him, craving attention with sniffing muzzle. He started off round the paddock, Sheba still at his heels. Each time he halted, the pony went through the same nuzzling act.

Willie made a great pretence of repelling these attentions but it was easy to see that he was delighted by the pony's show of affection. When we were stabling Sheba, he said to me:

'The wee mare's bulging with brains. You can see that, Jim? There'll be no trouble in the world breaking her to harness. It's just a matter of going easy and not rushing her.'

So for a week Willie and the pony performed their circus

act each afternoon in the paddock, with Mrs. Nesbitt, Cassie and myself for audience. Mrs. Nesbitt, a bitter-tongued old wasp gave out the pay as we stood at the gate watching.

'Boys-a-boys, thon's a queer looking yoke,' she said, out of the side of her uptwisted toothless mouth. 'I'll hould ye yon lady never cut a furrow or drew a load of dung. A plaything of the gentry, that's what she was.'

'Willie says he'll have her hauling before the end of the summer,' I said.

'I'm telling him to bring her back and take what he can get for her. He could plead he had a sup of drink taken when he made the bargain. I don't doubt he could even law them for fraud forby.'

'Maybe he's going to enter her for some of the Shows. There's big prizes to be won, they say.'

'Would you hould your tongue about Shows. He's wasted time enough on that daft creature without you putting ideas intil his head.'

Cassie never spoke. She stayed watching till Willie took the bridle off the mare, then ran back to the house.

Willie tackled me about her.

'You should give me a knock-down to her,' he said. 'When the old one's not around.'

He scratched his head thoughtfully.

'I'll tell you what we'll do, Jim. I'll try out the mare with the long reins in the morning. I've a notion she'll take to them. If she does I'll bring her down to the strand the morrow night. Let you pass the word to the wee cuddy.'

I gave her the message that night. She was sitting, as always, hunched over the dying fire, stuck into a paper-backed romance. Mooching around the kitchen I had rooted out a package of cream crackers and was buttering a rising column. I spoke over my shoulder:

'Willie's trying Sheba out on the long reins tomorrow night. Down on the strand. He thought you might like to come.'

I slapped the last of the butter on the one remaining biscuit.

'D'you think would there be a hunk of cheese in the joint, Cassie?' I said.

'He wants a knock-down to you,' I said.

There was no answer. Flinging down the knife, I turned round. The book lay open on her lap. As I watched, a leaf swung slowly back from left to right. She made no move to turn it back.

'Is there wax in your ears?' I said. 'Or are you struck dumb with longing for some silly old story-book hero?'

'There's cheese on the top shelf of the pantry, Master Jim,' she said, without budging.

I moved to the back of her chair.

'What's in these ruddy books anyway that keeps you re-reading every page as if you were revising your homework?'

I reached over her shoulder to flick back the vagrant page. Our heads were close together, her hair soft against my cheek. I froze into an attitude of attention, my outstretched fingers on the open page, repeating to myself the ridiculous words that caught my gaze:

'Love is the tenderness of the morning, not the madness of the night.'

I kept up the pretence of literary criticism even when she turned back to speak to me and I could no longer see the book.

'What sort of chap is he, Jimmie?' she asked, her voice purring from deep in her throat.

My mouth was jammed against her cheek. I pulled back my head to reply.

'Who?' a high voice, surely not my own, squeaked.

She craned further back so that her cheek was once more pressed against my mouth.

'Don't be a silly goose. Willie Nesbitt, of course,' she said.

Her skin smelt of soap and rumpled pillows and the plunge-room after a match.

'Oh, he's all right.' My dry lips grazed her cheek as the shameful voice croaked out a reply.

I felt I was being swallowed by an exotic jungle flower from one of my science fiction stories.

'Has he a girl?' she persisted. 'Is he in love with anyone?'

Dazed and stupified, I could only quote the words dancing across my closed eyelids.

'Love is the tenderness of the morning, not the madness of the night,' I said, hardly able to hear the silly words through the singing in my ears.

She swung round in her chair and faced me, her eyes all pupils, her lips puffed out like frost-stricken birds.

'You're a one,' she said, 'you sound like a story-book.'

Casually, as though I were a begging dog entitled to an encouraging pat for my cleverness, she leaned forward and kissed me full on the lips; calmly; expertly; leisurely. She got up, yawning and stretching. I stared hungrily at her tight-stretched nippled jumper. The blood hammered impatiently on my ear-drums: my insides weaved and lurched drunkenly. I felt shaky and weak. The cannibal flower had at last engulfed me, squeezing the very marrow from my bones.

'Ten o'clock,' she said, making for the scullery. 'The spuds still in their jackets and not a wean in the house washed.'

She moved with a slow voluptuous swagger, still twisting and flexing her arms. Drugged with emotion, I slunk off. Before I closed the kitchen door she called out:

'Tell your pal I go for a walk along the beach every night.'

Willie was delighted when I gave him the message next day.

'We'll take the pony out this evening,' he said. 'I tried the gear on her this morning and she was as quiet as a lamb.'

Sure enough, when he took Sheba, already tackled with bridle and girth, down to the strand, she stood quietly while he tied on the rope reins and threaded them back through the metal eyes on the girth. Willie walked back the full length of the long reins, shook them gently and chirped:

'Get up, Sheba!' he said softly. 'Get up, honey!'

The pony's ears pricked up. Willie waited.

'Get up!' he coaxed and chirped again.

Still the pony refused to budge.

'Get up there, you silly girl! Stop acting the mohawk!' he pleaded, shaking the reins very gently in time with his words.

She started off at a brisk gait. We were forced to trot to keep up with her, until the soft sand forced her to a plodding walk. Out on the hard sand she still kept to walking pace.

Cassie was dawdling along at the edge of the tide. Long before we were near her, Willie commenced to rein Sheba in.

'Whoa there, Sheba!' he called, easing back on the reins. 'Whoa, girl!'

The pony pulled up abruptly, nearly tripping Willie up.

'She has a good mouth,' he said. He was evidently disgusted at his failure to bring the mare to a halt at Cassie's side.

Cassie ignored him altogether when she reached us. She began patting Sheba's neck, rubbing her face against the pony's muzzle.

'Hullo, Pretty-puss!' she said. 'D'you think now would Willie let me handle you?'

She looked up.

'Your name's Willie, isn't it?' she said.

He reached out the reins to her.

'Here you are,' he said. There was a sappy grin on his face. 'You've had truck with horses before?'

'Wasn't I reared on a farm in Donegal!' she said.

He stayed close to her as furiously she shook and plucked at the reins, urging on the unheeding pony with clicking tongue and shouts of:

'Come on away! Come on away there!'

'Give over,' he said at last, taking the reins from her. 'You'll have her mouth torn to shreds if you keep on at that caper. You'd think you were bawling a drove of bullocks to the Fair.'

He turned to me.

'Will you chance your hand?' he said.

No matter how I tried – chirping, wheedling, twitching the reins – I could not stir the pony to more than a toss of the head.

Cassie was disgusted.

'What that Jezebel wants,' she said, 'is a lick of an ash-plant.

That would put some of the notions out of her head.'

'You'd never train Sheba that way,' he said. 'She's been petted too much. One belt of a stick and she'd never work for you again.'

'You're too soft-hearted, Willie. My father used to say that no horse was ever rightly broken in till your name was inscribed with an ash-plant on its side.'

'I never whaled a horse yet. And I've put a brave few through my hands. It's wrong. Don't you know what the poet says?'

He cleared his throat and commenced to intone:

> If I had a donkey and it wouldn't go,
> Would I belabour it? No! No! No!

'You're as mad as a March hare, Willie Nesbitt. Coming out with that silly nursery rhyme. As if there was ever an ass foaled that didn't need a proper flaking before it would budge a foot!'

It was terrible to see the abject look on Willie's face. Like a cringing mongrel set on licking the boot that kicked it. Before he could disgrace himself further, I handed him back the reins.

'Take over yourself, Willie,' I said.

It was uncanny. One chirp and Sheba was off again. No coaxing, no fuss. And once more Willie assumed dignity and authority.

For an hour he schooled the pony up and down the strand, concentrating solely on starting off and pulling up. As soon as she showed signs of ignoring his signals, he untied the reins.

'We'll knock off,' he said. 'No use working on her when she's getting browned off.'

'You have the patience of Job,' Cassie said. 'I don't know how you keep your temper with that saucy madam.'

With outstretched neck the pony sniffed and nuzzled at Cassie's face.

'Don't be trying to get round me, you old plaster,' she said, scratching Sheba's forehead. 'You'll not find me as soft as your boss.'

We started back up the strand with the mare pacing sedately behind, Willie holding forth non-stop.

'If you lift a hand in anger to a spoiled article the like of Sheba, you're goosed. You'd be well advised to sell her to the first man puts a price on her for she'll never do a day's work for you. No! This wee mare has got to be convinced that you're a class of a god – a decent kindly god that wouldn't rake her ribs with thunderbolts or start swearing at her out of the sky.'

By this time we were out on the metalled road.

'I'll leave yous and love yous!' said Cassie, branching off for the house.

Willie caught his breath.

'Eh?' he said.

'I'll maybe run into you the morrow night if you're below on the strand schooling the pony,' she called back.

While we were brushing down the mare Willie kept coming back to her last remarks.

'Did you hear what she said? She made a date for the morrow night. Isn't that what it amounts to, Jim? Eh? And what d'you think of her saying: "I'll love you and leave you". That sounds good, doesn't it? We'll have to be out on the strand brave and early to not miss her.'

I never in my life heard such mushy talk. The silly smirk on his face sickened me about proper. On top of everything didn't he say to me as I left:

'Put in a good word for me will you, Jim? Like a decent man.'

When I got as far as the kitchen, Cassie was sitting, book on lap, as if she had never moved since the previous night.

'He's a gas man, the bould Willie,' she started off immediately. 'He thinks of nothing but his blooming old pony. I thought he would never stop talking about her.'

'Does he never go with girls, Jimmie?' she asked.

Hands gripping the back of her chair, I was leaning over her in what I hoped was the correct attitude of a practised libertine. I said:

'You've nice curly hair, Cassie. Is it all your own?' My voice sounded normal enough but I was breathing like a beaten runner.

'Find out for yourself, Mr Curious Cat. And don't forget what happened to *him* when he became inquisitive!'

With the outstretched fingers of one hand, I started combing through the curls on the back of her neck, watching them coil up again like the little furry caterpillars we call Hairy Mollies.

'Why are you always asking after Willie?' I said. 'Have you a notion of him?'

She shook her head free.

'It's queer notions I'd be having, falling for the likes of him!' she said. 'Sure I suppose his old mother wouldn't let him look at a girl?'

'If Willie brought a girl into her kitchen, Mrs Nesbitt would split her with the tongs,' I said.

I reached down and turned back the page of the book, as I had done the previous night.

'You're not making much headway with your home-work,' I said.

She twisted round, grinning.

'Maybe you should give me a hand with it,' she said.

This time I did not wait for her to take the initiative. Closing my eyes I made a grab. Cassie squealed and fended me off.

'Are you trying to pull the head off me?' she said, rubbing her neck. 'D'you think you're bottling a calf or what?'

'You'd be the better for a little practice,' she said.

I could feel my face burning.

'Put your hands behind your back!' she commanded.

I did so.

'Now!' she said, leaning back, eyes closed, mouth puckered.

There I stood, bolted to the ground with shame, until she opened her eyes. The mocking curl of her lips shrivelled up the remains of my self-respect. She jumped up from the chair.

'Nine o'clock. Better for me to ready the supper,' she said.

As she passed me on her way to the pantry, she suddenly flung her arms round my neck, kissed me and whispered in my ear:

'I must keep in with Jimmie, mustn't I? It's not fair to be teasing him.'

Before I had time to gather my wits, my aunt's voice called from the stairs:

'Jim! Where are you?'

'I'm here, Aunt Mary. In the kitchen.'

'Don't be staying up late now. You know your mother warned you not to!'

Cassie turned at the pantry door, pointed dramatically at the calling voice and whispered:

'He shouldn't be collogueing with the kitchen staff, should he, Ma'am?'

She stuck out her tongue derisively.

Aunt Mary's voice came again, further up the stairs.

'You could bring up the supper. It will save Cassie the trouble.'

There was the faint sound of a closing door. Cassie whistled – a long sibilant tribute.

'She's got you taped, Master Jimmie. I'll better give you the tray before she comes down and takes you up by the ear.'

As she opened the kitchen door for me she said:

'Tell Silly Billy I was asking for him,' and in a whispered rush of words: 'D'you think could he ever be prised loose from that old vampire of a mother of his?'

The next few weeks are blurred with a haze of happiness. All my time seems to have been divided between Sheba and Cassie, though I must have gulped down three meals a day and bathed, fished and explored much as usual. Willie, drawing turf from the moss with a borrowed horse, was busy till tea-time so I had Sheba to myself all day. I spent hours in the paddock trying to coax the pony to do for me the things she would do so freely for Willie. I would give a finger-whistle every bit as shrill and curt as Willie's. The pony

70

would merely lift her head, look at me with disinterest and go back to her grazing.

When, after lengthy stalking, she allowed herself to be caught, there was no doubt of her affectionate response to my petting. Yet halter her and she would neither lead nor drive. She would graze her way round the paddock attached to me by a dangling rope. At the slightest pull of the halter, up would go her head in the effort to tear the rope from my fist. Never was I permitted any control over her movements.

Cassie had no better luck. She would stand at the gate coaxing and cajoling. The pony only lifted her head when Cassie's voice rose to a shout.

It was different when Willie put in an appearance after ricking his last load of turf for the day. Before ever he reached the gate of the paddock, the mare's head was up and she was whinnying with excitement. Still she never stirred till Willie whistled her up. Sometimes he kept her waiting deliberately, perhaps lifting his fingers to his mouth to deceive her, until he had her pawing the ground with impatience. Then, at the sound of the liberating whistle, she would break into a gallop and finish up snorting into Willie's face.

She was becoming accustomed to the daily schooling on the strand. Already she had mastered the signals for starting and halting. She would stand motionless for minutes on end waiting for the chirp or the twitch of the reins that would start her off again along the strand. Willie was confident he would have her working in harness before the summer was up.

Cassie joined us every night she could get away. She always fell in on Willie's free side and always the conversation opened in the same stilted, ceremonious manner.

'Well! How are times, Cassie?'

'Not so bad. And how is it with yourself?'

'Can't complain. A body must take the rough with the smooth.'

'Aye! True for you, Willie. You might as well keep the good side turned out.'

You would think they had not seen each other in six months. We would tramp along in silence behind Sheba for a while but before long the harping would start.

'How's your mother, Willie?'

'Oh, as well as can be expected. She's a hardy old warrior, that one.'

'She's getting no younger, though. She should be taking it easy at her time of life. It's a mystery to me how she keeps going!'

'Och, she manages well enough. It would take a lot to put *her* on her back.'

'I don't know. An old woman is no manner of use round a farm-house. It takes a sturdy young country girl to get the work done.'

Cassie was always getting herself worked up about the hard lot of the old people.

'It's a crying shame, that's what it is. Old creatures the like of your mother, forced to slave on where even a working horse'd have been put out to pasture.'

At this stage Willie generally produced a bar of chocolate or a bag of sweets. While Cassie was munching he would explain:

'No use in wasting your sympathies on that old hairpin. Sure she might as well be out in pasture for all she's doing.'

Cassie was not going to be down-sayed by this class of talk. She harped on:

'Isn't that just what I'm trying to tell you. A man come to your time of life should have his family reared instead of being still tied to his mother's apron-strings. You should think shame of yourself, Willie Nesbitt!'

At this Willie would shake the reins.

'Get up there, Sheba! The women get the last word, don't they, girl?'

Stabling the mare he always quizzed me about Cassie:

'How old do you think is she?' 'Would she have a boy of her own back in County Donegal?' 'Do you think would she be a steady girl that would settle down on a farm?'

Silly questions like these get my goat. I told him he had a

right to ask Cassie himself and not be trying to use me to ferret out information for him.

'I just thought you might know,' he said. 'You and she being so pack.'

I let that pass.

'Don't forget to keep her in mind of me, Jim. D'you hear now?'

'I'm never done talking to her about you,' I said.

'I know that. You're a good pal.'

Sure enough we talked about him, Cassie and I. And about Sheba and old Mrs Nesbitt. There was little else to talk about.

To be exact we did little talking. Most of our time was spent huddled over the kitchen range, acting out a charade that never got further than the first syllable. In bed each night, I planned its completion in a whirlwind seduction based on the scanty lore picked up at school from my fellow neophytes. Yet it only required a mild rebuke from Cassie: 'Where d'you think you're going with no bell on your bike?' to quell my cravings.

When my cowardly hands had surrendered their hard-won advantage and I had resumed my role as disinterested friend or bored voluptuary, she would close the book and say:

'I doubt they teach you more than your manners at school, Master Sly-boots, judging by your old-fashioned habits.'

The truth was, the stakes were too high. It meant risking my present small but certain happiness for the possibility of becoming a figure of distinction among the braggarts of the school jakes. And so, content enough with short rations, I made do with the small coinage of love – the strokings and nuzzlings and sudden casual pounces of affection that sent me reeling to bed when Aunt Mary called me.

Every night the call seemed to come earlier and from a lower step so that I kept my ears cocked for the creaking stair that would be the last warning of her approach.

Before I left for bed Cassie always said something like:

'Give the bronco-buster my love.'

73

Or:

'Tell Romeo that he has me put to loss with his attentions.'
Always I replied:

'Fat lot of use that would be! All Willie cares about is the pony. And his old mother, of course.'

*   *   *

The coming of the policeman with the census papers changed the routine of our ways. He stood for a solid hour talking to Cassie at the kitchen door – a tall young fellow, smiling and very sure of himself, hardly bothering to use the sheaf of census papers as an excuse.

That night, instead of giving me a message for Willie before I left the kitchen, Cassie said:

'What d'you think of Herbie?'

'Herbie who?' I said.

'Herbie Gibson, of course, the fellow doing the census.'

'Is it that peeler you were gassing to at the door? You weren't long worming the christian name out of him!'

'I could hardly call him "Constable Gibson" and him mad to square me for a date.'

'Do you mean to say he was trying to date you up and you only after meeting him?'

'He has me asked out for the morrow night. D'you think should I chance my arm and go out with him?'

'Well, if you are badly in need of exercise, a night on police patrol might limber you up.'

'Quit the codding Jimmie and pay attention!'

She was leaning towards me, scowling with the effort cf concentration.

'Do you know what it is?' she said, speaking very fast. 'I'll go clean daft if I have to stay any longer cooped up in here every night. Sitting waiting for your friend, Willie, to pluck up the courage to ask me out. If I don't make a move very shortly I'll find myself sitting on the shelf.'

She paused for breath.

74

'If I went out with Herbie a couple of nights,' she went on, 'do you think would it put the skids under Willie? There must be some way to get him out of his pooshey habits.'

My mouth was so dry I could not answer at once. Eventually I managed to say in a breathless croak:

'Willie is so taken up . . . breaking in the pony . . . that he'll never notice . . . that you're gone. Or who you're gone with.'

'Oh, it will come to his notice all right. Trust that scheming old mother of his to nose it out and dish it up to him for breakfast, dinner and tea.'

'But isn't that what you want?'

'Och, you don't understand. What really matters is *who* he hears it from.'

She eyed me with the steady, tilted gaze of a bird.

'Now if *you* were to tell him it would be different,' she said. 'You could give it the right twist.'

'There would be no need of any of this hunker-sliding if you were to give that Herbie guy the brush-off.'

'But maybe I want to go out with him. After all he is a bit more exciting than cagey Willie. What do you think, Jimmie? Will I chance it?'

I tried to moisten my lips with the strip of linoleum that was once my tongue. When I spoke I found myself gobbling with rage.

'Little-heed-you'll-pay-to-any-advice-you-get.' I drew breath. 'You'll just do what suits your sweet self.' I managed to break off without adding: 'No matter who it hurts.'

Cassie flung her arms round me, murmuring:

'Is Mummy's darling feeling cranky? Perhaps sugar plum has wind in his poor wee tum-tum?'

She commenced to pat my back and make clucking noises. Aunt Mary's call saved me from further indignity. I broke free. As I started up the stairs, she put her head round the kitchen door.

'Psst!' she beckoned urgently. I leaned over the banisters. 'Don't forget to tell Willie my side of the story.'

For the next three days Willie had me deeved with

enquiries about Cassie: 'What sudden notion has she taken to go walking into the village every night?' 'Could it be she's fashed about something?' 'Maybe it's because the pony won't take to her?' On the fourth day he heard the news.

I was helping Willie clean out the byre when Mrs Nesbitt came to the door. She stood watching us in silence, a humpy old witch, with crying red eyes and long grey hairs straggling over lips and chin, mumbling away at her toothless gums like a horse munching hay. At last she piped up:

'Postman's been!'

Willie ignored her and went on with the work.

'Letter from your sister. Four pages of excuses for not sending home any money. She was aye one for putting on the poor mouth.'

Willie grunted.

'Postman says he saw your friend Miss Fly-by-night walking the road with a polisman. I'll hould you it was the young blade was round with the tally sheets. He was chatting her for the best part of an hour the day he was here.'

Stupidly Willie stared at her, the dung-laden sprong, lifted to waist level, shedding its load unheeded.

Mrs Nesbitt went on:

'These mountainy young ones are woeful easy carried away. I dare swear nothing less than a uniform will do her now. She'll be too big in her boots for the like of a small farmer any more.'

She waited, munching furiously. Willie screwed up his eyes as if he had stared too long at the sun.

'They say in the village,' she continued 'that thon young polisman is the right blackguard. Does nothing from dawn to dusk but follow women. He's put down for poling Martha Fleming, yon sappy creature from the Crooked Bridge that finished up in the Mental Office. It's to be feared she's not the only silly young goose that'll be forced to hatch out that young fellow's goslings.'

She turned back to the house. Willie spat on his hands and commenced forking dung furiously.

'We'll start ringing Sheba this evening,' he said.

For the next fortnight he worked on the pony for a couple of hours every night. He would start Sheba up the strand. After a hundred yards or so he would put the pressure on one rein. Gently: steadily: he coaxed the pony until he had her wheeling around full circle, with himself as hub. Pivoting so that he always faced her, he signalled his instructions, calling or chirping, getting his results with an economy of effort that never failed to thrill me. A spell of walking, cantering, trotting, all in the same direction and he straightened out the mare once more. Again he gradually eased her round till he was ringing her in the opposite direction. Behind us we left a string of ploughed up circles for the incoming tide to wash away.

During all this time Cassie never appeared. Each evening after tea she would slip off up the road in the direction of the village. I have no idea what time she sneaked back. There was never anyone in the kitchen when I collected Aunt Mary's supper tray.

When I tried to speak to her betwen meals, she kept dashing about, plunging from kitchen to pantry, scullery to wash-house, banging saucepans, clattering delph, running taps – a picture of dedicated industry marred only by the all-too-frequent pause – standing perhaps over the scullery sink, plate in one hand, dripping cloth in the other, staring into the distance, the corners of her mouth quirked up in the beginnings of a smile, whether in recollection or anticipation I never waited to find out.

Meanwhile Willie, hurt at Cassie's continued absence, no longer ringed the pony within sight of the entrance to the strand as he had done the first days she stayed away. Instead he took Sheba to the Long Strand, a deserted beach a good mile round the point.

Here, with no sound but the soft padding of hoofs, the occasional ring of metal as the pony shook the bridle, the gasping of wavelets as they collapsed in exhaustion on the sand, Sheba circled the pair of us.

Her madly heraldic appearance as she paced around with determined thrusting head and high-stepping hoofs, her cream and gold skin gleaming like porcelain, the furious sweep of her long tail lashing her fly-tormented flanks: all these things combined to lull me into a speechless stupor. Willie too must have been affected the same way, for only when he had Sheba straightened out between rings did he speak. Bitter complaining talk.

'She's a lazy lump, that one,' he would say of his mother. 'Scrooging over the fire all day, with her muzzle cocked into the heat like a crippled old hound. Wouldn't rise off her hip to get you a sup of tea. A man has a poor time in a house the like of that I can tell you. There's no fear of him bursting his breeches with the burden of food he'll have to contend with. And to crown and complete all, there she is the day long, sitting in the corner chawing and champing at her gums till it would put you mad with the hunger looking at her.'

Or he would start giving off about the police, never singling out any particular officer.

'They are a nosey lot of boys, those. Aye sniffing around after something. If it's not tail-lights on bicycles or the lack of a dog licence, it's the poaching. Plowtering along the brew of the river at all times of the day or night. You'd wonder what they expect to find when you would hear the clatter of them a mile away. Cute hawks, too. Catch one of them jokers marrying a girl in service. Not likely. It's a school-teacher or someone the like of that they want, with a job and a bit of money in the Bank. You'd wonder the young cuddies haven't them taped long since.'

Never once did he mention Cassie.

He did not take out his bitterness on the pony. In fact he was even more gentle and tolerant with her. It seemed to me he had come to rely on Sheba's affection as a prop for his tottering self-esteem. Each day at the paddock gate the pony's boisterous welcome, once a casually accepted tribute, became a more and more necessary demonstration of love and loyalty, and her ready obedience – a proof of devotion, not of intelligence. Perhaps that was how it was for, though Sheba refused to work for me, in less than three weeks schooling Willie had her weaving from side to side at the

78

slightest pressure of the reins and obeying his reiterated: 'Back up there, girl!' without ever squinting round in distrust.

At last a day came when Willie was able to announce:

'It's time the mare was put hauling. She is well enough mouthed by now. We'll try her out in the paddock this afternoon when I get back from stripping the snares I set last night up at the shooting lodge.'

'Why the paddock?' I asked.

'The strand is too heavy going. She might only lose heart,' he said.

I was so excited I rushed off at once to tell Cassie. She was in the kitchen making an apple pie for the dinner. I stood watching the deft hands knead and roll out the pastry on the bake-board. Her sleeves were pushed up, her bare arms dusted with flour so that the fine hair stood up in a white fuzz.

She looked round.

'Has the cat run away with your tongue?' she said. 'I thought by the way you rushed in here that you were bursting with news.'

Face flushed and beaded with perspiration from the heat of the kitchen, she stared at me. I could feel the blood swishing round my head, thudding in my ears like the plunger of a churn. I ran an arid tongue round my mouth.

'You should come to the paddock this afternoon,' I said. 'Willie is going to try the pony out hauling.'

She turned back to the bake-board, lifted the flattened pastry and draped it over the apple-filled dish like you'd spread out a wet bathing suit to dry on the rocks.

'What's wrong with Willie Nesbitt delivering his own invites?' she said. 'He has not spoken a civil word to me these two weeks.'

With a knife she trimmed the fringe of hanging pastry, shaped it into narrow strips, and set about decorating the pie-top.

'Willie did not send me,' I said. 'I just thought you would like to see Sheba working, now she is properly broken in. You used to like watching once . . . before you . . .'

Cassie lifted the pie-dish and brushed past me to the range. I waited for the clang of the oven door shutting.

'Well,' I said. 'Seeing that you helped to train Sheba –'

Cassie laughed.

'Who do you think you're codding?' she said. 'Sure the pony never paid a bit heed to me.'

'You will come anyway, won't you Cassie?'

Behind me I heard her move. Her bare arms, warm and sweet-smelling, were wound round my neck. She whispered, her lips tickling my ear:

'I'm sorry, Jimmie. I won't be able. It's my afternoon off. I have to go into the village to do a bit of shopping.'

'Honestly,' she added.

I broke free from the coaxing arms.

'I may get back in time,' she called after me.

'Back in time!' I shouted before I slammed the kitchen door. 'That will be the day to go down in history.'

*   *   *

Dinner over, I went down to the beach. The tide was far out, the sand mucked up with dead jellyfish. I gave up the idea of bathing, climbed a dune overlooking the paddock and scraped out a cool trough for myself in the roasting sand.

It was the hottest day of the summer. Oily whorls of heat, swaying and twisting like tendrils of seaweed, reared up from the baked ground. Everything you looked at shivered as if reflected in rippling water.

Below in the paddock Sheba stood listlessly, head drooping, tail swishing feebly. An old sheep-dog of Willie's cowered under a farm cart, tail and lolling tongue flat to the ground. Belly deep in the tide, a trio of wretched bullocks faced out to sea, cudgelled to exhaustion by the drover-blows of the sun. The sea, flat and milk-white tracked by a stretch of leaping sparks as though swept by the flames of a welding lamp. A world of torpor.

Yet I had but to close my eyes and all was seething, clamorous life. Overhead a plague of larks with their shrill, interminable monologues. Sea birds screeching, wailing, moaning. A solitary corn-crake clearing its throat monotonously. In the background a throbbing drone of insects.

Sleepily I lay, chin knuckle-propped, soaking up the warmth. I watched Cassie, fresh and cool in a lemon frock, set off up the road to the village, breaking into little spurts of running like a wagtail and later I kept my blinking sunsodden eyes open long enough to see Willie start off across the sandhills, fresh snare wire coiled round his neck, a bunch of rabbit traps slung from one shoulder.

I woke up dazed with the sun and made off for the shelter of the house. From room to room I prowled, opening doors and cupboards, leafing through family photograph albums of trapped and glaring relatives, reading old letters that told, in the same scrupulous fashion, of weather or holidays: sickness or death. I read the titles of the sober leather-bound volumes in the bookcase: shook, without much hope, the locked drawer of my aunt's writing-desk: examined the hall-marks on silver, the pottery marks on china. I took a swig of sherry from the opened bottle in the liquor cabinet.

There remained one room I had never yet rummaged. Taking off my sandals, I started up the stairs, taking them in quick rushes of three or four steps at a time, being careful to avoid treading on the creaking ones. Cassie's room was at the end of the corridor, beyond the closed door of my aunt's room. To reach it I had to negotiate a stretch of loose floor-boards, one so noisy that the cat used to flinch when it padded over it.

I stuck close to the wall, balancing against it with my finger tips, trying to creep along as close to the skirting-boards as possible. I went flat-footed, placing the advancing foot down gently, slowly easing the body weight onto it, ready to shift back to the other foot at the slightest sound.

Teeth clenched, breath held in, I sidled past Aunt Mary's room, taking advantage of every cough or rattling bedspring that would cover the sound of my progress.

At Cassie's door, I gripped the handle with both hands

and turned it very, very gently till it would move no further, all the time pulling the door towards me so that the latch could move soundlessly.

At last I pushed inwards. The door gave. It was unlocked.

The curtains were drawn back from the open window: sunlight and the tang of seaweed filled the room. An iron bed, a chair, a table with ewer and wash-basin, a curtained alcove: that was the extent of the furnishings. Yet nothing was left lying around. A line of shoes were arranged neatly under the wash-stand, whose four corners held, like rooks on a chess-board, a covered soap-dish, a glass containing tooth-paste and brush, a plastic hair-brush and comb, both scrupulously clean, a folded face-cloth with the nail-brush placed in the exact centre. A suit-case was pushed under the bed.

Quietly I slid it out. It too was unlocked.

There was just time enough to note the neatly folded under-clothes and the transparent plastic bag with its meagre reserve of rolled-up nylon stockings before my aunt's voice put an end to my ferret-work.

'Cassie!' she called. 'Is that you?'

Under cover of her repeated calls, I pushed back the suit-case, scuttled out of the room leaving the door ajar and padded to the head of the stairs, where I faced down and cried:

'Commmm-ing!'

I dragged the word up from the back of my throat and tried to make it sound as if it was rising from the staircase well.

Waiting a few seconds, I marched up the corridor, burst open my aunt's door and poked my head into the room.

'Were you calling?' I said.

The huge darkened room, with its high canopied bed and littered furnishings seemed close and oppressive after the bright austerity of Cassie's room.

'Oh, is that you, Jim!' she said. 'I thought Cassie was back. I could have sworn I heard her moving about in her room.'

She was sitting up in bed, pillow-propped, a green bed-jacket draped round her shoulders. Her hair, that I had discovered to be really bronze, was fluffed out madly over the pillows and she stared at me with such wide-eyed tragic intensity that I had to restrain an impulse to pull away the pillows and let her roll stiffly back with rattling eyeballs clicking shut and chest bleating: 'Maaa-maaa!'

'Darling,' she said. 'Would you mind terribly bringing me up a glass of milk? My throat is parched.'

I must have moved into the room slightly for she suddenly said:

'What is the idea of the bare feet? Were you snooping around again?'

'The sandals were hurting me,' I said, making off as quick as I could.

I was worried. Aunt Mary was as cute as a cut cat and I did not relish the way she said: 'Again.' Going downstairs I tried to figure out a way to distract the probing I was almost certain to get.

The inspiration came to me as I was buckling on my sandals in the hall. Aunt Mary was due the special treatment reserved for visitors. So when I returned to her room I carried a tray containing the sherry bottle, a wine-glass and a plate of digestive biscuits.

'They say a change is as good as a rest,' I said, edging out space for the tray amongst the jars and bottles on the bedside table.

'Our science master,' I said, 'is always preaching that nature intended cow's milk for calves.'

Aunt Mary was transformed. She was suddenly young and pretty, the lines of fret and worry swallowed up by a cheeky school-girl grin. She said:

'I am not a science teacher but I know it reflects on the quality of one's hospitality if a guest must sup alone. Run down darling, and bring up another glass.'

So I found myself sitting on the edge of the bed, sipping sherry and munching biscuits, whilst my aunt chattered on and on about her school-days, dreamily at first but soon with increasing bitterness and I watched her grow old again and the edge creep into her voice and I wondered could I get away before she started reefing me.

I was just getting to my feet when she said:

'How often must I tell you, Jim, that you should not sit on the edge of a bed.'

I eased myself up, trying to ignore the peevish protest of the mattress.

'You know perfectly well it is bad for the springs. You could even damage the base. I'm always warning Cassie about that.'

Here we go, I thought. Next stop – Paul Pryland.

'And when we are on that subject,' she continued, 'I would be thankful if you would spend less of your time in the kitchen. You have been haunting it ever since Cassie came.'

I smother a sigh of relief. As Willie would put it – better bad than worse. Aunt Mary had spat up a bone that must have been stuck in her throat these many weeks past. I said:

'I don't know when I was talking to Cassie last. She has been out every night for the past three weeks. God knows where she goes to!'

What matter how many roosters I put crowing by my denials. It was a case of: 'Man mind thyself, woman do thou likewise.' And Cassie was well able to do that.

Aunt Mary was off again:

'Too much familiarity – that is how the best of maids are spoiled. They must be taught to keep their distance. Be polite and considerate to them, of course, but beyond that –'

She eyed me significantly.

'Yes, Aunt Mary,' I said civilly, wondering to myself what hare she was trying to rise.

'It is a bad thing for two persons of very different states of life to become over-friendly. It leads inevitably to the moral corruption of one or the other.'

Well! Well! So I was caught at last. Aunt Mary had unmasked the irresistible seducer who was preying on the kitchen staff. Corrupting an innocent country girl with hardly enough sense to come in out of the rain. What a pity it was not true! Still no one could accuse me of not trying. I shut my eyes tightly, not to avoid my aunt's accusing gaze but to close out the shameful picture of my defeat and disgrace.

My aunt's voice went on relentlessly:

'You know perfectly well that while you are in this house I am responsible to your mother for your moral welfare. What *are* you making silly monkey faces about?' She belched gently.

'Excuse me!' she said.

'It must be the sherry wine,' I said, opening my eyes. 'I feel dizzy.'

She was dabbing her mouth daintily with the edge of the sheet.

'I am not going to allow you – Oh, thank you!' she said, as I heeled up the bottle into her waiting glass. 'I cannot allow you to be demoralised by a shameless chit of a girl from the wilds of Donegal.'

I could hardly believe my ears. Here was I after wearing myself out trying to debauch my aunt's maid, being held up as a model of christian virtue and decorum, whilst Cassie –

'Aunt Mary,' I said. 'You have got Cassie figured out all wrong.'

My speech seemed curiously thick. I tried to scrape away with my tongue the biscuit grit clogging my mouth.

'She is no piece of cake, believe you me –'

This was not what I meant to say at all. I started again:

'She is the sort of girl –'

How could I ever civilise the scurrilous language used at school to describe a tease who manages to remain an unrepentant virgin.

'She's . . . She's . . . '

I gave up.

Aunt Mary was watching me, her face gone all mushy and wet-eyed.

'You are a good boy, Jim,' she said. 'A loyal honourable boy,' She belched again – without apology. 'But I am afraid we may have to send Miss Cassie back to her native haunts if she does not mend her ways.'

'Listen, Aunt Mary. I'm trying to tell you –'

What was I trying to tell her anyway? That by a system of trial and error I had proved Cassie to be a modest virtuous girl, worthy of respect and capable of exercising the franchise in a manner befitting her station in life? That I was a clumsy, bungling operator, unlikely to bring to ruin the silliest, most susceptible pinhead of a kitchen maid? Or that –

'You could not do it!' I burst out. 'You could not possibly kick Cassie out just because the two of us were civil to each other?'

Aunt Mary's eyebrows rose.

'If I have to let Cassie go,' she said, 'it will be because I consider her unsuited for the job.'

'Morally unsuited,' she said.

This groundless accusation had to be rebutted.

'Aunt Mary,' I said. 'Cassie is a good girl, as straight as a die.'

I squirmed at the pompous words, so like a grudging testimonial. Surely I could do better.

'A finer girl you could not meet. Not if you were to scour the country from end to end.'

Insincerity oozed from this declaration. What could I say that would have the bite of truth?

'If you sack Cassie on my account, I'll not stay a day in the house after she goes.'

Unmoved at my ultimatum, Aunt Mary put her empty glass back on the tray and commenced picking biscuit crumbs from the sheet. Without looking up she said:

'You must, of course, do as you see fit, Jim. But I think you are carrying loyalty a little too far.'

She was now picking crumbs from inside the neck of her night-dress. She so resembled an industrious monkey, crouched in concentration in a corner of its cage that I could not help giggling. Glancing up she caught my eye. Immediately we were both gathered up in helpless laughter; though what Aunt Mary was laughing at, God alone knows. We hooted and shrieked and wheezed. We swayed to and fro with shaking shoulders. In a frenzy of delight we pointed at each other's face, twisted up and streaming with tears. Doubled up in pain we clutched our aching sides.

Each time I tried to stop, Aunt went rooting around after another crumb, starting me off again worse than ever.

At length Aunt Mary managed to gasp out, between fits of coughing:

'You'll be the death . . . of your poor old Auntie . . . with your crazy fooling.' She pointed to the tray. 'Take down those things and put them away. And don't forget to wash the glasses!'

I stood looking down at her, unable to muster the energy – or perhaps the courage – to take up once more my defence of Cassie. I picked up the tray.

'You do not have to stay cooped up in the house just because of me, darling,' my aunt said, as I moved to the door.

*   *   *

It was now late afternoon. When I went outside my eyes winced at the glare of the sun. The heat and clamour of the day seemed intensified, the high-pitched raucous sounds of summer drilling into my skull. I started to walk towards the paddock, dragging my sandals on the dusty ground, too uncaring to shake out the pebbles that gathered under toes and heels.

To my surprise Willie was working at an old sawn-off tree-stump that lay smothered in rank grass and weeds in a corner of the paddock.

'You're back early,' I said.

He did not look up.

'So 'twould seem,' he said, the words sizzling like tobacco spits landing in the heart of a turf fire. 'Gimme a hand with this.'

He had wound one end of a long chain round the crutch of the V-shaped log. I strained against the timber arms whilst he tightened a running noose on the chain.

'That'll hold well enough now,' he said, still in the same sour tone. 'We'll try Sheba out hauling this old baulk of timber.'

He picked out the swingle-tree from the harness heaped nearby, hooked it up to the end of the chain and placed it carefully on the ground so that the chain was at full stretch.

'Now!' he said straightening up and putting his fingers to his mouth. At once Sheba, grazing in pretended indifference at the far end of the paddock, flung up her head.

Willie ignored her. Rooting among the harness, he lifted the bridle and shook it violently as though rattling a tambourine. At the jangling of the metal bit, the pony's ears pricked up. She pawed the ground with a fore-foot.

When the shrill whistle came at last, Willie was nearly knocked over by the butting, nuzzling, impatient animal. His face was wet with slobber but the sour look had gone from it. He rubbed his cheek against the pouting muzzle. I heard him mutter:

'A body would fare better sticking to his friends. Wouldn't he, girl?'

Without fuss or bother he slipped on the bridle, forced the bit into the pony's mouth, pulled the head-strap over her ears, tightened up the throat-band.

'How many rabbits did you get?' I asked.

'Hold her by the bridle now,' he said, 'and don't let her stamp on my corns.'

With that surly voice, it was a walking certainty that the fox had beaten him to the snares.

'I saw a flight of mallard yesterday up at the wee lake,' I said. 'Did you see any sign of them?'

Gripping the bridle-strap, I steadied the pony's head while Willie fitted and strapped on collar and hames. He worked smoothly and swiftly.

'Did you rise any game at all?' I persisted.

He was now tying the rope reins.

'A brace,' he said.

'Pity you hadn't the gun with you. You might have got a shot at them.'

He broke off threading the rope-end through the metal ring on the hames. He looked at me over the mare's neck.

'They were sitting targets,' he said. 'It wouldn't have been right to shoot them.'

'Sitting targets?' I repeated.

'Aye,' he said. 'A brace of love-birds.' He spoke quite softly, in a voice loaded with bitterness.

'Where did you come on them?' I asked. Right well I knew what he was driving at.

'Bring over the back-band and the traces while I finish off this job,' he said.

When I came back, the reins were neatly coiled over the peak of the hames. I watched whilst he slipped the narrow leather back-band over the pony's back, working it to and fro till he was satisfied with its position.

'Where were they?' I demanded.

Sheba started stamping impatiently with a hind-hoof.

'Get up to the mare's head,' he said. 'D'you want her to make a shambles of my feet?'

I went back to holding the pony's bridle but my imagination was ranging the length and breadth of the district.

'Were they in the hunting lodge?' I whispered.

Willie had picked up the traces. Quickly he moved round the pony, clipping the chain-rings to the hooks on hames and back-band. He did not answer till he was back at the far side of the mare, with the traces hooked up in readiness for hauling. Once more he faced me over the neck of the horse.

'Where else but in yon derelict hut would they get cover for their dirty capers?' he said. He was staring at me blindly, his eyes busy on their work of reconstruction.

'I heard the noise and me passing the hut and I pushed back the shutter a piece to see what it was. There they were, as God is my judge, lying out full stretch with nothing between them and the floor-boards but a length of dirty old sail cloth. Not a stitch of clothes on the pair of them, no more than on the shameless heathen, coupling like animals in the jungles of Africa. I tell you ... '

Willie's disclosure came like a blow in the stomach, leaving me breathless, sickened, numb. I broke in on his tirade:

'If you only got a glimpse of them passing the window, you might very easily be mistaken.'

'There was no mistake about it. Amn't I telling you I stood at the window looking in at them.'

'But sure they must have seen you?'

'They were too busy with their wicked antics to bother about me.'

I tried one last question. A forlorn hope.

'How are you so sure it was Cassie?'

'Wouldn't I know her yellow dress a mile away? And the policeman's tunic flung across the stern of the old duck-boat? Yon man's only half-human, that's what he is. With a mane of hair as thick as a badger's running down the small of his back. He would put you in mind of a stinking old conger squirming about in the bottom of the boat, trying to jook every belt you make at him with the butt of the tiller before you'd give him the sea-bed.'

The vision this evoked was too horrifying to credit. I let go of the bridle and stood back.

'Look here, Willie Nesbitt,' I said. 'It's a bloody shame telling this vicious pack of lies about Cassie. She's a stranger here with no one to stand up for her. You are only making up this lousy rotten story to get your own back on her because she would not go out with you.'

'I'm not saying a word against . . . ' He scratched his head in agitation. He began again: 'You've had no truck with girls. You don't understand these things.'

He shook his head violently as though trying, like Sheba, to dislodge the cloud of flies now swarming about us. The pony – ears gesticulating madly, mane and tail in constant furious motion, her flanks a crawling, twitching focus of activity – had now taken to stamping indignant hooves in her efforts to dispel her tormentors.

'The flies are driving her frantic.' I said. 'Would you not be better to wait till the cool of the evening?'

'The midgets will only be starting about proper then,' said Willie. 'Hold her steady till I yoke her to the swingle.'

He carried the traces back and harnessed them to either end of the swingle-tree making sure that each chain was of equal length. Moving up to the pony's head, he gathered up the reins.

'Get away back to the swingle,' he said. 'Start hauling on it and come with the mare as I ease her forward. Don't let go of the bar till the slack of the chain is taken up. That way there will be no jerk when she gets the pull of the log.'

I picked up the swingle-tree, moved back till the traces were clear of the ground and lay back in the dangling chains.

'Right you be!' I called.

Willie chirped.

'Get up, Sheba!' he coaxed. 'Get up, pony!'

The traces tautened. I began to shuffle forward, lying back on the wooden bar like a surf-rider. It was easy to imagine that I and not Willie was in charge of this sleek, unpredictable force.

'Give a shout when the chain leaves the ground,' Willie called back.

I watched the dwindling slack till the last loop uncoiled. When the chain straightened out and commenced to lift from the ground, I called:

'Easy now! Take it easy, Willie!'

As the log began to take the strain I released the bar and stood back. The pony jibbed at the extra pull of the lifting tree-stump.

'Quiet now, girl!' said Willie, patting her neck soothingly. 'I think we'll leave you standing a wee minute.'

We waited, Willie and I, while Sheba shifted about uneasily, the chain dipping and rising with each movement, but never quite reaching the ground. Willie, the reins held slackly, was staring at the swaying chain, his brows drawn down in a frown of concentration. When he spoke, it was in a droning voice with as much meaning to it as the tiresome buzz of the flies still swarming around us.

'What would take you to the fair,' he said, 'is the way a decent modest girl could make such a disgrace of herself. To be found stretched out in your pelt on the floor of an old deserted hut and it littered with every class of slaughtering accoutrement from harpoon to punt-gun and an array of decoy ducks ringed round you like a squad of Peeping Toms and you in the company of a black-avised Judas the like of yon –' He shook his head slowly. 'It's beyond the beyonds.'

He brushed away a fly that had settled on his nose.

'Women are the rare oddities too,' he continued. 'In the midst of all the turmoil, hadn't she readied up her clothes and shoes. Laid out neatly they were – as if she were going to bed in her own room.'

He dug deeply into one ear with his finger.

'As if she was going to her bed,' he repeated in a puzzled voice. 'In her own room.'

I fixed my gaze on the chimney ledge of my aunt's house and tried to concentrate, to the exclusion of all else, on a crow waddling back and forth as if on patrol duty. It was a seedy bird with balding head and plumage dusty, frayed and ill-fitting. Its ungainly body was mounted on feet as large and flat as any station sergeant's. At each end of its beat it halted and twisted its beak rapidly to either side, the victim of a lifetime of suspicion.

When it had made certain the coast was clear, it hopped up on the centre chimney pot, its wings tucked tight to its sides, as though it had thumbs hooked in the breast pockets of a uniform. There it perched, gazing down the shaft, its head swivelling around so that each eye in turn could survey its depth.

The side-cocked head had a knowing look that told of a chimney worth investigating. Whose room, I wondered, did it lead down to? Perhaps to Cassie's bedroom. I remembered the shoes stowed away under the wash-stand. If there had been a fireplace in the room Cassie would certainly have her shoes neatly arranged along the bar of the fender. Just as her clothes would be folded away tidily, no matter what the circumstances.

The grotesque scene described by Willie unrolled itself before my eyes. The derelict hut, its hinged shutter ajar. A space in the centre of the floor cleared of litter and covered with sail cloth, round which squatted rows of wooden ducks, their painted plumage dull and faded, their round incurious eyes fixed on the neatly piled garments and on the two figures . . .

For the second time that day I was forced to squeeze my eyes tight shut on something I could not face.

It was at this moment we heard the footsteps coming up the road and the gay chatter, broken by bursts of laughter. We waited motionless, watching where the road curved inland and disappeared towards the village.

Round the corner they came; the tall rangy policeman stepping it out, uniform cap pushed back from his forehead, tunic slung over one shoulder, shirt sleeves rolled beyond the elbows; beside him Cassie, clinging with clasped hands to the crook of his arm, skipping and dancing like a school-girl. You had only to look at her as she snuggled against him, wriggling with happiness and staring up at him with admiring gaze to realise that Willie's story was true. It was easy to picture her, with swollen lips and eyes as black and glittering and sightless as they were that first night in the kitchen, yawning and stretching herself as she padded across the floor of the hut to the little heap of neatly folded clothes.

Squirming with disgust, I considered the full extent of my humiliation. Night after night I had cringed after her, grateful for the casual caress you would give without thought to a fawning nuisance of a dog. I had swallowed rebuff and ridicule that only gawky ignorance could have stomached. My projected epic of a debauch so sumptuous, so gross, as to merit narration in the school bogs, had shrunk, under Cassie's scorn, to the capers of an unfluffed kid from prep-school.

Cassie was the first to speak when they stopped at the paddock gate.

'Hullo, boys!' she called across. 'How's the work coming on?'

'Don't you see they are hard at it?' Constable Gibson said.

Willie ignored them. He beckoned me up, gave me the reins and went round methodically testing the straps on both collar and hames, checking on the traces where they hooked to hames and swingle-bar, tugging at the chain fastened to the tree-stump.

'We'll haul,' he said taking the reins back.

He chirped.

'Get up, Sheba! Get up there!' he said.

The pony moved forward till she felt the pull of the timber. She jibbed again.

'Easy now, Cassie! Easy, girl!' he said.

Gibson laughed, a piercing cackle that put Sheba's ears pricking.

'Did you hear that, Cassie?' he said. 'You never told me he calls the four-footed friend after you.'

'Behave yourself, Herbie!' she said.

Willie's face reddened. He rested Sheba for a few minutes before urging her on again.

'Get up, girl! That's a good lass,' he coaxed softly, chirping encouragement.

Still Sheba jibbed.

'Maybe a stick of dynamite would shift her,' Gibson jeered.

Willie flinched. And no wonder. The river had been dynamited in the early spring and the police were said to be still trying to pin the crime on some of the habitual poachers.

Ignoring Cassie's timid appeals, Gibson kept up his teasing, apparently intent on riling Willie:

'Crank her up, you boy you. Her battery's down.'

'You've left her standing too long. Will we give her a push?'

'Och, sink her in a bog-hole and buy a tractor.'

Willie was getting flustered. His voice was louder – wheedling, urging, abusing. His hand was heavy on the reins, jerking roughly where once the merest twitch had sufficed. His movements – always slow, cautious, knowledgeable – had become fussy and agitated.

Sheba, infected with his uneasiness, was turning sour – sidling and backing to avoid the pull of the traces, jigging peevishly from side to side, tossing her head violently in her efforts to escape control. Nothing would persuade her to haul. In fact Willie was put to the pin of his collar stopping her from backing into and fouling traces, chain and swingle-bar.

I was so immersed in the duel that the sudden shrill whistle gave me the same jolt as it did Willie and the mare. Sheba swung round, head up, ears cocked, gazing expectantly at the grinning malicious face of Gibson, who was slouched over the gate, fingers still dragging at his lower lip. Willie, pale with rage, jerked on the reins, striving to pull the mare's unwilling head around. Sheba resisted stubbornly.

I heard Cassie say:

'Stop it Herbie! You'll only frighten the mare.'

Gibson laughed.

'Hey there, Useless!' he called. And whistled again.

Hesitantly Sheba moved towards the beckoning sound. At once Willie wrenched back her head. Shortening his grip on the reins, he hauled her forward till chain and traces were at full stretch again.

The pony stood trembling. A lather of foam fringed her mouth. Sweat darkened her neck and flanks. Her ears were laid back. Her eyes rolled in their sockets with terror and shock.

Willie was breathing heavily. He shook the reins.

'Get up there!' he shouted, his voice hoarse with fury.

Sheba did not move. Her ears were still flattened. Her eyes slanted back at the threatening figure with the unfamiliar voice.

Willie's free hand came up with the slack of the reins. He moved in closer to the mare.

'You stubborn bitch!' he whispered, staring across Sheba's back at the paddock gate. 'You silly, stubborn, betraying bitch!'

He brought the rope reins down smartly on her flank.

'Up –'

Sheba, plunging forward, seemed to pluck the word from his mouth at the same instant as she ripped the reins from his unwary hands.

What happened next had the remote ineluctable quality

95

of a nightmare, where spectator and participant are one, and screams of warning are as soundless as the cotton wool that must be floundered through.

Helplessly I stood watching the pony gather speed. Willie ran a few crouching steps beside her, groping wildly for the whirling reins, regardless of the charging tree-stump behind him.

It was his undoing. The bouncing twisting timber caught up with him, dealing him a swinging blow on the legs that sent him staggering forward in a sprawled-out heap. The impact caused the pony to swerve: it did not check her panic-stricken flight.

There was a nightmare logic about Sheba's flight that absolved me from intervention. I should have shouted a warning to Willie. Perhaps I even did – a soundless nightmare scream, part of the cotton wool silence through which the bolting pony fled.

Gibson's hyena laugh unmuffled the sound of snorting breath, of thudding hooves, of rattling trace chains.

'Oh-Oh-Oh! Sweet suffering saviour, did you ever in all your born life see the beat of that?' He indicated, with wagging finger the sprawling form of Willie.

'Behold the decline and fall of Buffalo Bill, the wonder horseman of the Pony Express!'

'If you don't stir yourself Nesbitt, your pony will be half-way back to the prairies of America,' he said.

By this time Sheba was stretched out in full gallop, mane and tail fanned out in splendour, a creature grown to twice her span by the speed of her going, flying hooves and threshing timber butt drumming the ground.

She was making straight for the paddock fence, a chest high construction, formed of three strands of rusty bull-wire, spliced and sundered and spliced again, attached to wooden paling posts so old and decrepit that some, freed by decay from their roots in the ground now hung between heaven and earth, like so many tethered souls condemned to the windy wastes of purgatory.

'She's going to tackle the fence!' Gibson shouted. 'Go on,

you girl you! Nesbitt never reared a jibber! Becher's Brook itself would hardly daunt you!'

There was a sound of cracking timber, snapping wire, flailing hooves.

Gibson said:

'Well, the curse of God on you for a thick, ignorant cowardly Clydesdale. Baulking at a couple of feet of fencing. Trying to barge through it like a bloody bullock. I tell you if I was near you I'd rise you over it with a boot to your backside.'

Mashed against the wire by the tree stump, the pony squealed with rage and fear, rearing itself up in its efforts to free itself from the wire.

'You've made a right pig's diddy of that job, Nesbitt. Look at the cut of that silly get wrapped up in bull-wire like a Christmas parcel. The man that told you you could school horses should get his head examined.'

Willie was squatted on the grass, arms clasping one leg, his face – twisted in pain – pressed against the knees of his blood-soaked pants.

A tearing, splintering clatter. Once more the sound of thudding hooves. The spliced wire of the fence had unravelled and the mare was through, scattering wide a skein of twisted fencing.

Off she galloped, dragging after her, besides the bouncing tree-stump, a length of severed fencing that had somehow got entangled in the tackle and now stretched out, writhing, jerking, flapping: a kite's tail of bull-wire and uprooted paling-posts.

'Holy jumping Jeezus!' Gibson screeched. 'Give me a mouthful of air before I choke myself!' He was wheezing and coughing, one hand held over his mouth, the other smacking his thigh.

'Do you know what it is, Nesbitt ... You'd only want ... a band of yodelling Indians ... a bloody stage-coach ... and that rusty old shotgun of yours ... to make your bucking fortune in the pictures ...'

He drew in a deep whistling breath. Pointing a finger he said:

'Would you take one look at yon careering creature and admit like a man that she'll never stand between shafts.'

Willie was scrambling slowly to his feet, watching with dazed eyes the progress of the pony as it headed into the sandhills, trailing after it the absurd string of leaping paling-posts.

Fouled by some obstacle, the timber hulk shot high in the air, snapping free the chain that linked it to the swingle-tree and carrying with it the length of fencing. By the time the last paling post had joined the confused twitching heap, the pony was gone – rid at last of her alarming burden.

Gibson let a great shout out of him, squeezing his hands to his sides.

'Oh, merciful God, have pity on my poor twisted guts.'

He moaned gently.

'Should I live to be as old as a cannibal pike I'll never see the like again.'

Willie was stooped down, holding back the torn trouser cloth and the torn bloodied underpants, examining the lacerated flesh of his injured leg.

The mocking voice kept rasping on:

'Did no one ever tell you that you never rise your hand to a spoiled slut the like of yon? Don't you know what old Spokeshave, the poet, said about beating dumb brutes?'

He cleared his throat and intoned:

> *If I had a donkey and it wouldn't go,*
> *Would I belt hell out of it? No! No! No!*

Cassie wailed:

'Herbie, didn't you promise me solemnly not to repeat –'

She broke off and faced around.

'Are you badly hurt, Willie?' she said. 'That was a sore toss you got.'

Gibson said:

'Saving your presence, girl, and not to put a tooth in it, he must be shook to the core of his lily-white agricultural arse.'

He threw back his head and laughed, a long drawn-out,

seagull-screeching laugh.

A ball of anger rose in my throat. I looked at Willie straightening himself up painfully, at Cassie wretched with anxiety, at the torn fencing and the deserted sand-dunes. I looked at Gibson's swarthy face, alive with malice, grinning at his victims. Surely someone should give this vicious, snapping brute a clout of the tiller to curb his flailing antics. Wildly I sought for words.

I said:

'Shag off, you bib cackling jackass! You'll have little enough to laugh about if you have poled Cassie as you poled that poor silly ghomey from the Crooked Bridge.'

Willie spoke back over his shoulder, his cold indifferent gaze fixed on the two figures at the paddock gate.

'Are you coming, Jim?' he said.

Without waiting for an answer he started off, limping with surprising speed, making for the gap in the fence.

Crippling along, one shoulder up to his ear, fisted hands held stiffly to his sides, blood-soaked long-johns hanging from the torn trouser-leg, he should have looked ridiculous. Instead there was something tough and resolute in his bearing that made you forget he was balding, chinless, splay-footed: that lent inches to his puny stature and dignity to his limping gait: that sent me trotting proudly after him, deaf to Constable Gibson's bitter tirade of abuse and threats, heedless of Cassie's wailing curlew cries, unmindful even of the cool wind now fanning my cheek – a warning that the hot endless days of an endless summer were at last over.

Interlude

It all started – the engagement, I mean – the morning that the landlady's fourteen-year-old daughter came bursting into Molly's bedroom to call her for work, shouting as she opened the door:

'Eight o'clock. Time to get –' Her startled gaze fell on me.

I was sitting on the edge of the bed, nothing on but my jockey briefs, scratching my armpits and yawning.

'Oh hello, Mr Doyle,' she said.

A muffled groan from Molly showed that I was going to get no assistance from *that* quarter. She had rolled the bed-clothes over her head and was now coiled up against the wall.

I cupped a hand over each bare knee, cocked my head aslant and gazed at the intruder with, what I hoped was, a quizzical stare.

'Hello, Babs,' I said. 'You're up early this morning.'

She eyed me up and down with bright, black, suspicious eyes.

'You're early yourself,' she said.

I drummed my fingers irritably on my knee caps, very conscious that the rest of my clothes were scattered round the room and that I was in a poor position to carry on a sustained conversation.

'I didn't sleep too well,' I said. 'I had a big feed of fish and chips before I went to bed last night.'

'Which bed?' Babs said, as she turned to go out.

Molly's head shot up from under the bedclothes; her face was scarlet.

'Stop her, Jim,' she begged. 'Don't let her away like that.'

I rushed out into the corridor.

'Babs!' I called.

The small, sturdy figure disappearing down the stairs halted.

'Yes?'

'Come back up a moment, will you.'

'All right.'

When I got back to the bedroom, Molly was sitting up, wrapped in a bed jacket. Her fair hair was fluffed out. Her eyes heavy with sleep. She was breathing like a beaten runner.

'Think, Jim,' she gasped. 'Quick. We'll have to tell her something.'

I had grabbed up my trousers and was struggling into them. My mind was in a whirl. What was there to say? How make respectable sense out of the circumstances in which we had been discovered?

'You talk to her, Molly. I can't think of anything to say.'

There was a discreet knock at the door.

'May I come in?'

Molly's lips mouthed a silent epithet.

'Yes, darling,' she called.

Babs sidled into the room and remained standing at the door, one hand swinging off the door knob.

A long silence ensued. Molly's lips opened and closed. Soundlessly. In desperation, I said:

'Look here, Babs, it's not what you think at all.'

She stared at me, a sly grin on her face.

'No,' I continued. 'It's just that . . . I happened to . . . I thought I would . . . I thought I'd make sure that Molly hadn't . . . hadn't slept in . . . '

Oh, what was the use of trying to fake up an explanation when Babs's keen eyes were already taking note of shoes, socks, shirt, tie, jacket, littered about the floor. Still –

'She's a heavy sleeper, you know,' I blundered on. 'I thought perhaps –'

Suddenly Molly cut in:

'Why make a secret of it, Jim? It's bound to leak out sometime.'

I gazed at her in amazement.

'M-M-Make a secret?' I stuttered.

Eyes gone soft and mushy, as I'd seen them so many times in the grey light of morning when I kissed her before creeping back to my room, she turned to Babs.

'He's terribly shy,' she explained. 'Doesn't want anyone to know about it.'

'In the name of God, Molly, are you gone –'

She interposed:

'I told you, Jim. It's something we just can't keep to ourselves.'

Babs was listening, open mouthed.

'Come here, Jim,' Molly commanded. She extended one arm full length, beckoning me with a finger. Like a stoat-seduced rabbit, I shambled forward, allowing her to grasp my hand. She leaned across the bed towards Babs.

'*You're* the first to be told,' she said, softly, confidentially.

She dragged me a step nearer. Waited till Babs, agog with excitement, had moved to the bedside. Announced triumpantly:

'We're engaged.'

I flopped down on the bed. My mind a blank. All my thought processes atrophied. Without interest I watched them hug each other. Heard them babbling:

'Oh, how wonderful.'

'Isn't it great?'

'When is it to be?'

'It's not settled yet.'

'Where will you go for your honeymoon?'

'We haven't decided.'

At last Babs made for the door. Molly called after her:

'Remember, darling, you're to keep it to yourself.'

Over her shoulder, Babs hissed:

'I won't tell a soul.'

I listened to the footsteps running down the stairs. To the sound of a door opening. And slamming shut. Dry-mouthed,

I croaked:

'I suppose you know where she's gone?'

'Of course I do. To tell her mother.'

Molly was sitting up very straight. Quite composed. Cheerful even, if I could believe the crinkle under her eyes that was always the prelude to a grin.

'You bloody idiot!' I exploded. 'What the hell possessed you? Look at the ridiculous situation you've created.'

'It's surely better than the situation we were found in?' She gazed at me blandly, eyebrows raised in enquiry.

'I'm damned if I see how you have improved matters by giving out that we are engaged.'

'You don't?'

'No. That Babs one is going to blurt the whole thing out to her mother. And what Mrs Mullen will say when she learns we were practically caught in bed together, is not hard to guess. We will probably both be chucked out of the digs. It will be the talk of the village for weeks.' I groaned. 'My God, what a bloody balls up.'

Molly was studying the finger nails of her left hand.

'Babs will be so excited with her news,' she said, 'that she won't bother with the details. After all, it *is* a bit of an occasion. The two boarders suddenly deciding to get engaged. After ignoring each other studiously for the last six months. Maybe it was too cute we were entirely.'

'To hell with casting up. It will get you no place. Better for you to figure out what we'll say when Mrs Mullen gets to hear –'

'And what if she does?' Casually she polished her nails on the soft wool of her bed jacket.

'My God, are you gone clean cuckoo?'

Molly looked up.

'You've got a lot to learn, Jim,' she said. 'Don't you know that engaged couples are allowed certain . . . certain liberties? People are more indulgent towards them than they would be towards ordinary couples. Mrs Mullen, when she finds out we are engaged, will not question our conduct. At most, she may hint at discretion. But that is all. The prospect of a fully-fledged romance breaking out right under her nose will be too much for her. You'll see I'm right.'

'You mean you're going to go through with this engagement business?'

'We have no other choice.'

'But people will get to hear of it. They'll be asking questions. What are we going to say?'

'That we intend getting married, stupid. What else can we say? Now, clear out of here until I get dressed. I am late enough as it is.'

I gathered up my clothes from the floor and went back to my own room. As I was dressing, I tried to figure out what should be my attitude to this grisly situation. A polite but evasive acknowledgement that the rumour was true? A jaunty nonchalance as though it were not to be taken too seriously? A grim resignation to the unavoidable?

Molly was right about Mrs Mullen. At lunch time she bustled around making a fuss over the pair of us, anxious to know if the soup was hot and the beef tender enough, if Molly had had a busy day in the Post Office and I a tiring round of Insurance calls, if we would care for a second helping of stewed apples and prefer biscuits to a nice slice of cake. When she brought in the coffee, she stood looking down at us, her brown spaniel eyes misted with emotion.

'I suppose,' she said, 'you'll not be here for tea tonight?'

Molly looked at her in astonishment.

'What makes you say that?'

Mrs Mullen stooped down, her sallow features creased in a conspiratorial smile.

'You'll be having a bit of a celebration somewhere, surely to goodness.'

She moved to the door. Wheeled around. Whispered:

'And don't do what I wouldn't do.'

The door closed on her throaty chuckle.

'Did you hear that?' said Molly. 'Isn't she the bad-minded article?'

'Though she's right about the celebration,' she added. 'We'll have to act the part of an engaged couple from now

104

on.'

'Maybe,' I said. 'But we can do that nice and quiet. No celebrations.'

'All right, honey. No celebrations.'

But there were celebrations. When I got back from work, Dick – Mrs Mullen's husband – was lounging against the bar door, waiting for me.

'The sound man himself!' he shouted, as soon as I got out of the car.

'Hello, Dick.'

'I hear you've done the bould thing.' He held out his hand. 'Well, it had to come some time.' Vigorously he shook my hand. 'It'll take the nyah off you, if it does nothing else.'

I did not like the sound of this talk. God knows what he would come out with next.

'It is supposed to be unofficial,' I said. 'We were only going to tell a few friends.'

He gave a great shout of laughter.

'God send you sense. The Missus spent her whole day chatting the neighbours. By this time there's not a dog on the street doesn't know of it.'

He pushed open the door.

'Come on in,' he said. 'This calls for a Papal blessing.'

He poured out two bumpers of whiskey. Held his glass aloft.

'Happy days, Jim! That you may never regret it.' In one swig he emptied the glass. 'There'll be no more outings with the boys. You're spancelled from now on.'

'Aw, it'll not be as bad as that, will it?'

'Sparing up for the big day, you'll be. So busy putting them on their edges that you'll give all your friends the go by.'

'Not a chance of that, Dick.' I didn't like the turn the conversation was taking. Finishing my drink, I said:

'A small similarity.'

When the drinks were filled, he leaned his elbows on the counter and rubbed his unshaven chin.

'I was just thinking,' he said, 'that maybe we should have a little party tonight. The Sergeant, Joe Harris, just a few of the

105

boys. It's an occasion for a jar or two, wouldn't you say?'

'Before you go on the dry,' he added, baring his yellow fangs in a smile.

There was little use arguing the point. It was apparent that all he wanted was an excuse for a night's carousing. Besides, I had a strong suspicion that he knew all about the goings on of this morning. Maybe a good deal more. It would pay to keep in with him.

'I suppose it would be in order,' I said.

We finished our drinks and I went down to the dining-room for tea.

Molly was delighted at the idea of an engagement party.

'But look here,' I said. 'I thought we were to keep the whole thing as quiet as possible. This party will broadcast it. And give it the appearance of a real . . . of an official engagement.'

'I had nothing to do with the arranging of a party. It was yourself and Dick Mullen.'

'Didn't I tell you I couldn't refuse. I was walked into it.'

'Then why blame me?'

'Nobody's blaming you.' I was properly nettled. 'It's just that you're . . . you're making a skit out of this ridiculous affair . . . taking it too . . . a bit too lightly.'

With finicky precision, she aligned the knife and fork on her empty plate. Pushed it away. Dabbed at her lips with her napkin.

'You're mistaken, Jim,' she said. 'I'm not taking it too lightly at all.' Thrusting out her flattened left hand, palm downwards, she brandished it under my nose. 'There!'

Only then did I notice the three-stone ring on her third finger.

'Wh-Wh-What are you doing with that yoke?' I demanded.

She held up her hand towards the naked bulb overhead, wriggling her fingers, so that the diamonds sparkled in the light.

'Nice, isn't it? It was my mother's, God be good to her. Until you get me a proper one, it will have to do.'

106

Suddenly she pointed an accusing finger.

'If you could just see yourself, Jim. Sitting there so dour and desperate and woebegone. Like a condemned man.'

Leaning over, she ruffled my hair.

'Cheer up, sour puss. I'm not the hangman. Just your fiancée. The little girl you asked to marry you this morning. Remember?'

She began to laugh, a wry stifled laugh at first, but soon she had her head back crowing with half hysterical laughter. Against my will, I joined in and soon the pair of us were hooting and screeching and spluttering with helpless laughter.

Mrs Mullen poked her head round the dining-room door, an indulgent smile on her face.

'Isn't it well for you?' she said, as she backed out, closing the door softly behind her.

Molly wiped the tears from her eyes.

'Didn't I tell you, Jim,' she gasped, 'that the romance of the situation . . . would be too much for her . . . she is probably taking credit . . . for bringing the two of us together.'

'An odd sort of a matchmaker, if you ask me.'

Again we laughed, this time contented, happy laughter. And why not? Weren't we leagued together against the world of meddlers, a vast conspiracy of busybodies intent on our destruction? Our only hope of survival was the bond that coupled us.

I reached over and patted her hand.

'Do you know what it is? We might very well turn out to be a creditable enough combination.'

Her face lit up, eyes glittering from unshed tears, quivering lips clogged with unspoken words. At that moment it was borne in on me that she was heartbreakingly beautiful.

'I wish,' she said, at last. 'Oh, I wish –'

'Yes?' I prompted.

'That was the nicest thing you ever said to me,' she finished, but I knew it was not what she had been about to say.

Tea finished, we sat on either side of the fire, our eyes locking as we glanced up occasionally from our reading. Talk was unnecessary as was the need even to touch each other. After all, what was the urgency? Ahead of us there was time enough and to spare for all that had to be done and said. When Dick shouted in to me to come down to the bar, I obeyed reluctantly.

The sergeant and Joe Harris, cashier in the local Bank, were already there.

'Well, here he is,' said the Sergeant, putting down his glass. 'So you're taking the big step.' He shook me vehemently by the hand. Put his lips to my ear. Whispered: 'A grand wee girl. You're making no mistake there.'

Joe Harris, his bald head already sweating, lumbered across.

'Congratulations,' he boomed, his swarthy simian face unsmiling.

'Isn't he the right villain, Joe?' the Sergeant said. 'He wiped *your* eye about proper. Doing a steady line on the Q.T. and not letting on to a sinner. Oh, he's worth the watching, all right.'

'Large whiskies, Boss,' ordered Joe.

Drinks in hand, we waited whilst he held the glass to his nose. Sniffed eagerly, like an impatient terrier. Lifted the glass perfunctorily in my direction.

'Luck!' he grunted and gulched back the whiskey greedily, holding the inverted glass to his lips till the last drop was gone. Smacking his lips noisily, he replaced the glass on the counter.

'Aaaaaaaaaaah!' he sighed.

We stayed there drinking – the Sergeant and I, bottled stout; Joe Harris, whiskey – until closing time when we all moved down to the sitting-room where Molly and Mrs Mullen were awaiting us.

Joe, by this time nicely thank you, insisted that the ladies join us in large whiskies.

'Settles the stomach,' he said.

I tried to warn Molly to refuse but she was too excited to

pay heed. Face flushed, eyes sparkling, she took the glass from the tray of drinks and raised it aloft.

'Your very good health, Mr Harris,' she said.

She drank, making an involuntary gesture of loathing at the first sip.

'Aaaaaaaaaah!' Joe banged his empty tumbler on the table. Molly laughed.

'It's well somebody enjoys the stuff,' she said.

Joe smacked together his out-thrust lips.

'You can't whack it, Ma'am,' he said. 'The real Ally Dooley.'

The rounds of drink began to come up middling quick. The Sergeant and I went back to Guinness, Dick and Joe stuck to the whiskey, the ladies turned to gin and tonic. Soon we were all talking at the same time, leaning forward to shout across the room at each other. Groups formed and dissolved as people with a weighty message to deliver found themselves forced to act as audience. Patriots held forth, politicians explained, newsmongers enlightened.

'What I say is –'

'What he actually said was –'

'What they're all saying is –'

Molly was sticking it out well. Waving her arms about a little too much, perhaps. But that was all. When the chance occurred, I would catch her eye and signal encouragement. The way she smiled back, a contented, trusting, completely defenceless smile, made me square my shoulders, push out my chest and sink whatever was left in my glass.

At the first lull in the pandemonium, the Sergeant called out:

'What about our charming hostess giving us a song?'

'Oh no, Sergeant,' Mrs Mullen demurred. 'Don't ask me. I'm out of practice. Haven't sung a note since God knows when.'

Overborne by the insistent clamour, she at length consented and took her seat at the battered-out piano.

'What shall I sing?' she mused, rippling out a few preliminary chords. She struck the base of the keyboard twice in a decisive manner. 'I know,' she said, over her shoulder. 'I'll sing you something from *Il Trovatore.*'

She played the few opening bars with the melodramatic action of a trotting pony, lifting each hand high in the air, wrist curved down and holding it poised threateningly for a moment before slamming the spreadeagled fingers down on the keyboard. I had heard her sing the song a dozen times but was still flabbergasted at her interpretation. As long as the melody remained in the low register, she gabbled out the meaningless Italian words with a reckless, an indecent haste, battering out a TUM-*tum-tum*, TUM-*tum-tum*, accompaniment on the piano. Only when the high notes were reached did she get a proper chance – as she phrased it herself – to display any brio.

Striking a chord on the base and treble, her hands extended to either side, she bent over the keyboard, shook her head violently as she gnawed and worried at the precursory note and then, like a terrier throwing a rat in the air, hurled its mangled remains at the ceiling. At last with back-flung head and mouth stretched wide, she attacked the high note.

It was an appalling sound, a hoarse rasping screech, rendered more agonizing by the piteous quaver in the voice. Sustained until there was no breath left in her lungs and accompanied by a vibratory barrage from the outstretched fingers of both hands, it set the ornaments on the mantel-piece jingling.

Clutching my empty glass, I stared into its depths and tried to arrange my features into an expression of stunned appreciation. I noticed that Molly was holding her bowed head in one hand and that the Sergeant was gazing into space with a curious stricken look on his face. When Mrs Mullen, panting triumphantly, brought her solo to an end with a series of chords executed with crossed hands, I found my forehead beaded with sweat.

We clapped and applauded and begged for more. Dick, his lips drawn back in a wolfish smile, said:

'You're in great voice tonight, Bridie.'

But she was adamant.

'That will be all for now. Maybe later on. When the rest of you have all done your party pieces.'

So Dick recited *The Green Eye of the Little Yellow God* and I belted out *The Irish Rover* and Molly sang in a pleasant contralto *The Snowy Breasted Pearl* and the drinks kept coming up for further orders.

By this time we were all getting a bit mouldy, but poor bloody Joe was properly fluthered. He was crouched down in an armchair, his face knotted up in a scowl of bewilderment, his gaze fixed, as far as I could make out, on Molly's crossed legs. He kept blinking away the sleep and his mouth continually opened and closed in what could only be abortive speech. But his drinking arm was still working, though when he swallowed back his whiskey there was now a despairing note in his usual:

'Aaaaaaaaaaah!'

We were all surprised when, without taking his eyes off Molly's legs, he burst out, in a thick Kerry accent:

'Ach, doze old songs! Dey're a t'ousand years old. Is dere notting better to sing than dat?'

In one quick glance, the Sergeant had the situation sized up.

'I'll tell you what I'll do, Joe,' said he. 'I'll sing you a wee love song.'

He went over to the piano and whispered in Mrs Mullen's ear. She strummed the opening bars of *Annie Rooney*. The Sergeant sang:

'She's .. my .. sweet .. heart .. I'm .. her .. beau
She's .. my .. Molly .. I'm .. her .. Joe.'

He stopped, as if searching for the words, whilst Joe struggled to his feet. Eyes closed, feet sprawled apart, clenched fists held up, he roared:

'Soon .. we'll .. marry .. wah-wah .. wah-wah
Wah .. wah-wah –'

The bellowing ceased. Swaying on his feet, mouth open, brows drawn down in a scowl, you could see him trying to rake up the words. At last he gave up.

111

'Can't remember,' he muttered.

The Sergeant took up the melody again:

'*Soon . . we'll . . marry . . never . . to part*
Pretty . . little . . Molly . . is my . . sweet . . heart.'

Waving his arms wildly aloft, Joe shouted:

'Again!'

And we all started to sing:

'*She's . . my . . sweet . . heart . . I'm . . her . . beau*
She's . . my . . Molly . . I'm . . her . . Joe.'

On weaving legs, Joe went staggering across to where Molly sat on the sofa. As she made to get up, he clutched at her for support and they both reeled back amongst Mrs Mullen's hand-embroidered cushions. Nothing could be seen of Molly beneath his huge bulk except one frantically kicking leg. His arms gripped both couch and occupant, his legs were sprawled out, one on the sofa, the other on the floor, his face was buried in a cushion from which his muffled voice still bellowed:

'*Wah-wah . . wah-wah . . Molly . . is my . . sweet . . heart.*'

An elbow jogged my ribs. It was the Sergeant. A worried man by the look of it.

'Better get him up out of there, Jim, before he has her ravished. He's just about –'

Dick interrupted:

'Myself and the Sergeant will handle him. You take Molly out on the floor for a dance. That'll keep her out of harm's way.' He waved towards the piano. 'Keep playing, Bridie.'

While the two of them tugged and hauled at Joe, Mrs Mullen struck up *Annie Rooney* again. It's a catchy air and by the time Molly was freed, I was humming away at the melody, my feet tapping out the beat on the lino.

'Come on, girl!' I said, grabbing her up.

Off we wheeled, leaning away from each other the better to gather momentum.

'That was a whirlwind courtship,' Molly gasped. Her face was flushed, her hair tossed.

'Aye, Joe's manners aren't the best when he's mad a-horsing.'

112

We bounced off the sideboard.

'Don't blame Joe. It wasn't his fault.'

'Begod, the Sergeant thought he was going to lepp on you.'

We crashed into the table.

'If the Sergeant hadn't started teasing Joe, it would never have happened.'

'Teasing Joe?'

'Yes. Changing the words of the song.'

She flung back her head and sang to the music:

'*She's . . my . . Molly . . I'm . . her . . Joe.*'

Her foot caught in the fender and she staggered forward. Only that I had a firm grip on her, she would have fallen.

'Sorry,' I said.

It was borne in on me that Molly, who only rarely took a drink, was half tiddley. Somehow or other, this endeared her to me. As though she were in need of protection. And the support of an older brother.

'Let's take it easy,' I said. 'I'm getting winded.'

We slowed down till we were merely shuffling and swaying to the beat of the music. Molly took up the melody again:

'*Soon . . we'll . . marry . . never . . to part.*'

She squeezed my hand.

'Wouldn't that be nice, honey?' she said.

'Uh-huh.'

'You don't sound too enthusiastic.'

I whirled her round a few times, barking my left shin against the leg of a chair.

'Joe seems to have quieted down,' I said, slackening once more to a shuffle. 'The notion must have gone off him.'

'Never mind Joe. It's yourself we're talking about.'

Softly I hummed the catchy air:

'*Daah . . Deeh . . Daah . . Deeh –*'

'Give over, Sly-boots. You're engaged. Remember?'

'Of course.'

'Well, do you like it?'

'Sure.'

She clutched me with both arms, crushing herself frantic-

113

ally against me.

'Is that any better?'

I tried to push her away but she only clung the closer.

'Go easy,' I begged. 'They're all watching us.'

'Relax, Jim. This is what they want to see. Come on!'

Swinging to the music, she sang:

'She's .. my .. sweet .. heart.'

Lured to the tingle of warm breath on my neck, entrapped by the tang of heady sweat and hungry flesh, beaten and overwhelmed by the accusing eyes, clouded surely with love, I buried my face in her hair and sang:

'Soon .. we'll .. marry .. never .. to part

Pretty .. little .. Molly .. is my .. sweet .. heart.'

Soon the others joined in, with Joe's discordant bellowing dominating the rest, until at length Dick shouted:

'That'll do, Bridie.'

Once more the company fragmented, with the ladies exchanging whispered confidences on the sofa, the Sergeant, Dick, and myself sitting round the table arguing politics, and Joe, slumped down in the armchair, chin sunk on chest, arms dangling between outspread legs, snoring and grunting in a drunken stupor.

Drinks were still coming up at rapid intervals. I tried to persuade Dick to leave Molly out of the round, but he only jeered at me.

'It's early on you're getting to act like a married man.'

He, too, was beginning to show signs of wear and tear. His tread was heavy and deliberate. He handled the glasses with exaggerated caution. He blinked continuously in the effort to steady his unfocussed vision.

The Sergeant and I still stuck to Guinness. It was in powerful order and neither of us had any difficulty keeping the drinks from piling up as they are very apt to do at the tail end of an evening. In fact my thirst seemed to increase with every tumbler I sank. I had the glass up, ready to dive into a fresh one, when I heard Molly call:

'Jim!'

I looked round. Harris was half-kneeling, half-squatting,

on the floor beside Molly. He was sprawled across her lap. She seemed to be put to the pin of her collar thrusting away the hands clumsily pawing at her legs. He was muttering hoarsely:

'De people in dis town talk too much. Dey all know too much about deir neighbour's business. We'd need to go away. For a holiday. Somewhere like Scarrrr-borr-ough. *Dat's* de place. Nobody bodders about you dere.'

'Stop it! Please!' Molly begged.

'It's a grand place, Scarrrr-borr-ough. Dere's cinemas. Dere's t'eatres. And dere's dance halls. And grand swanky hotels dat would house an army.'

'Will you behave yourself, Mr Harris!' she pleaded.

'D'you know what it is,' said the Sergeant. 'I'd nearly go to yon place for my summer holidays, he makes it sound so good.'

'He's making a hames of the party,' grumbled Dick. 'We'd better break it up before there's trouble.'

'A fine healthy place too, Scarrrr-borr-ough. De sea air is like a tonic. You could put up your hand and *squeeeeeze* the salt water out of it.'

Molly screamed.

'Take your filthy groping hands off me!'

She struggled to her feet. Stood swaying uncertainly.

'Jim,' she said. 'Will you look after me?'

'She's tired out, poor thing,' said Mrs Mullen. 'Better get her to bed, Jim.'

I went to her.

'What about the hen roost, honey?' I said, putting an arm round her.

'All right.'

At the door she turned.

'It was a lovely party. Thanks a lot,' she hesitated. 'Everybody.'

'He's a horrible man, that Joe Harris,' she said, as I helped her up the stairs. 'Did you see the disgusting antics of him?'

She missed her footing on a stair and stumbled forward. I just grabbed her in time.

'Take it easy, darling,' I said.

'It's all very well for you to say that, Jim. You didn't hear the . . . the . . . the outrageous suggestion he came out with?'

'No, dear.' We were nearly at the top of the stairs.

'He wants me to go with him for a holiday, to some evil low-down haunt. He's a nasty old man, that's what he is.'

'I dunno. He's just a poor sod who has fallen for you.'

'It's sweet of you to put it like that, Jim.' She stumbled to a halt as we reached her door. 'But then you've been very sweet all evening.' She wound her arms round my neck. 'You should have heard Mrs Mullen. She couldn't stop talking about you. Such a nice boy. Easy to see he's a gentleman. It's lucky the girl that gets him. So quiet and well behaved. She doesn't know you the way I do, you blackguard.' She drew my head down and whispered: 'Aren't you glad now? Glad you decided to get engaged, I mean?'

'Of course,' I conceded, giving her an encouraging hug.

'We belong to each other now, don't we? There's no one else in the whole world that matters. Only the pair of us. Isn't that right?'

'Uh-huh.'

'Sure?' she insisted.

'Sure I'm sure.'

Impatiently I grasped her, lining with urgent hands her body against my own. I kissed her, lips mashing on teeth till the taste of blood was in my mouth. Groaning with desire, I buried my face in her hair, her neck, her rudely exposed breast, whilst the blood pounded madly in my ears.

Struggling fiercely, she broke away from my arms.

'Now-now, Jim,' she panted. 'Behave yourself.'

She backed away from me, hurriedly putting to rights her disordered clothing.

'You're every bit as bad as Joe Harris.' Her outstretched hands groped behind her for the door handle.

'Molly,' I whispered, edging closer. 'Will I wait till they're all gone to bed or will I slip in now?'

'You'll go straight to your own room this minute, that's what you'll do. Like a good boy.'

'So you mean . . . you're not –'

'I'm not. I'm locking my door tonight.'

I tried to gather her once more into my arms but she pushed me firmly away.

'No, darling. You're not going to get round me that way.' She kissed her finger-tips and put them against my lips. 'Good-night, love. Happy dreams.'

I grabbed her hand.

'But why?' I begged.

'We're engaged. That's the why.'

'I don't see why that should make any difference?'

'Don't you? It means no more to you than that?'

'You said yourself that engaged couples were allowed liberties that . . . that . . . other couples don't get.'

'Not that sort of liberty. Where would you finish starting off like that?' She pulled her hand away.

'You mean that from now on we're to go round together like a couple of craw-thumping penitents?'

'I do. And stop shouting at me.'

'I'M . . . NOT . . . SHOUTING,' I hissed. 'I'm merely trying to din into you that we're too far gone in our ways to make a change now.'

'Speak for yourself. I've none of your old-fashioned habits.'

'My God!' I was flabbergasted. 'Would you listen to her! And she every bloody bit as bad as myself.'

'Now you're swearing. And wagging your head like a school-teacher. You're losing your temper, as usual.'

I took a deep breath.

'No wonder,' I said. 'Making out that I'm the culprit. And you leaving the door ajar any night you wanted nookey.'

She took a step towards me. Her cheeks were blotched, her brows gathered in an ugly frown, her lips a thin resentful line.

'No gentleman would make a remark like that.'

'It's true enough though, isn't it?'

'You're hateful.'

'There were times you were eager enough for my company

117

when, God knows, I'd have been better off in my own bed getting a proper night's sleep.'

'Oh!' she gasped. 'You've gone too far this time.'

'Well, if it means the end of this ridiculous sham we've been carrying on, so much the better.'

'It isn't ridiculous. And it is no sham. And it's about time I broke it off, the way you are behaving.'

'I like that. Making out that you're breaking it off.'

'Of course I am.'

'Are you codding yourself, girl? Don't you know damned well that there was never anything there in the first place for you to break off?'

'There was! There was! THERE WAS!'

'Keep your voice down. There's no need to screech.'

'I'm not screeching. I'm just not letting you away with that last crack.'

'You mean you've forgotten already that this phoney engagement was rigged up because you were discovered in bed with the cock lodger?'

'How dare you say such things?' she screamed, slapping me full force across the face.

My reaction was immediate. I let her have it. In the double – Smack Smack – on each cheek, watching her face jerk to either side as my right hand swept back and forth across her face.

While you could count three we stood, horrified, staring dumbly at each other. She was panting heavily, her whole body rocked with agitation. Her face was blanched except where palm and knuckles had inflamed her cheeks. Her eyes glittered with tears.

'Look, Molly,' I began.

'You brute!' she burst out. 'You cruel, callous brute. Never did I think you would turn out to be so mean and bitter and treacherous.'

She buried her face in her hands and wailed:

'Ooooooh! Oh, what am I to do? I'm ashamed and disgraced. Ooooooh!'

Rocking her body to and fro, she sobbed and cried.

118

Hesitantly I reached out. Patted her shoulder. Before I could say a word, she brushed away my hand.

'Take your filthy paws off me!' she screamed. 'I want nothing more to do with you. I'm finished with you. D'you hear? Finished with you. For good.'

Once more she broke into a frenzy of weeping. Crying out, between sobs and moans, in a rush of broken speech:

'What am I to do . . . never hold up my head again . . . it's a disgrace that can't be lived down . . . leading me on like that . . . letting me tell everybody . . . even having a party to celebrate . . . what am I to say to people . . . Ooooooh.'

As, bewildered and distraught, I strove for words of comfort, I heard from the well of the stairs, a dry, throat-clearing, apologetic cough.

'Hush!' I whispered, but Molly, sobbing and lamenting, paid no heed.

Appalled and panic-stricken, I would have fled to my own room but I knew it was imperative that the eavesdropper be identified. There would be no peace of mind for either of us unless this was known.

On rubber legs, I tiptoed the few steps to the banisters, the creaking of the floor boards muffled by a wild outburst of weeping from Molly. Cautiously I peeped over.

Below me, huddled on the stairs, was a group of figures, their upturned faces floating in the gloom of the stairwell like phosphorescent masks. Silently they stared at me. The Sergeant, Mrs Mullen, Joe Harris, Babs. And a few steps above the rest, Dick.

For an agonizing moment I was impaled by their impassive stares. Then Dick's head bent further back.

'Are you all right up there?' he enquired politely.

119

Rise Up, My Love,
and Come Away

All graveyards are depressing places. Even the New Cemetery out the Glen Road, with its row upon row of tombstones and statuary set out in orderly files and eyeing each other across railed-in plots containing glass-domed wreaths or carefully tended flowers or pebbled chips of gleaming white marble. That is why I found it so difficult to understand how I came to be in Ballysillon graveyard, soaking wet from head to foot, my stockings laddered, my shoes plastered by muck and clay, my new grey skirt ruined by slimy green stains.

Of course, Ballysillon graveyard would destroy anyone's clothes. Unkempt and neglected, a wilderness of weeds and nettles, briars, and scutch grass, it is the oldest graveyard in the parish, catering alike for Catholic and Protestant and refusing refuge to no one. Rarely used now for burial, there had to be good reason for such an impertinent intrusion on its dead. It was no place to find oneself on a day like this, with overhead a dull leaden sky and a watery sun trying desperately to break through the slowly moving rain clouds.

And yet breakfast – how long ago now? – had been such a gay meal, with John, usually so quiet, chattering to the children, teasing me and clowning like a young fellow, so that he was nearly half an hour late starting off for his work in the bog. Very kind and considerate he was, even remembering not to ruffle my hair when he stooped down to kiss me goodbye. When he was gone and the children packed off to school, I could only sit in happiness at the table and thank God for my good fortune.

So what had gone wrong? I waded aimlessly through the long grass towards a marble angel, leaning dispiritedly against a stubby cross. The angel's nose was chipped off, as was one eye and a large section of the left wing. The face was mottled, the robes disfigured by stains – green, grey, and brown. It was erected, so the legend read, to the memory of James O'Neill, who died March 12, 1878, aged 56. R.I.P.

Even doing the housework, I moved around in a glow of happiness. Clearing away the breakfast things, washing the dishes, making the beds, scrubbing, dusting, tidying – everything I did seemed to have a special significance as if sanctioned and ordained by God. At least, looking back on it now, that is how it seemed. As I went from room to room, picking up soiled clothes from floor or chair or bed, emptying chamber pots into the slop pail, putting away books and comics littering the bedside chairs, I hummed and whistled and sang. I even broke into a few shuffling steps of a dance routine. Not even the discovery of a cigarette butt in the fireplace in Jackie's room, could disturb me. And why should it? John loved me. The children adored me. I was loved and I had a heartful of love to bestow in return. How could I be anything else but happy?

Or was I? It all seemed to have happened so very long ago that you could not be sure of anything. All I knew now was that I felt terribly, terribly tired – as if I had walked for miles. A few yards away was a fallen tombstone. I pushed my way through briar and nettle till I reached it and flung myself thankfully down on the rough granite. Idly I began to spell out the worn inscription.

Erected in loving memory of my dear wife
Judith Barnes
Who died June 6, 1844, aged 20
'The Lord giveth and the Lord taketh away'

What a dreadful tragedy! To be cut down at that age. After only a few months or maybe a year of married life. The poor thing! People are not half thankful enough to have their health and their family and their friends. No matter how bad things are, they could be worse. John was always saying that. And God knows it is a true saying. He is a good man, John. Attends the sacraments regularly. Smokes little and drinks less. Always kind, affectionate, and understanding towards me, when there must have been many times, goodness knows, that I was a trial. I am a lucky woman to have such a husband. So what prompted me to act as I did? What sudden impulse sets a body veering about like a weathercock?

I read on.

Also her husband, Amos Barnes
Who died of fever, March 15, 1846, aged 27

He had not survived her long. Just two years. It must have been the famine fever that carried him off. Some people would say that it was a fitting thing for a husband to follow his wife so soon to the grave. But I think that is wrong. I would like to think of John living happily for many, many years, not just to care for the children but to remember me always and ever with love. Never to let my memory wither. That would make me very happy.

The rest of the legend ran:

Also their son, Matthew Barnes
Who died May 3, 1928, aged 84.

How awful! Judith must have died in child-bed giving birth to this doddering old monster. How unfair that he should outlive for all these years the person for whose death he was responsible. And now, the fragile brittle crumbling remains of age are heaped on the sturdy bones of youth. I shivered. Got up from the tombstone and wandered off towards the small building, cupola shaped, that must have been used as a kind of mortuary chapel. Tripping over mounds and hollows, climbing grave railings, for no paths were evident, forcing a passage through the dense under-growth, I reached the building and flopped down on the stone bench running round the inside wall.

What, I wondered, had caused my sudden confusing change of mood? One moment, happily carrying on the housework; the next, sitting morosely in the bedroom gazing down at the laced fingers of my hands. Lonely, depressed, frightened, I sat there and it seemed to me as if every blind in the house were drawn, the carpets up and the furniture gone. I was in a deserted, a forsaken house. My family had abandoned me. Perhaps never to return. I would be forced to spend the rest of my days in this airless gloomy house. With not a sound of shout or of laughter or of scampering feet. Only the creaking of old boards, the squeaking of mice, the rattle of window blinds.

It was then I decided to dress up. After long pondering, I laid out on the bed the grey tweed skirt. My nice pale-blue woollen twin set. My best pair of stockings. And my black court shoes. I decided also on fresh underwear.

Filling a basin with warm water, I stripped off to the pelt and scrubbed myself with sponge and soapy water till my skin glowed. Then I dressed up, taking extra pains over my appearance. I spent a long time at the mirror making up my face, even using a little rouge to put a bit of colour in my pale cheeks. At last, with my wiry dark hair brushed out and a final dab of powder on my nose, I examined myself in the mirror. Satisfied with my efforts, I folded up and put away my discarded clothes and made off for the porch where I slammed behind me the front door. I stood, looking up at the lowering sky with its threat of rain, uncertain what I should do.

Getting up from the stone bench, I wandered restlessly around the mortuary chapel. It was quite small – about six paces wide – with one deeply embrasured window, curtained and clotted with spiders' webs. These were so covered with dust that it was impossible to see out. On the sill of the window I discovered an inscription. It ran:

This graveyard was given and walled in to the people
of Ballysillon and the surrounding district by the Rt.

123

Honourable Wm. Conyngham at the expense of twenty pounds and ninepence.

What an absurdly small sum. The stonemasons and the labourers who built the wall must have worked for almost nothing. And yet this great gentleman saw fit to have the cost of his gift chiselled on stone for posterity to wonder at. A skinflint, that's what he must have been.

There was an angry buzzing from the recessed window. A large bumblebee had got itself entangled in the folds of cobweb. It beat its wings frantically, plunged and threshed around, wading, by dint of sheer strength, through clusters of webbing until its whole body was encrusted and wound about with dusty strands of gossamer. Sometimes its wings would become trapped. At once the buzzing would rise to a higher pitch as the insect sought to free itself of the constricting folds. At last, partly freed, it would lurch forward again with long gossamer trailers whirling like spray from its beating wings.

In one corner of the window a large spider crouched, sunk deep in its folded legs. Twice it rose, ran down the webbing and moved cautiously round the entrapped bee. At a safe distance it stayed, watching the struggling insect. Then retreated back to its earlier position at the top left-hand corner of the window.

Meanwhile the bee, by now swathed in a clinging pall of dusty cobweb, had thrust its way downwards towards the bottom of the window. At last it reached the sill where it lay quiescent for a few moments. Its head was smothered in webbing as though in a diver's helmet. From this casque protruded one feeler. Its whole body was festooned with threads of gossamer. Gossamer flapped from its slowly moving wings, twined about the hairy feet, wound itself in chains around the parti-coloured belly.

How long I stood at the front door before deciding to go on my bicycle, I do not know. But once I had made up my mind, there was no stopping me. I went to the turf house. Rooted out the bike.

The two tyres were flat. I pumped them up. Somebody had lowered the saddle. I found a spanner and shifted it up to the right height. The chain was bone dry. I got an oil can and oiled it. By the time all this was done, the first drops of rain were falling. I had to stand for the most of a quarter of an hour in the turf shed before the rain stopped. Then I started off.

The bee moved forward across the sill, crawling on partly pinioned legs, its outstretched wings trailing at either side. Its body was humped in the effort to propel itself forward. Every so often it blundered against the sucked-dry body of a dead discarded fly. Then it would stop. Investigate the body with the single free feeler. Attempt to nudge the dessicated corpse out of the way. Crawl on once more with the dead fly trailing after it, attached to a strand of gossamer. Sometimes the bee would stagger into a matted cable of tethered cobweb. Push and thrust and bullock its way clear, emerging often with much of its wrappings torn off. Once it rolled over on its back and jerked its legs about, trying to free them from their shackles. Never did it succeed in ripping away the webbing that encased its head. And always it moved blindly towards the edge of the sill. It had not a chance. Stumbling and lurching forward, it toppled over the edge and fell with a squelch on the stone floor. For a few seconds it lay on its back, waving its unentangled legs feebly. I stayed till they had ceased moving. Then I went and stood at the doorway.

I cannot think why I decided to take the Knocklangan road. For it is a hilly road. Very different from the metalled main road. It means pushing the bike up the hills and braking with both hands going down them. Of course the road goes through lovely country. Vivid green pasture land dotted with the pale gold of corn fields and here and there plantations and shelter belts of trees. The rain had brought out a rich heady tang in the air. Larks sang overhead: robins chirped in the bushes: blackbirds screeched as they fled at my approach. The sun was trying to break through the clouds. And yet I was sunk deep in despair as I walked and cycled and walked again.

At Corrigan's Cross I met Mrs Leary coming against me. Driving a herd of Herefords. I had to get off the bike to pass.

'It's turning out nice after the rain,' she said, stopping.

'It is that,' I said, edging forward to get past.

'Though God knows, we could do with a sup of rain. The country's parched for the lack of it. I'm just walking these animals down the road to the Water Field.'

The bullocks had spread across the road and were grazing the grass margins.

'That was a good shower a while back.' I edged a few steps further forward.

'Not worth a curse.' She drew nearer. Her black beady eyes looked me up and down. 'You're all toveyed up. Where are you for, if it's a fair question?'

Another cautious step forward. Where was I bound for anyway?

'I'm heading for the lake. Knocklangan Lake.'

'And what's taking you there, in the name of God?'

'There's a picnic. I'm going to a picnic.'

I was clear now. Up on the bike and away with you.

'I must run now or I'll be late.'

As I pedalled madly away, I heard her exclaim:

'God and his Holy Mother, what's the world coming to?'

Still overcome by depression I pushed and pedalled and braked. With the fields getting scrawnier and scrawnier and the rocks beginning to get above ground and the hedges and bushes and bits of trees all lying the one way on account of the wind that is blowing all the time from the south-west and the day getting darker and darker with the threat of rain. Till at length I reached the foot of Knocklangan. Got off the bike and left it propped against the ditch.

I stood there in the doorway of the mortuary chapel, looking out at the scattered tombstones, almost hidden by the tangled grass. They had the bedraggled appearance of a defeated army. Tombstones sagging wearily forward ready to collapse with exhaustion. Tombstones arched back so that wind and rain and bleaching sun had long since scoured away the chiselled lettering. Tombstones tilted over crazily as though time itself had shrivelled and contracted the muscles of mountain granite. Or sunk to their rounded shoulders in the soft ground. Or sprawled their length in the rank undergrowth, face up or face down it mattered not in their last indignity. And over all the strong musty odour of nettle and briar and scutch grass.

It is a long climb from the road, up through the foothills to the lake. The most of three good miles. There is no recognizable path. Only sheep and rabbit tracks. And these wind their way round rock and bramble patch, pools of water and stunted trees, so that you feel that you are not making an inch of ground. The climbing too is discouraging for no sooner have you struggled to the crest of one hill than you are sliding down the slope on the far side to face once more a panting floundering ascent. At no time can you glimpse the entrance to the lake; all that can be seen is the towering peak of the mountain.

Once in a while you rest, leaning against a boulder. Sucking the cold mountain air into your racked lungs, you look back down the slope and draw some comfort from the tiny figures of man and animal, the ribbon of road and the dolls' houses scattered about below you. Far in the distance, the sea bounds the horizon and the smoke of an unseen ship is pencilled against the sky. All around you stretches the gloomy dun-coloured waste, broken only by mountain tarns and out-crops of grey granite rock. The loneliness was made more lonely by the occasional cry of a seagull muted by height and distance to a pitiable puling wail.

There was a trampling of feet on the road leading towards the cemetery. Many feet. And the low hum of a bevy of slow-moving cars. I waited, listening. As the cars drew nearer and the shuffling footsteps more distinct, it was borne in on me that it was a funeral cortege bound, without doubt, for Ballysillon cemetery. It was only then that I noticed in the far corner of the graveyard, almost hidden by a towering clump of nettles, a mound of freshly dug clay. I moved back inside the mortuary chapel, taking shelter in the corner farthest from the door. There I waited nervously.

The climb up Knocklangan had become steeper. The mossy ground slippery underfoot from the recent rain. Twice I lost my footing, the second time laddering a stocking. Shoes and skirt were mired and stained. My underclothes were sticking to me with sweat. With sweat my eyes were blinded, my lips salty. But still I kept on, gasping and groaning, with the blood thumping in my ears. Up one hill and down the next. Making no apparent headway. Until suddenly, when I had almost given up hope, I was there. Standing at the top of a short slope, dropping sharply down to the lake.

It is cupped in a horseshoe of mountain, the slopes of which drop sheerly down to the rim of the lake. Only at the entrance is there any pretence of a beach. This consists of a narrow strip of grey gravelly sand, littered with a confusion of granite boulders. The lake, reputedly bottomless, rarely gets the sun and its smooth surface has the unhealthy pallor of a man who works underground. The immensity, the absolute stillness, the dull grey quality of the light, were awesome and scary.

I turned away to survey the route I had climbed. Far below me, stretching to the sea, lay the toy landscape of a child. The jumbled up checker board of fields – green, brown, golden. The diminutive houses with their red-roofed barns and sheltering trees. The tiny motionless animals set in position on the nursery floor. The minute figures crawling slowly around intent on their clockwork tasks. It was all so far away and unimportant.

On the horizon, the sea. A broad expanse of grim unpolished silver. At one point – where a cluster of houses indicated Claran Strand – an errant shaft of sunlight burnished the water.

Claran Strand. What a host of happy memories this splash of sunlight evoked. Long summer days stretched out on the beach, the warm wind stroking your limbs with feathery finger tips. The eventual bathe with icy water stinging scorched flesh. The cycle home in the cool of the evening, the wind of your going cooling the sunburn.

Marriage, the move inland, the coming of the children,

had changed everything. How many times were we at Claran Strand since we got married? Once. No, twice. The first time before Jackie was born. John hired a car and the pair of us set off for Claran. We bathed, splashing each other like children. We chased each other around the beach. We walked, arms round each other, along the cliffs where the pounding waves and the sheer drop alongside the path, made me cling still closer to him. Until the craving was too much for us. Over the ditch we went and John, usually so solid and staid, made love to me in the broad light of day. It was a cornfield. As we lay back afterwards, eyes closed, hunger slaked, you could hear the wind whirling through the stalks, cutting a swathe of rustles like the whirring of a flock of starlings or a long-eared dog shaking its head. Then sluggishly, linked hands swinging, we went back along the cliffs. Before we went home we had one drink each in Lacey's bar. A bottle pint for John: for myself a glass of sherry wine.

The second time was when? Let me see. Jackie was born, so was Phil. Marie was on the way. There was a strike on at the bog and John was at home, eating his heart out. No wages coming in and the debts mounting up and nothing to be heard from morn till night but a lot of old trade union talk. The two of us fought the piece out with rows and arguments that got worse every day. Eventually I could stick it no longer. I had over three pounds spogged away. Enough for a day's outing. The hired car cost two pounds. A picnic lunch was another ten bob. The remainder went to John for spending money.

We had a marvellous day. The kids took to the water like ducks. We paddled, bathed, built dykes and sand castles, played games, slept. At length, tired out, John and I sat on the rocks leaving the children to their own devices. John was filling his pipe. Leisurely, methodically, he tamped down layer upon layer of tobacco from the shredded heap in his cupped hand. Suddenly he looked up.

'What have they got now?' he said.

The two children were chasing something along the strand. Something black and white. And small. That

129

scampered ahead of them in little spurts.

It was a bird. A sea bird of some sort or other. There was a peculiarity about its gait as it ran and fluttered ahead of them. An awkward, unbalanced action that I felt to be unnatural.

John pointed with his pipe.

'That bird,' he said. 'It has got a broken wing, by the look of it.'

He was right. The left wing was trailing the ground whilst the other fluttered bravely in a futile effort to fly. It was this that gave it the lop-sided appearance.

'The poor thing,' I said.

Just then Jackie caught up with it. Stooped down.

'Jackie!' I shouted. 'Don't! Don't touch it, Jackie!'

The bird escaped his clutching hands. Wheeled about. Made for the sea, followed by the two screaming children.

'Jackie! Phil!' I called. 'Come back! Come back here at once!'

By this time, the bird had reached the fringe of the tide and was scuttling through the shallow depths of a receding wave. It had not yet started swimming when the next wave reached it. Caught up in the rushing surf, the bird was carried ashore whirling and tumbling helplessly about. The children rushed to catch it but it evaded them and scurried back in the wake of the retreating wave. Once more it was caught up by the oncoming breaker and swept to the shore.

The children were dancing with glee.

'Oh, Mummy, Mummy, come and look!' they chanted.

'Leave the bird alone, you young rascals!' shouted John.

At the third attempt the bird got through the foaming lather. Swimming strongly, it headed out to sea. But before it got very far, a comber broke over it. I thought it would never reappear. When it rose to the surface, I cheered.

'Oh, you beauty!' I cried.

Soon it was through the breakers and out to the open sea, I turned to John.

'Wasn't it wonderful?' I said. 'I am so glad it got away.'

He struck a match and shielding it, sucked at the pipe. Between puffs, he said:

'It's banjaxed . . . that broken wing . . . it'll banjax it entirely.'

'You mean it was all a waste of effort? That never will it fly again? That the poor thing will have to die? Oh, it can't be. It is too unfair.'

John flung away the burnt match. Drew deeply on the pipe. Blew from pursed lips a slow cloud of tobacco smoke. Shamefacedly, almost furtively, he reached out and caught my hand.

'There's not much fairety in this world, darling,' he said. 'Either for birds or people. If there was, you'd maybe not have had to punch in such a lousy spell as the last few weeks.'

The tears spurted out of my eyes. My throat went dry. A torrent of emotion rose inside me till I thought I would choke. I gripped tight at John's hand. Blinked back the tears. Clamped shut my lips so that I would not disgrace myself by shouting aloud for all the world to hear, that someone I loved still loved me.

I was happy. So very, very happy.

Over Claran the shaft of sunlight was quenched. The world was once more a grey and silent place. Bounded by gloomy mountains and a gloomier sky. So that you are shut in from everything and everybody. No longer able to beat your fists against the invisible barrier that encloses you. Moving further and further away from all you love. You may complete the journey. With your heart turned to stone and the gorge rising in your throat at the thought of turning back, what else is there left to do? Have not the shuffling feet come to a halt outside the cemetery gates. Are not the bearers already shouldering their burden? What need is there to linger? Listening maybe to a voice blown in the wind, intoning sombre, mysterious, terrifying words in an alien tongue? Or the scrape of shovel, clink of stone, thud of clay on hollow wood? Or perhaps watching the stricken desolate faces gazing, not at the open grave, but across at the distant mountains? The sweat of the long climb has put you shivering. Better that you get moving. Scramble down the short incline to the lake shore, your feet sinking in the gravelly sand. At the water's edge, stand a moment to draw breath. But not for long, for hesitation will undo all. Mouth dry and eyes blinded with tears, wade out into the lake, swaying, stumbling, staggering, unmindful of soggy shoes or clinging skirt and jumper, feeling the rising water press against thighs, groin, breasts, ever struggling forward to the final step into bottomless depths that will complete your pilgrimage.

In Ballysillon graveyard, the mourners are beginning to drift away, stopping here and there to gather in groups. Scraps of their conversation come to me, blown on the wind.

'A big turn-out . . . Half the parish must be here . . . Why, in the name of God, did she do it? . . . A shocking business altogether . . . Such a quiet inoffensive creature . . . How could she do such a thing? The husband near demented . . . You'd be sore at heart looking at the childer . . . Och, the poor angashore, what came over her at all? . . . Cycling the most of ten miles . . . Why? . . . Dressing herself up in all her finery . . . Why? . . . She shouldn't have had a care in the world . . . But, why?'

The wind is rising, coming in fresh from the east, flattening nettle, docken, and scutch grass with the rustle of starlings' wings. Flurries of rain come in its wake, driving the loiterers helter skelter through the cemetery gates. I shiver. Better for you to go now. Why delay? What is there to keep you here any longer?

Sally

I was mooching around the sitting-room, examining yet
again the familiar bric-à-brac – the glass-fronted cabinet
crammed with china and glass ware, the ebony elephants, the
large white egg suspended by a ribbon of fading red silk, the
souvenir plates from Bangor and Bournemouth – when Aunt
Mary called from the foot of the stairs:

'Jim, where are you?'

I replaced the glass ball with its shaken-up snow flakes still
whirling around the tiny model church.

'Here,' I called, moving out to the landing.

'What are you doing up there?'

'Nothing.'

'Tck! Tck! Tck! Why aren't you out taking the summer
sun? Much good the holiday is doing you. If you don't soon
get the results of your Leaving Certificate, I'd be half inclined
to pack you back home to Omagh. Apparently a village the
size of Drumkeel is too small to hold you.'

'Did you want me for anything, Aunt Mary?'

She sighed.

'Run across to McGahan's and get a pan loaf and a half
pound of streaky bacon.'

At the kitchen door, she turned and called up:

'I see Sally McGahan is home from the convent for
holidays. Like yourself she is waiting for the results of her
examination.'

She was sitting on the garden seat outside 'McGahan's
Grocery & Licensed Store' – a small sturdy girl with black
curly hair and olive skin. As I crossed the road she turned

133

her head away, gazing intently down the deserted street towards the range of hills enclosing the village. Too prim and proper, I decided, going past her into the shop.

Next day, I saw her again when I wandered down to the tennis court in the forlorn hope of being able to make up a set. The court was laid out in a wired-off segment of a large field bordering the road, about a quarter mile outside the village. She was alone, sitting on a wooden bench, nursing on her lap an ancient racket with frayed and grubby strings.

'Care for a knock up while we're waiting for someone to arrive?' I said, flicking the taut strings of my new and much too expensive racket.

'I'd love to,' she said.

Unheeding the way she stood at the base line, stooping forward intently, racket ready-poised, I dished her up a cookie. She drove it back cross-court, taking me off balance when I was moving up leisurely towards the net. A lucky fluke, was my verdict.

My next service was medium paced, deep to her backhand. Following it up quickly, I was mortified to find myself beaten by a sizzling backhand drive straight down the side line. Two swallows don't make a summer, I consoled myself as I went back to the base line.

This time I really laid into my first service, delighted as I ran up the court, to see the white dust rise off the bounce. To my horror, she moved up, took the ball on the half-volley and sent it steaming straight back at me. Instinctively I put up the racket to save my face.

'Bad luck,' she said, as the ball glanced away, yards out.

There'll be an end put to your gallop this time, I swore, steadying myself down for the next service. I dished it up to her medium paced, slicing the ball down the centre line and standing my ground for the return. The rally lasted nearly a dozen strokes, deep drives to the base lines – forehand, backhand, down the side lines, cross-court – until a return of Sally's, low and stinging, found an uneven patch of ground and skidded.

'Game,' I conceded.

'Sorry,' she said. 'The court is badly in need of the heavy roller.'

I retrieved the balls and tapped them across to her.

'Your service,' I said. 'You didn't waste your time at school, I'll say that for you.'

She grinned.

'Thanks. I was first string on the senior team.'

'The nuns made no mistake there. But we'll try and give you a run for your money.'

It was the last game she won. No longer did I attempt to match her in base line play. Instead I drew her to mid-court with chop shots, low volleys and short, well-placed lobs. Then when I had caught her out of position, I clobbered her unmercifully.

Once when she failed to reach a sneaky lob that landed a couple of feet from the net, she shook her head sadly.

'Oh, dear. You do play a mean, lousy game, don't you?'

After three sets we were fast friends. On the way back to the village she told me all about herself. Just turned seventeen. An only child. Strict but adoring parents. Not allowed out late at night. Never yet been to a dance.

'But I've been going dancing for two years now,' I said. 'And we're much the same age.'

'Lucky you. My folks say I am time enough to start dancing when I've got a job. And can pay my way.'

'Though, of course,' she added, 'we were taught ballroom dancing at the convent.'

'What do you do with yourself at night if you're not allowed out late?'

'Oh, I read a lot. Play chess with Daddy. And I do an hour or two's piano practice every night.'

'So you play piano?'

She stopped in the middle of the road. Pointed an accusing finger at me. Announced triumphantly.

'I'll bet *you* play too? Mean, sneaky piano playing just like your tennis?'

I nodded.

'I knew it!' she cried. 'I knew it! I knew it!'

Back in the village, she insisted that I come in and play the piano.

'Bit early in the day,' I objected.

'Come on,' she said impatiently, dragging me into the shop where she introduced me to her parents.

'He's a nephew of Miss Meehan's across the road. I want to see if his piano playing is as low down as his tennis.'

'Yes, dear,' said Mrs McGahan.

'Take him upstairs to the sitting-room,' said Mr McGahan. He called up after us as we mounted the stairs: 'I hope he doesn't play any of this new-fangled dance music. I can't abide it.'

The sitting-room was like Aunt Mary's only smaller and stuffier. The blinds were half drawn. Two china dogs glared at us from the mantelpiece. Family photographs lined the walls. The chairs and sofa were placed too tidily to have been recently used. But the piano lid was turned back and the keys were white and gleaming.

I sat down on the broad piano stool and rippled the keys. The action was light: the tone good. I tried the pedals. The soft was a little muffled: the loud just right. I flung back the piano top.

'What's it to be?' I asked.

'Anything you like. Only don't soup it up too much.' She pointed down to the shop.

'Right. If it's corn they want, it's corn they'll get.'

I waded into a medley of old time waltzes, starting off with *What'll I do?* Bumping out the hiccuping bass chords and swelling from soft pedal to loud, I poured out the syrup the way Charlie Kunz used to do. '*What'll I do . . . when you . . . are far away . . . and I . . . am blue? What'll I do?*' Pure bull and a yard wide, but the melody caught me by the throat and made me gulp.

I followed up with *Wonderful One, When You and I Were Seventeen* and wound up with *Always*, the corniest of them all. Hunched low over the keyboard, I really gave it all I'd got, squeezing out the last drop of juice from the keys. Sally was singing the words softly: '*I'll be loving you. Always. With a love that's true. Always.*' I could feel my eyes stinging. By the time I had tapered off the last echoing '*Always,*' high up in the treble, I was just about wrung out. When I looked up, I saw that Sally's grey eyes were moist with tears.

'Don't tell me that you go for that mush, Sally. Get a load of this.'

I swung into the explosive rhythm of *Jailhouse Stomp.* Before I had beaten out more than a half dozen bars, there was a thumping on the floor.

I stopped.

'Carry on,' she said. 'Don't mind Daddy.'

'The Management's decision is final in all cases,' I said, getting to my feet. 'What about giving us a stave yourself?'

She sat down, rested her fingers for a second on the keys and started off. I don't know what she was playing but I suspect it was the set piece for a music exam – an Etude in A Minor or some such guff. Her playing was technically perfect. Her fingers scampered over the keys and produced the sounds indicated on the score. But of feeling there was none. It was without heart.

'Banzai!' I called out when she finished.

She swung round on the stool.

'You don't have to pretend to like it. I don't care for it myself. Dance music is what I'd rather play.'

'Well, why don't you?'

'That's the why.' She pointed down to the shop below. 'I'm supposed to be studying for a degree in music.' She looked depressed. 'I'll probably finish up teaching music in a convent school.'

Idly I listened to the sounds leaking up through the floor – the murmur of conversation, the constant ringing of the cash register, the wheeze of the bacon slicer, the sound of a drawing cork.

'Hey!' I said. 'No reason why you shouldn't whale out a dance number now. They'll think it's me playing.'

She brightened up.

'I never thought of that,' she said.

'Well, go ahead.'

'But I can't play by ear. I'd need sheet music.'

So it was arranged that I would come back after tea with a few albums of dance music. Strictly corn, of course. Sally was to tell her folks that I was anxious to punch in a bit of practice on a first-class instrument, Aunt Mary's piano being a clem.

She was sitting out on the garden seat when I returned. She had changed from her white tennis frock into an orangey-brown affair with a white collar.

'What kept you?' she said. Before I could answer she got up. 'Come on.'

The curtains were still half drawn in the sitting-room, giving it an air of snug seclusion. In the gloom of early evening, the ornaments, photographs and gleaming brasses melted into the background. The china dogs no longer glared at intruders.

She sat down on the piano stool and leafed through one of the albums, stopping here and there to hum a few bars of the melody. At length she commenced to play.

You would imagine that anyone could squeeze a bit of feeling out of *Charmaine* – a number oozing with treacle. Yet Sally just played it as it was scored. Without warmth. Without lift. Without swagger. When she finished, I said:

'Cold as charity. You want to give it swing.'

I leaned over her shoulder.

'Like this,' I said, bouncing out a few bars of the melody.

Shifting across the stool, she motioned me to sit beside her.

'Play that again,' she said.

I crushed in alongside her and belted out once more a phrase from the treble.

'What about the bass?' she asked.

'Bump it out this way.' I played a couple of chords. '*Oom-pah. Oom-pah.*'

'Oh, I see.' She rested her right arm across my shoulders whilst she picked out the bass with her left hand.

'Now you've got it,' I said.

'If you were to play the melody,' she squeezed my

shoulder, 'it might be easier for me to beat out the rhythm.'

As I took up the treble with my right hand, she snuggled against me.

'Nice, isn't it?' she whispered.

'Yeah, we're getting the beat now.'

My left hand was hanging stiffly at my side. I shifted i cautiously around her waist.

'That's better,' she said, cuddling closer.

We played like a team, Sally hammering out a steady beat that gave me a chance to improvise. When we finished, she said:

'Let's play *Always*. It is a much nicer number.'

One-handed I riffled through the music till I found it. Propped up the album, tightened my encircling arm.

'Now,' I said, breaking into the melody.

Cheek to cheek we played, Sally strumming out the bass whilst she sang in a half whisper: *'I'll be loving you. Always.'*

Keeping her eye slanted on the music, she turned towards me until at last her lips were fastened on mine, her right hand keeping my head in position like a clamp. Somehow or other, eyes shut, fingers groping for the right keys, I kept the melody going, urged on by the remorseless *Baruhm-pom-pom* of Sally's bass. When I fumbled out the last two chords, high up in the register, she pulled away.

'Gosh!' I gasped.

'Isn't it nice?' she asked.

My head was spinning and I was breathing heavily. But I was still in there. Fighting.

'Yes,' I said. 'What colour is it?'

'What colour is what?'

I pointed.

'Oh, the frock,' she said. 'Tangerine. Do you like it?'

'It's cute.'

'Thanks.' She laughed ruefully. 'Though I don't know what for.'

'Wh-what d'you . . . what d'you mean?' I gobbled.

'Never mind,' she said. 'Up you get.' She pushed me to my feet. 'I'd better play something myself to show I'm still in the land of the living.'

She played another exam piece, deftly handling the difficult score and surely earning full marks for carriage and deportment. Then, easing herself across the piano stool, she patted the vacant space and said:

'What about another duet?'

Thus was the pattern set for the next three weeks – weeks of bewildering enchantment during which I moved in a fixed and fascinated orbit around Sally. All activity – the moody prowling round the house each morning that used to get on Aunt Mary's nerves: the lunch gobbled down with indecent haste so that I could rush across the street to McGahan's: the afternoon session of ruthless tennis, mitigated only by the occasional bout of wrestling, hair tousling or other horseplay as we changed sides after a set – all this was but the preliminary to the hectic, nerve-racking fraud we practised each evening in the sitting-room.

We became skilled at deception. Locked in each other's arms, lips pressed together, it only required an occasional glance at the score to churn out the corny tunes. Soon we learned to vary our technique – by turns stroking with tender exploring hands the proferred lips, eyes, cheeks or stealing a quick hug by pouncing on each other two-handed during pauses in the rhythm.

Sometimes Sally would perch herself on my knees and smother me with kisses whilst I strove unseeing to beat out a dance number with my encircling hands. Or I would stand behind her when she was playing one of her exam pieces and try to break down her mechanical proficiency by nuzzling her neck and hair or nibbling at the lobes of her ears. We kept the sitting-room door open so that we would have ample warning of approach and always we were on the alert for the sudden silence in the shop below that could mean danger. Altogether it was a performance – foolish, crazy, but wholly delightful.

So dazed was I with happiness that it did not at first register when one afternoon she told me as we sprawled together, our backs against the netting wire of the tennis

140

court, that she was being allowed to spend the week-end with a school pal in Bundoran.

'Oh, Bundoran,' I said, idly bouncing the racket-face against the toe-cap of my tennis shoe.

'Yes. Aren't you pleased?'

Puzzled, I turned to her.

'Should I be?' I asked.

'Of course, fathead. Didn't you say you wished you had the opportunity to bring me out dancing?'

'Sure.'

'Well, now is your chance. If you can manage to get to Bundoran on Sunday, we can go to the Astoria that night. My first ever dance. Wouldn't it be thrilling?'

During the next few days I made my arrangements. I was to go by bus to Bundoran on Sunday afternoon. I had no difficulty scrounging a lift back by car after the dance. Aunt Mary raised no objections. In fact she was super. She gave me the latch key. Warned me to come straight home after the dance, to be sure to shoot the bolt on the front door and to come upstairs to bed quietly. Milk and biscuits would be left for me in the kitchen. And finally:

'I suppose you have spent all your pocket money.' She opened her purse. 'Here.' She reached me a pound note. 'This will tide you over the night.'

So Sunday afternoon saw me stepping off the bus at Bundoran, preening myself like a newly-clipped poodle. Sally was waiting at the bus office, looking very sweet in a white tennis frock. With her was a freckly, carrot-haired girl.

'Hello, Jim,' said Sally. 'Meet Doreen.'

I held out my hand.

'So this is Wonder-boy!' Doreen staggered back a step, her hand to her mouth. 'The tennis playing Fats Waller. I'm quite, quite wild with excitement.' With polite tapping hand she extinguished a gaping yawn. 'You've been the sole topic of conversation since Sally arrived.'

'Don't mind her, Jim,' said Sally, gazing at her friend with affectionate tolerance. 'She goes on this way all the time.'

And so she did. She narked at me continuously as we

jostled our way through the crowded main street or wandered aimlessly around the amusement park. She kept up a stream of sarcastic remarks as we downed our Knickerbocker Glories in a milk bar. Even when we were lolling on the soft sand of the beach, with the sun pounding us into lethargy, she harped on, ignoring my grunted rejoinders. Did I find it tiresome being constantly besieged by admiring fans? Did I think country girls more manageable than city ones? Who did I count the world's greatest lover – Romeo, Abelard, Don Juan?

Sally continued to smile indulgently during this nagging onslaught. In desperation, I suggested a walk along the rocks.

I took them along the bottom of the cliffs, where the path ended and the going became rough. Edging along narrow shelves of rock with the waves battering and foaming beneath, clambering across stretches slimy and treacherous with weed, jumping from rock to rock of a causeway crossing a spongy beach, I urged Sally along, whilst further and further behind us trailed Doreen's bleating cries: 'Wait for me. Wait for me, can't you.'

At last we came out on the sand dunes. For a minute we stood watching, in the distance, Doreen claw her way on hands and knees along a narrow ridge of rock.

'Hurry up,' I shouted, waving her on. 'You're delaying us.' Then I dragged Sally to the shelter of the tallest sandhill.

Gasping with smothered laughter, we rolled about on the sand, hugging and kissing each other hysterically every time we heard Doreen wailing:

'Sally! Where are you, Sally?'

The cries seemed to come from every direction as though she were running wildly around, searching the sand dunes.

At length Sally pushed me away.

'We'd better show up, Jim,' she said. 'We can't afford to annoy her.'

'Annoy her?' I burst out. 'Hasn't she been larding into me all afternoon without rhyme or reason.'

'If she is going to the dance,' I added, 'she will ruin our night.'

142

'She's *not* going to the dance. That's the whole point. Her father would not give her the latch key. She is going to wait up for me.'

'That's different.' I put my hands to my mouth. 'Doreen!' I called.

Linked together, we ploughed our way across the sand-hills towards the answering cry.

The walk back, by road, to Bundoran, was a glum affair. Doreen sulked. Sally sought to pacify her. I tried to make a joke of the whole affair but was glared down. By the time we reached the house where the girls were staying, we had given up attempting to make conversation. Sally and I arranged to meet at nine o'clock outside the dance hall. I shook Doreen's limp hand.

'It's been nice knowing you,' I said.

'I suppose I'll get over it,' she grunted, before turning away.

After a cafe tea, I strolled through the streets until it was coming up on nine o'clock. By that time the crowd was already milling around the entrance to the Astoria. I stood at the door, tapping my foot to the beat of the music that swelled out each time the door to the ballroom was opened. The couples drifted past, chattering loudly, scattered a trail of perfume and tobacco smoke. The girls were dressed in a bewildering diversity that ranged from elegance to scruffy disorder. Sweatered slacks, brilliant summer frocks, slinky ball gowns, shabby jeans. Yet all had one thing in common – they were worn as unself-consciously as an animal wears its pelt. The worst dressed of them looked jaunty and attractive. So caught up was I by the gay crowd and the lift of the music that Sally was at my elbow before I was aware of her coming.

'Hi, Jim!' she said. 'I'm not late, am I?'

She had changed into an orangey-brown frock with a white collar. It had short sleeves, a belt of the same material as the frock and it sagged, drab and depressing, to just below her knees.

'No,' I said. 'I've only just arrived.'

I gazed at the frock. It was dowdy – painfully, incredibly

dowdy – making of her a hick, a real dyed-in-the-wool country hick. She intercepted my gaze.

'I put it on specially for you.' She smiled knowingly. 'You said you liked it. Remember?'

'Uh-huh,' I took her arm. 'We'll go in.'

The band – a seven-piece combo – was playing a real cool number. I could feel my feet picking up the beat even while we were pushing our way through the crowd standing around inside the door. The hall was a blaze of light. Too early yet for the spotlight fanning the darkened hall and the crystal ball gleaming overhead.

Out on the dance floor with Sally in my arms, her warm hand squeezing mine, her hair brushing against my lips, I was already gathered up in the pulsing rhythm. Body swaying to the swell of the music, I waited impatiently for space to weave into the stream of dancers. At last it came.

In the first few steps, I found that Sally did not fall into a loose prowling stride. Her body remained stiff and unyielding as though it resented being propelled forward. I shifted my grip on her back trying to squeeze the slinky rhythm into her reluctant limbs. Instead of yielding to my pressing hand, she took over completely, lugging me after her as you would drag a stubborn child.

I wheeled her round recklessly in an effort to loosen out and control her unruly limbs. I cleared a space on the floor by cannoning into all comers until at last, dizzy and panting, I was forced to stop. At once Sally took over again, propelling me backwards, marching with a Guardsman's stride. At last I knew what I had let myself in for. It was all too clear that Sally, as befitted the star athlete of the convent, had been forced to assume the male role in the weekly dancing lessons. Now she was so used to acting as the dominant partner that she was totally incapable of dancing like a normal girl.

I suffered myself to be pushed and pulled around, with little more than token resistance when I was spun about in the corners of the ballroom. Very conscious I was of people staring at us, especially those we bumped against. But Sally paid no heed, continuing without a break to sing the words

144

of the melody in a loud and cheery voice. Two encores had to be punched in before the band leader called: 'Next dance.'

'Isn't it marvellous?' she said. Her face was flushed. Her eyes sparkling. 'The band. The floor. The crowd. Absolutely super.'

'Let's cool off,' I said, heading for the mineral bar.

After two bottles of coke, I began to cheer up again though every time I got the impact of the orange frock, I would wince. It was really the ultimate in squalor. The sort of thing you would see at a village hooley. The glances of passing girls swept over it with condescending smiles that made me angry and ashamed.

Half way through my third coke, the band struck up a quick-step.

'Let's dance,' said Sally. 'Shall we?'

Gulping down the last of the coke, I followed her, with sinking heart, back to the ballroom.

Out on the dance floor, my fears were more than justified. From the word 'go' she tried to take control. Only by hoisting up my right arm until our two elbows were at a level with my shoulder, was I able to loosen her grip on my back. I could do nothing with her right hand. Time and again I attempted to loosen its clutch but I might as well have tried to wrench a tennis racket from her grasp.

Under her tutelage I rushed round the dance floor, colliding with all and sundry, my face burning with shame as I apologized for my clumsiness. Soon I came to feel that every eye in the hall was turned on us. That passing couples discussed our absurd appearance on the dance floor: 'Who is the young fellow dancing with the girl in that dreadful orange frock?' 'Oh, some country boy from the back of beyond. Like herself.'

Though I consider myself a good dancer, I found I could not deal with the situation. I lost confidence. Like a beginner on the dance floor, I tripped and stumbled, tramping on Sally's toes as she was tramping on mine. For both these offences I kept saying mechanically: 'Sorry.'

The ballroom had become really stifling. Sweat rolled

down my face: my hands were damp: my shirt clung to my back. Never had I felt so uncomfortable. Sally too was suffering from the stuffiness. Through the frock I could feel her body seething with heat. It was as if I held in my arms an enormous baked apple, pulsing and sizzling, fresh from the pan. Her face was flushed, her hand sticky. But still she clipped along untiring, humming or hissing through clenched teeth – an inexorable marionette.

At length, overcome by heat, exhaustion and embarrassment, I gasped:

'This place is like a ruddy oven.'

'Sure is.' She did not slacken speed.

'Let's rest up.'

She leaned back. Studying me.

'Don't say you're tired. After all that tennis practice.'

'I'm properly banjaxed. Whacked out.'

She released me.

'Dear-dear. He mustn't overtax his strength, the poor darling.' She patted my back soothingly.

'Come on, lunkhead.' I gripped her arm and steered her through the crush of dancers to a seat near the now propped-open door.

'It'll be cooler here,' I said, hovering over her uncertainly. The band brought the number to an end with a crashing climax.

'Next dance,' announced the leader.

'Excuse me,' I muttered. 'Have to go places.' I waved my hand in the general direction of the door. 'The loo.'

'Don't be long, Jim,' she called after me as I made off through the scattering throng of dancers.

In the lavatory, I moved around slowly from wash-basin to wash-basin, running the taps, examining the soap, staring at myself in the mirrors. I pulled down the towels on the automatic dispensers until all displayed a freshly-laundered loop. I stepped on the weighing machine, in the hope – unfounded – that the previous penny was jammed and the scales were weighing for free.

At length I dawdled back to the ballroom, going no

further than the door, where, through the press of bystanders who stood watching the stream of dancers move past, I peered cautiously round, in the hope of seeing Sally out on the floor with another partner. Through the shifting pattern of dancers, in the exact spot where I had left her seated, I had a glimpse of an orange frock.

Back in the lavatory, I picked the cleanest wash-basin and turned on the hot water tap. Hanging up my jacket, I soaped and scrubbed my hands with scrupulous care. Let off the soapy water and steeped my hands in freshly run hot water. Then with my nail file, I dealt with each finger nail, forcing the softened cuticles back and scraping clear the ragged loosened skin. I was slowly combing my hair and patting it meticulously into place when one of the cubicle doors opened and a voice addressed the mirror into which I was peering:

'Well, if it isn't the hard man himself!' I got a slap in the back that doubled me over the basin. 'Hi'ya, pal?'

In the mirror, an amiable monkey face grinned back at me. It was Bill Baxter, who lived beside us in Campsie Avenue. He was a medical student, with the usual addiction to Guinness and girls.

'Hi'ya, Bill,' I said. 'What are *you* doing here?'

'Spending a few days on holiday. And yourself?'

'I'm only here for the dance. Getting a lift back to Drumkeel tonight.'

'What's the dance like?'

'Oh, a grisly crowd. Mostly country clod-hoppers.'

'Any talent?'

'The hall's reeking with it. Chancy characters fresh in from the grass.'

'Ah!' He smacked his lips. 'Goody-goody!'

I waited in the cubicle for a quarter of an hour before returning to my vigil at the ballroom door. I spotted them at the top of the hall, near the orchestra, dancing together with furious abandon. Somehow or other Bill had escaped Sally's possessive grip and held her away from him, one hand firmly grasping her shoulder. In this position they capered around

147

like children, kicking up their feet, wriggling their bodies, brandishing their clasped hands aloft. They banged into other couples: trampled on toes: butted, collided, stumbled. But so gay and relaxed did they look, so completely isolated in themselves, that I was tempted to cut in and finish the dance with Sally myself. Instead I dodged back to the lavatory where I immured myself once more in one of the closets.

Soon the faint insistent beat of the music, setting my toes tapping on the floor, proved too much for me. I decided to go back to the ballroom. After all, I argued, if Bill could curb Sally's headlong flight, there was no reason why I too could not call a halt to her gallop.

The floor was jammed with dancers when I returned. I stood at the door scanning the couples as they moved slowly past. There was no sign of Sally, but this was not surprising as it was only possible to view the fringe of the crowd.

During the interval, the crowd seemed as thick on the floor as before. I pushed my way through the press, glancing around for a sight of the orange frock. The band struck up the next dance before I was more than half way down the hall. Once more I took my place amongst the onlookers gazing at the heaving, struggling mass. Still I could see no sign of Sally.

At the next interval I did the round of the ballroom, forcing my way through the swirling, chattering crowd. I picked up a partner and danced, quartering the hall like a working gun dog. I went up to the balcony and stayed there for a good half hour watching the seething throng of dancers. I tried the cloak rooms, the mineral bar, the street outside: Sally was not to be found. Nor was Bill.

The awful possibilities latent in this gross betrayal were not to be thought of. Despairingly I rushed back to the ballroom. With such a mob, it was just possible that Sally and Bill were there all the time. I had but to root them out.

This time I fine-combed the hall, shouldering past protesting dancers, peering through gaps in the surging crowd, alert for a glimpse of a frock similar in colour to Sally's. Like mushrooms, orange frocks sprouted up around the dance floor. I had no sooner checked on one than I had to struggle half the length of the hall to find I was again mistaken. Once I fought my way through the mob to the far end of the ballroom where an orange frock sat in lonely accusing solitude. Again I zigzagged across the dance floor in pursuit of a yellow frock with a white collar.

I went up to the balcony, leaned out over the railing and studied the shifting heads and shoulders. For fully half an hour I stayed there, scanning the groups that collected in different parts of the hall, the rows of wall-flowers patiently waiting for partners, the fresh couples pushing their way on to the floor. Dotted everywhere were frocks like Sally's — amber, golden, saffron, copper. None of them had Sally's black hair and olive skin.

At length I got up and hurried out. By this time she must surely be in the mineral bar where everybody drifted at some time during the dance.

For the next hour I shuttled between the balcony and the mineral bar, constantly consoling myself that my quarry had only just then departed. But every moment my mouth became drier and my stomach more unsettled. By the time I met Charlie Foster leaving the ballroom, I was really panic stricken.

'Do you still want a seat home to Kilkeel?' he asked.

'I do, Charlie.'

'Right. I'll meet you out here after the dance.'

He made to move off. Paused.

'Aren't you friendly with young Sally McGahan?' he said.

I could feel my face reddening.

'Uh-huh.'

'You didn't bring her to the dance, by any chance?'

'I did.'

'Well, if I were you I'd get back to the ballroom and cut in on her. She's dancing with a queer-looking character. A right young pup, I'd say.'

Without waiting for a reply, he passed on towards the cloakroom.

149

For a moment I stood there, my head whirling, the taste of disaster in my mouth. Then I started off slowly towards the ballroom.

The band was playing a blues number, dragging out the sultry sluggish rhythm. The lights were dimmed, only the whirling crystal ball dangling from the ceiling gave a measure of dispersed and flickering luminosity. A spot light swung round among the dancers, changing colour as, here and there, it lingered lovingly on some tightly clasped couple.

I pushed through the crowd at the door until I was in the forefront. Almost at once I saw them. They were only a few yards away, on the fringe of the dance floor. Locked in each other's arms, they moved forward slowly.

Just level with me, the spotlight swept across the heads of the dancers and snared them in a flood of crimson light. I could see that Sally's eyes were closed and her lips parted in a tiny smile. No longer stiff and unyielding, she nestled in her partner's arms, her body supple and pliant, swaying in unison with his.

The spot changed to amber as, caught in the crush, they came to a halt beside me. In the golden glow, Sally became a wild raven-haired beauty, her tangerine frock clothing her in a mantle of flame. Bill's ugly face had become hawklike and imperious. They were surely the handsomest couple in the ballroom. With absorbed faces, they clutched at each other whilst Sally flung back her head as though demanding to be kissed. Bill was stooping over her when the spot changed to white.

Trapped in the harsh glare, which deepened the bruised shadows under their eyes and heightened the pout of their avid lips, they drew apart. Bill glanced swiftly around. Spotted me at once.

'Psst!' he signalled. His face was wreathed in a delighted, a self-satisfied grin. He raised his right hand in salute, circling the thumb and forefinger. Leaning out towards me, he whispered:

'Deadly!'

Three is Company

As he changed gear and swung into the terrace of houses overlooking the village and the wide sweep of ocean glittering in the summer sun, he realized, with sickening disappointment, that the car, usually parked on the grass verge opposite number five, was gone. Surely Julian and Maeve had not forgotten. Cleared off someplace for a bathe perhaps, mindless of their arrangement to go sailing with him for the day? He had hired the boat: the fishing tackle was in the back seat of the car. They would never renege without letting him know.

He changed down to low gear to avoid the pot-holes. Of course, they could have been called away unexpectedly, he argued. Something urgent. like the death of a relative. It was hardly a business call for they were on holiday from the city. Could there have been an accident? A car smash, maybe? The headlines formed before his eyes.

COLLISION WITH PARKED LORRY
PROFESSOR AND WIFE BADLY INJURED

It was with a feeling of relief that he discovered, on pulling up outside the gate, that Maeve was sitting on the door-step reading a book.

He rolled down the window.

'Hullo there!' he called. 'Are you ready for the road?'

'Give me two minutes, Frank.' She got to her feet. 'You can be turning the car while I get my things.'

By the time he had the car turned, she was waiting, beach

bag in hand, at the gate.

'Where's Julian?' he asked.

She got in beside him, slammed the car door and settled herself comfortably on the seat.

'He's not coming.'

He gazed at her in astonishment.

'Not coming?'

'No. Something annoyed him yesterday and he broke out. Didn't come home till four this morning. Footless.'

He found it hard to picture Julian – cool, reserved, cynical – staggering home, pale face flushed, hair sweat-soaked, keen eyes bleary and bloodshot, a flabby smile twisting the thin lips.

'But-but-but where is he now?'

'He took off in the car a few hours back. To cure his hang-over. Heaven knows when he'll be back.'

Impatiently he tapped the steering wheel.

'We can't go without him,' he said.

'Of course we can. He insisted, before he left, that we go ahead with the sailing trip. There was no use arguing. You know Julian.'

He revved up the engine viciously.

'It seems a dirty trick going off like this and leaving poor Julian to stew in his juice.'

'Don't be silly. Julian can take care of himself.'

'Maybe. But I am his friend. It just doesn't . . . seem right . . . to . . . to – '

'To go sailing with you in broad daylight? Within scream-ing distance of the shore? Come on, Frank. Don't let's waste the whole afternoon.'

Not till they reached the main road did he break the silence.

'How long does he stay on the . . . does he stay drinking?'

'It hits him like a hurricane. The only thing to do is to wait till it blows itself out. Could be as long as a week. Maybe longer. He drinks until he has to take to the bed.'

'Does it not interfere with your work? The worry and so forth, I mean?'

'No. When I am writing, I shut myself off from everything. I could work through the Day of Judgment without knowing or caring.'

He pulled in to the grass margin to allow an oncoming turf lorry, swaying with its top-heavy load, to pass. The road clear again, he said:

'Where does he go? I didn't see his car round the village.'

'He doesn't drink in the village. He makes for a country pub, as far away as possible. Sometimes he drives till his tank is empty.'

'But why? Why on earth doesn't he –' His sidelong glance took in the lifted chin and the whitened knuckles of the clasped hands.

'Because every so often he finds himself hating us all. He can no longer abide the drivelling nonsense talked by his wife –' she paused '– or his friends. And so he goes where he can be sure we won't catch up with him. He will sit on a half-barrel in the bar all day long and as far into the night as the publican will allow, buying drinks for all hands whilst he discourses on political and social philosophy until he has drunk himself into a state of stupor or his disciples have all slunk home to their beds. Laughing their heads off at the improvidence and garrulity of the Professor.'

He stared at the road ahead. It was difficult to believe that Julian, always so aloof and austere, could behave in such a stupid fashion. Harder still to accept that the lean olive features, lit up with animation, as he listened to the nightly arguments on literature, masked an intolerable boredom. Every summer for the last three years the debates had continued. Whilst they were out fishing, sun-bathing on the beach or sitting around the kitchen range sipping cups of Julian's exotic soup, they had talked about nothing but books. He felt his face redden at the memory.

The car topped a hill. Before them stretched the coast road, winding along on the verge of the cliff tops, ducking out of sight where the tiny bays and inlets were eaten out of the rock. Tall Atlantic breakers laced the base of the cliffs in a smother of foam and raised a curtain of mist high above their crumbling tops. Far out to sea the Island lurked, skulking behind a shimmering heat haze.

He swung across to avoid a group of scrawny cattle grazing along the side of the road.

'Should be a good day for sailing,' he said, his voice cracking on the last syllable.

'Looks like it.'

No more was said till they pulled up on the cement pier at Creevan Bay. Jimmy Dhu was waiting for them, sitting on an upturned fish box, mending lobster pots. His boat was pulled in to the steps, sail already set and flapping in the wind.

'Hi, Frank!' he called, as they got out. 'Hullo, Ma'am. Where's the Professor?'

'He's not coming,' said Maeve.

'Pity. It should be a right day for the mackerel.' He waddled over to the guard rail of the steps.

'Where would be our best chance?' asked Frank, as he collected the gear from the back of the car.

'Seal Bay would be the likeliest spot.' Jimmy had the mooring rope unloosed and was stumping down the steps. His disembodied voice came up to them.

'You'd want to stay middling close inshore to catch fish the day.'

He crouched on the lowest step, top-boots knee-deep in water, holding the stern of the boat, whilst they climbed aboard.

'Using spinners?' he said contemptuously, nodding his head towards the reels.

'Why not?' said Frank.

'The way the fish were taking this morning, you could have caught them with your bare hands.'

He thrust the small boat out from the quay wall.

'Away with you,' he said.

Frank shook out the sail and grabbed the tiller. As they drifted away from the pier, Jimmy called after them:

'I threw in a couple of mackerel for bait. You'll maybe need them if the spinners fail.' He waved. 'Good luck, boy.'

Clear of Hawk Head, in the open sea, they started to fish.

There was a mackerel breeze blowing – enough wind to keep the lines stretched out astern with the sinker the proper distance below the surface. They had almost reached Seal Bay before they started to kill.

At first they fished two lines, waiting for the quick double tug, before hauling in. But soon the mackerel were taking so greedily that Frank lashed the tiller and cast out two more lines, securing all four to the thwarts. They worked both sides of the boat, Frank in the stern, Maeve in the bows, dealing with two lines each.

They hauled and cast out in a frenzy of haste, without even checking if the lines jerked. Why should they when the mackerel were feeding? All around them the sea boiled with activity as the tiny sprat, driven to the surface by the hunting shoal, leaped frantically in the air to escape their pursuers. The air was filled with a loud rustling noise, like the hiss of rain sweeping a cobbled street, as the myriad of small bodies flopped back into the sea. Above them, cackling and screaming, the gulls dived, not only on the sprat but on the struggling mackerel as they were dragged the last few yards to the boat, capering madly on the surface of the water. Once a gull swooped down and grabbed up a mackerel Frank was hauling in and he was forced to pluck the fish away from its beak when it was already mast-high in the air.

Hands and clothes plastered with slime and blood and scales, Frank and Maeve kept hauling in the catch, ripping hooks from gaping mouths, tossing the wriggling fish aside, before flinging the sinkers back into the sea and leaning across to haul in the alternative lines.

The take ceased as suddenly as it had started. The seething water calmed as the shoal moved away with the screaming gulls in tow: the thrumming lines stretched out impotently in the wake of the boat.

'Will we go after them?' asked Frank.

'No. It is nothing but butchery.' She studied her hands, her jumper and skirt, her bare, blood-spattered legs. 'Eugh! Look at the state I am in. Let's get back to Creevan Bay and have a swim.'

They reeled in the lines and heaped the dead mackerel into a battered soap box they discovered in a locker in the bows. By the time they had finished and Frank had unlashed the tiller, the wind had died down. Still, whatever was left was a following wind and they crept before it with slackened sheet and sail flapping and only the tiny whisper of water on wood to indicate movement.

Sprawled in the stern, Frank steered a course for the look-out tower on Hawk Head, letting the boat yaw now and then to get a glimpse of Maeve, sitting up very straight in the bows, gazing back at the long stretch of coastline reaching out far into the sea with its range of distant mountains, blue-hazed by the evening sun. Each time he caught her gaze, he would grin back at her out of the depth of his happiness. At last he spoke.

'How is the novel going?' He writhed in embarrassment at the polite tolerance in his voice.

She laughed.

'You make it sound like a book of stories for tiny tots.'

'I'm sorry, Maeve. I didn't mean to sound patronizing. It's just –' He watched a gull rise from the water as they drew near. It flew a few lazy wing-beats farther out to sea and slowly settled down again, feet dangling, wings raised high, easing itself into the water as though it were an element foreign to it. 'It's just that I have no idea what . . . exactly what you are really doing. You have never shown me any of your work, you know.'

'Maybe some day I will. When I feel you are in a charitable mood. You can be as severe a critic as Julian when you choose. And you know how he despises me for wallowing in a mess of emotional syrup.'

The sun was now low over Hawk Head. Already the lengthening shadows of the cliffs reached out, turning the sea to a pool of molten moss. On the horizon, the Island was still steeped in sunshine, the heat haze lingering over it so that to Frank it looked like a reptile drowsing in the steaming mud of some tropical swamp. Hawk Head and Glen Head, on either side of him, dozed too, their massive muzzles tucked between outstretched paws. Sounds had become muted to the whisper of the surf and the distant wailing of the gulls.

The sea stretched around them in an oily calm with shifting whorls of colour – green, red, purple, grey – moving over its surface. It had a curious soothing effect as though the swimming colours were cast upon eyelids closed against the glare of the sun. At the same time, there was a nagging compulsion to seek out and clothe in words – perhaps in a single line of poetry – the exact descriptions of those coloured spirals, dappling the surface of the sea like huge, myopic, staring eyes.

'At this rate,' said Maeve, 'we'll not get back before dark.' She was leaning over the side, dabbling her hands in the water. 'Wouldn't we be better to row for a spell?' Lifting her hands to her nose, she sniffed. 'Eugh! They still smell.' She peered round the slackly flapping sail. 'Whatever are you staring at, Frank?'

'The fanned-out feathers of a peacock's tail,' he said, triumphantly. 'That's what it is like.'

'What on earth are you talking about?'

'The sea. It is dappled with eyes. Like a peacock's tail.'

Her gaze followed the gesturing hand.

'So it is,' she said. 'Like a peacock's tail, its fanned-out feathers dappled with eyes.'

Again she murmured the phrase.

Then with metronomic finger she tapped out the rhythm on the side of the boat.

'*The fanned-out . . . feathers . . . of a peacock's . . . tail.* It is too good a line to throw away, Frank. Why don't you – '

She hesitated.

He waited, gripping the tiller fiercely.

'Oh, what is the use?' she continued. 'Like Julian, you despise poetry.'

A cud of resentment rose in his throat.

'What makes you think –'

'Look, Frank,' she interrupted, pointing astern at the ruffle on the sea. 'The wind is freshening again.'

The tide was high up the steps when they got back to

Creevan Bay. Jimmy Dhu was waiting for them.

'Leave everything be,' he called, catching the rope Frank flung to him. 'I'm going out myself shortly for the evening rise.' He peered down at the soap box. 'You done middling well.'

'The spinners,' said Frank. 'You can't whack them, Jimmy. I'll leave you the gear and you'll maybe catch a couple of mackerel yourself.'

'I will in my bib. Are you not taking back any fish for the Professor?'

'Maybe we should, Maeve?' Reaching out, Frank gripped her hand and helped her out to the step beside him. 'You know how Julian loves them.'

'Idiot,' she whispered. Then looking up at Jimmy Dhu, she grimaced. 'Don't mention mackerel to me. I have had more than I can stand of them today.'

'I'm not dying about them myself.' With finger and thumb he blew his nose, neatly disposing of its contents by a quick, expert flick of the hand. 'They're dirty-feeding fowl. Though I'll grant you there's a powerful smell off them from the pan.'

'Just what I mean,' said Maeve. She moved towards the car. 'Look, Frank, we'd better hurry if we want to get a swim before sundown.'

'Where will we go?'

'Ballyvourney might be best. You get your depth quickly on a high tide.'

Jimmy, leaning on the guard rail, called over his shoulder.

'A lonely old strand. I never liked it.' He took out his pipe and examined the bowl. 'The lobster quit there twenty years back.'

Ballyvourney Strand was reached by a lane a quarter mile long, at the end of which was a derelict cottage, roofless and windowless, a padlock still securing the rickety door to the door frame. Nettles blocked the path to the house and spread themselves still high across its length. A grassy track led to the cliff ledge.

Slipping and stumbling, they climbed down the crumbling pad zigzagging down through successive ledges of fallen rock and clay till they jumped the last few feet to the beach. The tiny land-locked cove faced westward. In the confines of its crescent of tall cliffs, the accumulated heat of the afternoon sun still lingered. It was baked deep into the white floury sand into which their shoes sank ankle deep. It rose in shimmering waves from the gleaming granite of the scattered rocks. It glittered from the polished glass of a sea sheltered from the evening breeze. Its breath bore down on them, making them aware of the hampering clothes sticking to their sweating bodies.

Frank flung himself down on the sand beside a flat boulder.

'This will do me,' he said. He hauled off his shoes and commenced unloosening the laces. 'And don't be long,' he called as she moved round behind an outgrowth of rock.

He was pulling on his bathing trunks when she reappeared, running down the beach towards the sea. He pitched his shirt on the flat rock beside the rest of his clothes and raced after her. She moved with an easy loping stride, her slender body and long graceful legs and the anonymity of the simple black swim-suit, giving the illusion of sexless immaturity.

He overtook her at the water's edge, waded out rapidly and dived into the first breaking wave he met. A dozen strokes and he was treading water, watching her slow progress through the surf, jumping to avoid each wave until at last the rapidly shelving sand forced her to walk forward on tiptoe, arms held high above her head.

'Get in,' he called. 'Get in or you'll be dragged in.'

'Oh, don't! Please don't!' she pleaded.

At last, with the water up to her chin, she was carried off her feet by the swell of a wave. Launching herself forward, she swam out to join him, cutting through the water in a lazy effortless crawl.

'The length of the beach and back,' she challenged.

He was hard pressed to keep up with her. By the time they reached the rocks his arms were getting tired, his breathing laboured. It was with a sense of deliverance that he saw her

159

change over to a breast-stroke and face in towards the shore.

'I've had enough. I'm going in,' she called back to him.

They reached the shallow water together. Together they stumbled through the surf, flinging themselves down in the tepid water near the beach where they rolled and wallowed and splashed each other. At length Maeve got to her feet.

'We'd better get dressed.' She pulled off her bathing cap. 'It must be getting late.'

They started off up the beach, shaking themselves free of the salt water, their eyes stinging from the sea, their bare feet sinking into the hot powdery sand. In the sheltered cove, the late afternoon sun seemed to stir up the sweltering warmth of the day that still clung to clay and rock and sand. Dazed from the heat and tired after the swim, they moved in silence – slowly, eyes half closed against the glare of the sun. Sometimes their shoulders brushed: again they walked a few paces apart.

Once she stumbled and grasped at him for support. Instinctively he reached out to steady her, circling her shoulders with his arm.

'Sorry,' she murmured. 'I am dizzy with the heat.' Cool and moist, her hand still gripped his naked shoulder.

Linked together, they moved on unsteadily, their bodies grazing each other as their feet floundered and sank in the yielding sand. Gradually, in the silence of awareness, their flagging steps came to a halt. They swung round to face each other.

For the first time he saw her pale, heart-shaped face, almost Renaissance in its elegance, with its straight nose, firm chin and dark hair swept back from the high forehead. For the first time he met the cool appraising gaze of the deep-set grey eyes. Dry-mouthed, swallowing dumbly, he stared at her.

The quiet that isolated them drowned out the rumble of the surf and the fretful clamour of the gulls. Shrouded in heat, sultry languorous heat, they stayed facing each other, arms loosely twined around shoulders, like dancers awaiting the resumption of the music.

And then they were clinging to each other and her lips

were cool, moist, yielding and the fresh tang of the sea was on them and the taste of brine was on her eye-lashes and on the lobes of her ears and her hair was still damp from the surf and the fingers clawing at his back were urgent, avid, frantic and she was grinding her mouth against his and uttering little moaning cries and crushing her body against him and the taste of someone's blood was in his mouth and her bathing cap was clammy upon his back and if this sort of carry-on went on much longer –

'Sorry,' he gasped, pushing her away firmly. 'I don't know what came over me . . . ' Resolutely, trying to ignore the harsh, shallow breathing and the trembling body, he fixed his gaze above her left shoulder to where, a hundred yards out to sea, a cormorant had just dived. '. . . pure madness . . . try to forget it ever happened . . . how am I going to look Julian in the face . . . taking advantage when he was . . . ' The cormorant surfaced, much farther away than he had calculated. Now it was paddling around, moving erratically, its beak close to the water. ' . . . it is poor treatment for someone who trusts you . . . after all, he is my best friend . . . ' The cormorant dived again. ' . . . it was an unforgivable thing to do.'

'It is getting late,' she said. 'We had better get back to the village.'

He was dressed and waiting for her before the cormorant at last surfaced with a fish. Pushing its beak up, it juggled deftly with its struggling prey until it was gripped by the tail. With a quick flip the fish was swallowed back in one gulp. The cormorant then reared itself up in the water and commenced to fan its wings vigorously across its breast as though beating warmth into its body. At length it took off, running on the surface of the water, sustained by fast flapping wings until it gained height and flew, low and swift and with craning neck, out to the open sea where, with wings outspread in heraldic attitude, it perched on the peak of a massive rock guarding the entrance of the cove.

He was still staring out at the lone rock when the crunch of shoes in the sand aroused him. He looked round.

'Are you ready?' he asked.

She stooped to adjust a sandal strap.

'No hurry,' he said. 'There's no one rushing you.'

Still stooping, she glanced up at him coldly.

'We-we-we'll be home in twenty minutes,' he stammered.

She straightened up and moved past him.

In silence they trudged through the soft sand and scrambled up the cliff. In silence walked together to the parked car. In silence threw their bathing gear into the back seat and got in. Only then did he realize how important, how absolutely indispensible to him, had become the hunched-up figure sitting quietly beside him.

As he drove along, he touched with the tip of his tongue his bruised and tingling lips. He shifted around in the seat as he felt again the skin of his back crawl under frenzied fingers. Once more he heard the sound of tiny moaning cries and the hiss of shallow breathing. With sickening clarity he recalled each detail of his cruel and cowardly rebuff. The pompous phrases, the unctuous voice, the threadbare sentiments. Small wonder that, hurt and put to shame, she now shrank away from him resentfully.

A wave of tenderness, pitying and protective, swept over him. Breathless and with thumping heart, .he sought for words to express the emotion that had so suddenly engulfed him, but it was not until they pulled up outside the terrace house that he was able to put into halting phrases the distress he felt at the humiliation he had caused her and the subsequent discovery of his own feelings.

For a long time she did not speak but remained staring ahead at the scrawny sandhills encircling the bay. At length she roused herself. Collected her beach bag. Got out of the car.

She leaned in through the open door.

'Look, Frank,' she said. Her voice was level, her eyes expressionless. 'There is one thing I want to make very clear. Julian means everything to me. I have never loved anyone else. And never will.' She paused. Her voice softened. 'Forget all these silly romantic ideas of yours and remain, as you always were, our best friend.' Again she paused, eyeing him coldly. 'But if you are going to spoil things, Frank, it might be better if you stayed away altogether.' She straightened up and slammed the car door.

Head whirling, he turned the car and drove away.

For four evenings he lay on the top of the cliffs across the bay from the terrace, watching for the return of Julian's car. He would stay there till dusk fell and the light went on in the upper room of the house. The sight of this tiny light so far across the bay brought no comfort. Only a desperate, sickening loneliness. Sometimes the dreadful feeling of desolation and loss would so overwhelm him that he would become physically ill. Then with the bile still bitter in his mouth, he would stumble back down to the village to drink himself into a stupor.

On the fifth day, as he was having his tea, he saw the car pass. It was only a fugitive glimpse so it was impossible to tell what shape Julian was in. Still, Frank had a few quick drinks before venturing up to the terrace. Just in case. By then it was almost ten o'clock. The car was parked outside but the only light showing was in the bedroom upstairs. He was about to move off when he noticed that the front door was ajar. He pushed it in.

'Anybody home?' he croaked.

'Is that you, Frank?' Julian's muffled voice answered. 'Come on up.'

'You can close the front door now, Frank,' Maeve called down.

Carefully, by banister and wall, he pawed his way upstairs towards a narrow shaft of light coming from a door jamb. He fumbled for the door knob as he knocked.

'May I come in?' he said, opening the door.

The room was hot and stuffy: the air thick with tobacco smoke. There was little furniture. Maeve's work table: a wash stand with ewer and jug, carafe and glass: a small chest of drawers: a curtained alcove.

They were both in bed. Separate single beds. A chair between them held a stack of books and magazines, a scatter of cigarette packets, a lighter and an ash-tray already choked with quenched cigarette ends. On the floor was a case of beer, three-quarters full. Beside it a litter of empty bottles.

Julian was lying back, smoking, a glass of beer in his hand. He had flung off the bed clothes and was stretched out, stripped down to his underpants. His hair was damp and his tanned body glistened with sweat.

'Hope you don't mind the heat, Frank,' he said.

'It is Julian's way of having a Turkish bath,' said Maeve.

Clad in a flowered satin jacket, she was sitting up in bed, pillow-propped. A batch of typewritten sheets lay on her lap and others were scattered face down on the coverlet.

'Take a pew,' said Julian.

Frank looked around. The only seat in the room was being used as a table.

'Sit down here,' said Maeve, patting the edge of her bed.

Gingerly, he sat down at the foot of the bed.

'Where were you these last few days?' she said. 'We were beginning to think we had offended you in some way.'

Frank gulped noisily.

'I was nowhere . . . what I mean is . . . I was actually . . . to be honest . . . I was having a few jars.'

'Oh-ho! So you were on a jag?' Julian chuckled.

'Like His Holiness here.' She nodded across at him with a tolerant smile. 'He is supposed to be thinning off now. But you would hardly say he is in the odour of sanctity yet, would you?'

'Beer!' Julian sniffed. 'Open a bottle yourself, Frank.' He reached him an opener. 'When all fruit fails, welcome haws.'

Frank poured out the beer. Sat down once more on the end of Maeve's bed. He raised his glass formally.

'Good health,' he said. 'Or maybe it should be – better health.'

'You can say that again.' Julian took a long draught of beer. 'The way I feel at present, health is a thing of the past.'

'Is it as bad as that?'

'Every bit. My stomach is in a state of tumult that would –' He rifted, loud and prolonged. Stubbed out his cigarette. Sighed, 'that's better.'

'Where were you last night?'

'At a place called Cleggan Cross. In the heart of the Blue Stacks.'

'Byrne's pub, was it?'

'That's right. A decent man. A cheerful character too.'

'Smiler Byrne. No wonder you are feeling bad. That man would smile when he was serving you rat poison. He probably dished you up first run poteen, coloured with tea. A well-known antic of his.'

'So that accounts for it,' Julian murmured. He frowned into his half-empty glass. 'Now that I look back, there were times I was doubtful about the taste of the whiskey. And the smell seemed odd somehow.'

He groaned gently, as though the recollections of the previous night were too vivid. Leaning out of the bed, he placed the half-empty glass carefully on the floor. Burrowed his head into the pillow. Closed his eyes. Groaned again, drowsily.

Frank sat motionless, staring at the dozing figure. Julian was coiled up sideways, his head resting on one hand, the other dangling, the fingers almost touching the beer glass he had just left down. The silence in the room was broken only by the occasional rustle of paper as Maeve leafed through the typescript.

As the silence lengthened, Frank became more and more aware of her presence. Her body was so close to him that he could sense the warm flesh through the bedclothes that separated them. Every movement she made, seemed to him like a caress. When she reached down to lift a sheet of paper, he trembled, waiting for her touch. A breath of perfume filled him with a wild desire to bury his face in the fragrance of her hair.

So agitated was he that the sweat broke out on him and he was forced to grip his knees to steady his trembling hands. In desperation he cleared his throat noisily in the hope that Julian would awake. Again, more noisily, he cleared his throat.

Maeve laughed, a soft, husky chuckle.

'He can drop off to sleep –' She snapped her fingers.
'– Like that! Lucky Julian.'

'I've a frog in my throat,' said Frank hoarsely. He shifted round till he faced her. Lapped his dry lips. 'How is the work going?' His voice issued in a falsetto squeak.

'Another chapter finished. It needs a bit of brushing up.' She hesitated. Tapped her teeth with the end of the pen. 'Would you like to read some of it?' she asked, her voice very off-hand, very casual. 'I did promise, after all.'

She gathered up the typewritten sheets. Riffled through them. Picked out one and scanned it quickly.

'There you are,' she handed it to him. 'See what you think of it.'

His distracted gaze settled on the last line.

Once I saw the sea . . . like a peacock's tail.

Startled, he glanced up. Her grey eyes, cool and detached, were watching him. They were the clinical eyes of a surgeon.

He turned away and started to read. It was loose, disjointed work – the rambling thoughts, it would seem, of a dying man. Revealing. Self-accusing. Comfortless.

You, who lived in the body, are dying in the body . . .
and your heart is untouched . . . a stunted seed . . . riven
by longings and regrets.

He could feel her gaze fixed on him but he refused to look up.

He read on.

And yet, one September evening . . . you sailed into
the sun . . . and the calm water was dappled with colour
. . . like the fanned-out feathers of a peacock's tail . . .
and you were sick with hunger for you knew not what
. . . Did the seed stir then?

His eye fled down the page to the last line, where the

piteous cry was repeated, loaded with regret.

Once I saw the sea . . . like a peacock's tail.

He lowered the sheet and looked at her.
'Well,' she said. 'What do you think of it?'
He swallowed.
'It is . . . '
What was to be said? How put into words the feelings that overwhelmed him?
'It is . . . '
She had plundered his fancies for a phrase. *The fanned-out feathers of a peacock's tail.* It was to have been the springboard for a poem. But now it must be cast aside as a cull. For it was shop-soiled. Shoddied by misuse.
'It is . . . it is . . . '
He should have been warned when she said it was too good a line to throw away. Already she had decided to pilfer it. What else had she said? 'Like Julian, you despise poetry.' How could she possibly know? It was too personal a passion to reveal to anyone. Yet, but for a ruffle on the sea, he would have blurted it out to her. And now, not satisfied with pillaging his work, she must needs rub his nose in it like a dog in his newly-discovered filth.
Outrage overwhelmed him. Words, bitter and scathing, bubbled in his throat so that he groped helplessly for speech.
'I'll-I'll-I'll . . . tell you . . . wh-wh-wh-what it is –'
He broke off, gasping.
From the other bed there was a creaking. A dry cough. The chink of glass.
'Pull these, will you?' Julian reached out two bottles of beer. 'You sound like someone who could do with a gargle.'

Age, I Do Abhor Thee

'Never get old, child, I tell you. Never get old. There's a poor way on you when you do.'

Many's the time I heard Granny say that. And indeed there wasn't a word of a lie in it for she was a sad enough looking sight, sitting perched up straight on the edge of the armchair, her whole body twitching, the knitting needles clanking together in her shaking hands.

'You're a burden to yourself, Jim, and to everyone else.'

Her lower jaw trembled like mad. Except when she spoke.

'No one has time for you when you're getting on in years, that's the first and the last of it. Och, there's a poor way on you all right.'

The knitting was laid down on the jerky knees and the faded grey eyes stared hopelessly into space.

'Never get old, do you hear me. Never get old.'

It was queer advice to be giving and the house stuffed with old birdies like herself. Aunt Sarah, a little stoopedy creature with red eyes and a sharp nose – a professional cross-patch, always whinging and complaining about nothing. Auntie May, fat, frizzy-haired and hip-shot, who stumped around the house, puffing through her pursed lips and muttering: 'Where has it gone? In the name of God, where has it gone? You can leave nothing down for five minutes itself but it disappears.' And Hannah, the maid, a martyr to the pains, crouched over the kitchen range in the warmest day in summer, loth to get off her hip, as Aunt Sarah put it, to do a hand's turn for anyone.

Even my friend, Doctor Clark, who called to see Granny

every week, was old. Tall, gaunt, baldy: he would sit opposite her, one hand grasping her wrist, the other holding, opened out in the flat of his palm, a gold Albert watch. Silently he would wait, eyes half closed, lips constantly parting with a sound like water dripping from a tap, until suddenly he would snap shut the watch and replace it in his waistcoat pocket.

'Aye . . . Hmm . . . So.'

Eyes ajar, lips out-thrust, he munched each word thoroughly before letting it dribble out in a low croak.

'And . . . Mrs Farley . . . how have you been keeping . . . ah . . . this last week?'

'Poorly enough, Doctor. As you can see for yourself. Sure I'm only an old bag of bones waiting for a happy release.'

'She tries to do too much,' said Auntie May. 'And she's not fit.'

'Happy release!' He pursed his lips and through his nose blew out a long sniff of derision. 'I'm telling you now . . . as I have told you many times before . . . for a woman of your years . . . you are . . . ah . . . as sound as a bell.'

'But the headaches? The dizziness? The palpitations? The –' She glanced down at the hands trembling in her lap.

'My good woman . . . you must expect at the age of . . . ah . . . eighty-three –'

'Eighty-five.'

'Eighty-five . . . I only wish I had a heart as sound . . . and a body as . . . ah . . . youthful.'

She giggled.

'Well, now, Doctor. I think that compliment deserves a little something. Sarah!' She waved towards the sideboard where a bottle of whiskey and a carafe of water stood ready. 'May! The biscuits are on the top shelf in the pantry.'

'None for me, Mrs Farley,' said the doctor.

'Jim!' She turned to me. 'The doctor's glass.'

When I returned from the china cupboard with the cut-glass goblet reserved for these occasions, the doctor took the glass and said, with the closest approach to a wink that a man with his eyes near shut could hope to achieve:

'Thank you, James.'

From the feel of the coin he had slipped into the heel of my fist, I knew it was a two shilling bit. As always.

'You're getting to be . . . ah . . . quite a big fellow. Tall as your father . . . you'll soon be.'

'You couldn't keep him in clothes.' Granny was pouring out the whiskey, the bottle chinking out a tattoo against the glass.

'Ben-weeds flourish –'

'Now, Sarah,' Granny protested.

'He's becoming a spoiled young rascal,' insisted Aunt Sarah. 'Water, Doctor?'

'Just a splash, thanks.'

'Och, the poor little fellow is only a child yet,' said Granny. 'Living all these years in a house full of women, what else could he be? If his mother, God rest her, were alive it would be different.'

'Very true, Mrs Farley . . . young James misses a mother's . . . ah . . . shall we say, restraining influence.'

To listen to them giving off, you'd have thought I wasn't there at all. But that's grown-ups all over. Let you be standing over-right them and they'll talk about you as though you were stone deaf or the Invisible Man.

Aunt Sarah sniffed.

'If his father wasn't roaming the country with a broken down no-good travelling show, he could be at home looking after young Jim.'

'That's going a bit far,' said Auntie May. 'You could hardly call the Globe Repertory Company a travelling show, could you?'

'Any company that raffles a pound note in the middle of a cut-down version of *Hamlet* and concludes with a "laughable farce" is a travelling show, as far as I am concerned.'

'Even so, Michael has his own life to live.'

'That is a poor excuse for throwing up a good job and going off on this daft expedition. Reappearing once in a while from the back end of nowhere.' She grunted. 'Without as much as a by-your-leave.'

'He didn't throw up his job, Sarah. He was sacked. Because he wouldn't agree to give up his part-time work in the theatre.'

'Well, why didn't he look for another job? Instead of swelling his chest and announcing to us –' Aunt Sarah threw back her head and declaimed in a high mincing voice. 'This is my chance to become a full-time professional actor.' Her little red eyes gleamed triumphantly as they impaled poor Auntie May. 'Stupid proposals like that make me puke.'

'That will do now, girls.' Granny held up a shaking hand. 'And there is no need for vulgarity, Sarah, no matter how strongly you feel.'

'There you go again, Mother. Taking sides. As far as the pair of you are concerned, Michael can do no wrong.'

'After all,' said Auntie May, in a reasonable tone of voice, 'it's his own life, as I said. He must make the best he can of it.'

'I know! I know! I know! But that is no reason why he should go off and desert young Jim.'

They were off again ding-dong, the three of them, rehearsing the same old arguments I had listened to week in, week out, since the night a year ago that Father had glanced up from the slice of toast he was buttering and announced: 'You needn't call me tomorrow morning as I shan't be going to work.'

Without much interest, I sat on the sofa and watched them whilst the doctor sipped his whiskey in discreet silence. Aunt Sarah, her neck outstretched like a goose, a drop trembling on the end of her nose, addressed herself to Auntie May, though you could see that the burden of her complaint was directed at Granny. Auntie May listened attentively, one hand resting on her displaced hip, the other on her bent knee, her head cocked aslant. Stolid, wary, stubborn, an infantry-man braced for a cavalry charge, she managed to get in an occasional sensible remark when Aunt Sarah paused to draw breath, thereby infuriating the latter still further. Granny's head was tick-tocking from side to side in the effort to keep track of the cross-talk. At length she

171

interjected:

'Ah, well, Sarah, what's done is done. No use raking a dead fire.'

Aunt Sarah turned on her.

'That's just what I mean, Mother. He has no fire in his guts. What is he but a deep voice clothed in flesh? Forever booming out bits of Shakespeare. As an actor –' she snorted, '– he's a proper ham.'

This was more than I could stand. Heedless of the rule that bed was the punishment for butting in on the conversation of grown-ups, I cried:

'He's not a ham. D'you hear.' I stamped on the floor. 'He is a great actor. The best in the whole world.'

The doctor took my part.

'James is right.' The blinds were up on his eyes and he fixed Aunt Sarah with a pale blue glare. 'Perhaps a slight exaggeration . . . but no matter. His father is a good actor . . . as good as the best that's going.'

But you couldn't down Aunt Sarah.

'Oh, I knew you'd say that,' she snapped. 'Aren't Michael and yourself butties? Every time he comes home, the pair of you are off up to the hotel for a session.'

'Sarah!' warned Granny.

The doctor finished his drink.

'I must be going now.' He got to his feet. 'Goodnight, Mrs Farley. Take care of yourself and . . . don't be overdoing things.' He waved vaguely as he followed Auntie May to the door. 'Goodnight, all.'

'You shouldn't have talked to the doctor like that,' Granny said, when the door closed.

'And why shouldn't I?' Aunt Sarah exploded. 'Wasn't it he who encouraged Michael in this crazy escapade? If it hadn't been for Doctor Clark blowing him up with flattery, he would be in the job yet.'

'Och, sure the poor doctor had nothing to do with it. Michael would have been gone out of here regardless. After all, you're only young once.'

Aunt Sarah raised her hands high above her head and

172

addressed an appeal to the ceiling.

'Do you hear that? "Only young once." Is she beginning to dote?' Lowering her head, she stooped forward and hissed: 'He's wearing up to the fifty mark. You'd hardly call that young, would you?'

'He *is* young!' I chipped in before she could say more.

'And look who's talking now!' She was fit to be tied. 'The young boss! He'll be running the house before we know where we are.' Her lips twisted in a sour smile. 'But, of course! His father *is* young. They're of an age, the pair of them.' Like a snake about to strike, she reared up. 'And the one has as little sense as the other.'

'Sarah.' Granny was shocked. 'You shouldn't talk that way. It's not right.'

'And if the truth be told,' Aunt Sarah snarled, 'you've little enough sense yourself to be putting up with this whole carry-on.'

She flounced out of the room, slamming the door.

Granny sighed.

'Never get old, Jim. Amn't I forever telling you that? There's a poor way on you when you do.'

'But Father's not old,' I insisted. 'He's young.'

And so he *was*. You never thought of him as anything else but your own age. Though, of course, he was years and years older. With a moustache, side-burns and a fleece of curly black hair on his chest.

He didn't go all out to appear young. You never felt he was putting on an act when he suggested a game of Snakes and Ladders. Or a hand of Happy Families. If he wanted to help you lay a new track for the clockwork train, you knew he got more fun out of it than you did yourself. If you came across him working at your Meccano set, you learned that the thing to do was to slide quietly away and not let on you had seen him.

He never issued warnings or condemnations. Advice was something he never gave. In fact, more often than not, it was he who sought advice.

Off his own bat, he would never have discovered that

adhesive tape can mend anything from a ball-point to a shaving mirror. Or that most complicated juggling feats with a pared-down matchstick can be performed by a blue-bottle if its wings are plucked and it is impaled on the end of a knitting needle.

As for the Zoo, a familiar haunt of ours, you'd be mortified sometimes at the way he went on. He would come rushing up to where you were standing at the lion's cage trying to drive a blink out of the big yellow eyes by staring the brute down. Grabbing your arm, he would say:

'Come on quick, Jim. Wait till you see this.'

And then he would drag you across to where a spindle-legged idiot of a giraffe was licking at the branch of a tree with a tongue as long as your arm.

'Look, Jim. He's licking the bark off. That's a queer bit of work, what? He could strip wallpaper with that tongue of his.'

Or he would rush you past the reptile house with its crocodiles, toads, scorpions and slender, tangled-up snakes, motionless but for flickering tongues.

'Isn't that awful, Jim?' he would say, pointing to a silly old eagle with head back to front and dull scraggy plumage. 'That poor fellow was never meant to be cooped up in a zoo. He should be soaring high in the sky. Where he belongs. No commerce with groundlings except to scatter them with droppings.'

That sort of talk would put you looking over your shoulder to see if anyone was listening.

And yet he was so different when he was on stage. Padding across the creaking boards with the soft tread of an animal, to crouch on a stool near the wings where, with one high-booted leg stretched out, purple doublet crinkled as he leaned forward, chin resting on fisted hand, he murmured to himself, *'To be, or not to be: that is the question.'*

The words flowed over you, slow and benumbing, telling of fortune and trouble, heartache and shock, and there was no need to know the exact meaning, only everyone around you was, like yourself, frozen into stillness and, like yourself,

174

gazed spellbound at the eyes that glittered in the spotlight.

Even better was it in the morning to sit on the edge of the bath and watch him scowling, smiling, sneering into the mirror as he rubbed in the lather on his face, breaking off every so often to address the lean face with the tousled hair.

'For so work the honey-bees, creatures that by a rule in nature teach the act of order to a peopled kingdom.'

His lips shape the words with the same authority as, on the bake-board, Hannah's floury hands move deftly about – kneading, smoothing out, moulding into shape the pulpy dough.

His mirrored glance meets mine. He winks.

'I know what you want, old man, don't I?'

He opens the leather case containing the seven gleaming razors, each one with a different day of the week engraved on the back of the blade.

'What day is it?' he asks.

When I tell him, he picks out the appropriate razor, strops it and tests it on the palm of his hand.

'Here we go,' he says, gripping with his thumb the skin of his left cheek bone so that a smooth surface of creamy lather presents itself to the poised blade.

'To-morrow,' he intones, sweeping the blade down the tautened skin.

'And to-morrow.' On the other lathered cheek, in the wake of the reversed blade, a swathe of pink flesh appears.

Now the razor smooths a path from the uplifted chin to the jutting thrapple.

'And to-morrow.'

The spoken words, deep and rounded, drop like a stone into bottomless water and ripple into silence. I pray that he may keep repeating these astonishing words so that inside my skull the sound of the plunging stone may echo on and on. But I know what comes next.

Chipping at his throat with the razor, he declaims, *'Creeps in this petty pace from day to day, to the last syllable of recorded time.'*

Ever and always he keeps spouting silly gibberish like this

175

and always I listen, hoping that maybe once more a stone will fall. And sometimes it does.

Once I woke up from nightmare sleep, screaming my head off. Granny switched on the light and tried to soothe me but I could not, could not, could not break out of my dream. Only when the door was flung open and Father strode over to the bedside, did I stop screaming.

Tall as the ceiling, he stood there, hair rumpled, eyes blinking.

'What's this?' he demanded.

'Hush!' Granny said. 'The poor child had a nightmare.'

Cautiously he squatted on the edge of the bed. Felt my forehead, for some reason.

'We all have them,' he said. '*I could be bounded in a nutshell and count myself a king of infinite space, were it not that I have –*' He stooped down and murmured, so low that I doubt if Granny heard. '*– bad dreams.*'

The whispered words lapped on my closed eyelids.

'Leave him be now, Michael,' said Granny. 'Don't be filling his head with a lot of nonsense.'

I knew it was nonsense. But I knew also that he was the only one in the whole house who wasn't old and crabbed and contrary.

Just before Christmas a pipe under the bathroom floor sprang a leak, making a mess of the kitchen and putting everyone running with bowls and buckets and basins and crocks to catch the drippings from the spreading patch of damp on the ceiling. When the plumber arrived, I waited while he turned off the water at the main with a huge corkscrew affair. Then I followed him upstairs and stood watching as, with no hurry in the world on him, he proceeded to lay out his tools in an orderly fashion on the bathroom floor, checking them off to himself as he did so:

'Blow-lamp . . . stilson wrench . . . hammer . . . hack-saw . . . shifting spanner . . . file . . . '

'What's that?' I pointed.

Out of the bulging bag he extracted a grey sheet of metal,

folded up untidily. Like an old newspaper.

'This stuff?'

'Aye.'

'Lead sheeting. The wee lad wants me to make a keel plate for his sailing boat.'

'Doesn't look like the lead you get in pencils then.'

'It'll write every bit as good as the best pencil you could buy. Would you like me to pare off a strip for you?'

'Please. I'll hop off and get a sheet of paper.'

But when I got down to the kitchen, Aunt Sarah wired into me.

'Stay down here and don't go near the bathroom again. These tradesmen are only looking for the chance to drag out a job.'

'They don't like being watched at their work,' said Granny.

'The sooner he's gone, the sooner we can clean up after him,' Auntie May said.

It was near tea-time before the bathroom was pronounced fit for use. Armed with an old writing pad and a pencil, I rushed upstairs.

It was worse than I expected. Taps, porcelain, mirrors, window glass: all freshly burnished. Clean towels on the towel rail. The floor scrubbed, polished and swept clear of litter.

Without much hope, I ferreted around under the bath: in the hot air press and the soiled clothes basket: at the back of the lavatory cistern. I was about to give up when I suddenly thought of the heavy mirror hanging over the hand basin. Sure enough, when I pulled the bottom of the mirror away from the wall, out fell a narrow strip of lead sheeting. The plumber had not failed me.

I wasted no time examining the lead strip but tried it out at once on the writing pad, dashing off a faint, but clearly discernible, squiggle. By pressing down hard the squiggle became broader and darker but never up to the standard of a pencil scrawl.

Deciding that perhaps the metal strip needed paring and sharpening, I got at it with my penknife. To my surprise, the

177

blade sank into the lead and sliced off a shaving as easily as you'd peel a spud. So soft was the metal that it was possible even to scratch with a thumb nail the dirty grey skin that coated the surface. Soon I was busy scraping with knife blade and finger nails until at last the length of lead sheeting was restored to its original purity.

I turned it over and over in my hands – a gleaming silver trophy, brighter and certainly harder to come by than any coin ever minted.

Its pliancy fascinated me. It could be coiled into a liquorice twist or furled into a Swiss roll. It could form bridges, mountains and letters of the alphabet. It could be folded up again and again, each fold being squeezed into place by sinking my teeth into it. As there was no taste of any sort off the lead, there seemed a good chance that, if worked on long enough, the thin strip could be chewed into a solid plate. Or even into a shining metal ball.

Heavy going it was. And sore on the jaws. But I kept at it, confident that in the end a nugget of pure silver would be the reward for my pains. Continually I was running out of spittle with the sheer dint of nibbling and biting, chewing and gnawing. When I plucked out the lump of metal so that I could suck up spit and ease my aching jaws, it was discouraging to see how little progress was being made. Still, I consoled myself, look how it is pocked with tooth marks. All that is needed is patience and perseverance.

So I thrust the leaden caramel back into my mouth and began once more to chew vigorously. This was becoming ever more difficult as the chunk of metal seemed to be increasing in size so rapidly that soon all movement of my tired jaws would be impossible. I was slowing to a halt when Hannah opened the door.

'Your tea's on the table, Master Jim,' she said. 'Did you not hear me call?'

'Hmmnhgm hnwh.'

'Don't tell me you're eating sweets before your tea?'

'Hmhgm hnht.'

'Well, what have you got in your mouth so?'

178

By this time I was near puking point. Glad enough to be shut of it, I spat out the metal plug. Held it up, dripping with slavers.

'What's that? Let me see.'

Grabbing, she peered.

'Lead! My God, he's been eating lead!'

She hobbled downstairs, one hand gripping the rail, the other held aloft, waving her find.

'Lead! Lead! Lead!' Her screams rose higher and higher. 'He's been eating lead, Mrs Farley. The wee lad's been eating lead.'

I was met at the kitchen door by the whole drove of them. All shouting at once.

'What's this all about? . . . Aren't you the bold article? . . . How is it you can't behave yourself? . . . What's happened atall, atall? . . . When will you learn manners? . . . What was he doing, tell me?'

'Amn't I tired telling you?' Hannah gobbled. She waggled her outstretched hand. 'See! A lump of lead as big as your fist. He was going to swallow it when I managed to stop him. How much he had devoured before I came on the scene, God alone knows.' She paused for breath. 'Making a junk yard of his stomach. He'll never be the better for it.' Her face crumpled up. 'Oh, dear,' she wailed. 'The poor wee mite.'

They surrounded me.

'Open your mouth . . . Wider . . . Wider still . . . Head back . . . Further . . . Keep still.'

Prodding and peering, they crouched over me. Squinting down my gullet. Poking around my tongue. Running their fingers between teeth and gums. I began to feel sick. And all the time they kept firing questions at me.

'How much of that dreadful stuff did you eat?'

'Did you swallow it in lumps or chew it properly?'

'How do you feel?'

'Is there any stuck in your throat now?'

'You're not coming over weak, are you?'

To tell nothing but the truth, the walls were beginning to revolve. Not very fast, I'll grant you. But you could sense that they might start whirling anytime.

'I – I – I – ' Reaching out, I tried to halt the nearest wall.

'Are you all right?' said Granny.

'He's very pale looking,' said Auntie May.

'Are you going to be sick?' Aunt Sarah said.

They closed in on me. Half pushed, half carried, I was brought into the sitting room. Eased on to the couch.

'How do you feel now?' Auntie May laid her hand on my forehead. 'He's running a temperature, I'll swear.'

'If he doesn't sit up, he'll be sick.'

'Leave him alone, Sarah. He's better lying down.'

'If he gets sick, he'll puke on the carpet.'

'You've a heart of stone talking about carpets at a time like this.'

'I'm the one who'll have to clean it.'

'Shouldn't we send for the doctor?' said Granny.

In the sudden lull, there came a soft, excuse-me cough. Every head jerked round towards the door.

'Begging your pardon, ladies, and meaning no offence, but what the hell's going on here?'

It was Father. Dressed in a camel hair overcoat and a gaudy yellow scarf. We gaped at him in silence. The returned wanderer.

'Are you rehearsing *East Lynn*, by any chance?' he said.

Aunt Sarah was the first to recover.

'This is no laughing matter, Michael. We had the plumber in today fixing a burst pipe and he left a sheet of lead after him. Young Jim here is after chewing and swallowing back all of it. Bar –' she reached across and grabbed from Hannah the collop of lead. Thrust it out. '– this!'

Father took it. Turned it over gingerly. Glanced up.

'He has a better mouthful of teeth than I have myself.'

He came over to the couch.

'Well, aren't you the tough young tit! Not satisfied with swinging the lead, you start eating it.'

He stooped down till I could smell the whiskey off his breath. Whispered.

'Did you eat much of it?'

I shook my head.

'Half a hundredweight?' he suggested. 'Or maybe just a couple of bites?'

'I – I – I don't know.'

Nor did I. The fuss and turmoil had left me so groggy that I was not at all sure what had really happened.

'Hadn't we better get the doctor?' repeated Granny.

'Did you swallow any of the stuff at all?' Father persisted. 'You're not acting the candy man, by any chance?'

'I don't know . . . I – I could have . . . Mebbe I did.'

He straightened up.

'I'll get the doctor,' he said.

Out in the hall, I heard him asking Auntie May what plumbing firm had done the job, so that he could check up.

This bowled me over completely. Bad enough being in trouble myself. But getting an unfortunate tradesman hauled over the coals – perhaps even sacked – for smuggling me a wretched strip of lead sheeting –

'Oh, dear,' I moaned, as my stomach started to heave.

'Quick, someone,' Aunt Sarah cried. 'Get a basin. He's going to be sick.'

She put me sitting up straight on the side of the couch, my hands clasping my outspread knees.

'Bear up,' she said, 'till Hannah gets back, there's a good boy.'

I did my best, God knows. My stomach was churning. My forehead damp with sweat. The tears squirting out of my eyes. I clapped my hands to my mouth. Flung back my head. And with bulging cheeks, tried to hold out.

But the final spasm could not be contained. Through constricting fingers, the contents of my stomach burst forth, fanning out in a dreadful spray and engulfing all before it.

Aunt Sarah let a screech out of her.

'My good skirt! Sweet Mother of God, it's destroyed completely. It'll never clean off. And my shoes. And stockings. And, God grant me patience, take a look at the carpet, the state it's in. And . . . It's time for you, Hannah. You're never to be had when you're wanted . . . Here, boy. Hold that under your chin, before you spread ruin all round you.'

I pushed away the basin and lay back groaning.

'Sit up, Jim, and do what you're told.'

'Leave the child be,' said Auntie May. 'Can't you see he's ill?'

'No reason why he couldn't have manners.'

'Oh, Sarah. The poor boy could well be suffering from lead poisoning.'

'He's in a bad way surely,' Hannah chipped in.

'Shouldn't we look it up in the book?' said Granny.

The fat paper-backed volume – *1001 Medical Hints* – was produced. As it was in every household crisis. Granny, her poor fingers shaking madly, adjusted her spectacles and leafed through the pages, murmuring:

'Burns ... cats ... fainting ... hives ... jaundice ... lameness ... laryngitis ... here it is. Lead poisoning or plumbism, a form of poisoning due to the ... Oh, dear –' her voice quavered, 'to the introduction of lead into the system. A common form is lead colic which is attended with frequent ... frequent intestinal pains.'

Moaning softly, I harkened to my fate.

'The poison proceeds to generate obstinate constipation ... anaemia ... wasting ...'

'Stop it, Mother, don't you see he's listening,' hissed Aunt Sarah.

'Little pitchers have long ears,' Auntie May warned.

Granny paid no heed.

'Muscular tremors ...'

Already I could feel my arms and legs trembling and twitching. Soon my jaws would start clanking.

'And ultimate paralysis.'

At the sound of these dreadful words – a stone sinking into black and bottomless bog – the living daylights were scared out of me.

'Ooooooooooh!' I wailed.

'Now see what you've done.' Aunt Sarah snatched the book from Granny's hands. 'Didn't I tell you to stop.'

She wheeled round to the others.

'Warm up a glass of milk, Hannah. And May, bring a rug in from the hall.'

Soon, tucked up snugly and warmed with the hot drink, I lay, blinking the sleep from my eyes and trying to catch a stray word from the guarded whispers. Granny was sitting up very straight in her chair, an invisible volume gripped in her trembling hands. The sound of her chattering teeth could be heard above the murmuring talk. As I was drifting into sleep, I heard her mutter:

'You can do nothing right in this house. Try as you might. It's as I've always said – never get old. For there'll be a poor way on you when you do.'

The sound of voices in the hall awakened me.

'This'll be them now,' said Auntie May.

'And time for them,' Aunt Sarah muttered. 'Nearly two hours getting here. Easy to tell the form they'll be in.'

The sitting room door was flung open.

'Go on in, man,' shouted Father. 'Don't stand on ceremony.'

Doctor Clark poked his head round the door and peered about him, blinking rapidly. The silly smile on his face didn't cheer me up any.

'We were . . . ah . . . delayed a little.'

'So I see.' Aunt Sarah's voice was pure vinegar.

'Sure the doctor can't call an hour of the day his own,' said Granny.

'Come up to the fire,' said Auntie May.

Cautiously the doctor advanced into the room, one hand holding the bag to his waist, the other stretched out as though he were feeling his way.

'I learn . . . on the highest authority –' He lurched against the piano, setting the strings jangling. Steadying himself against the lid, he pushed himself upright.

'Sorry,' he said gravely, patting the piano top in a kindly fashion.

'My God!' Aunt Sarah breathed. She couldn't have been more horrified than I was.

Father bustled in, holding himself a little too erect, his

gestures a little too expansive. He went to the sideboard and lifted the bottle.

'You'll join me, Bill,' he said, already pouring. 'A little of what you fancy does you good.'

When he wheeled round with the glass, I noticed that his lips were damp and somehow flabby looking.

'Here we are,' he said.

The doctor was shuffling across to the couch.

'I think we must first examine the ... ah ... patient.'

He sat on a chair beside me, head flung back, eyes closed, lips smacking away as though in relish of my plight.

'They tell me you were trying to ... emulate Socrates.'

From his breast pocket he pulled out a slender metal cylinder. Extracted a thermometer. Shook it and popped it into my mouth.

'*A drowsy numbness pains my sense ... as though of hemlock I had drunk.*'

I could well believe it. Whatever he had been drinking, the wretched man looked to be asleep on his feet. He was in no fit condition even to treat the like of my granny let alone someone suffering from lead poisoning. Shivering with fright, I pulled the rug up around my chin.

'Most extraordinary . . . in all my years spent in the . . . practice of medicine . . . this is the first case . . . I have encountered of . . . ah . . . addiction to lead.'

It would drive you up the walls, this humming and hawing and beating about the bush when something terrible could happen any moment. He took the thermometer out of my mouth. Held it up before his closed eyes. You'd think it was a dog lapping up milk the way he smacked his lips.

'Tell me, James . . . as a matter of scientific interest . . . did you have much trouble . . . ah . . . engorging this stuff?'

'I – I – I don't know.'

Such silly questions. Wasting valuable time.

He put away the thermometer. Felt my forehead. Lifted one eyelid. Glanced into my mouth.

'All in order,' he said. No mention of my ravaged stomach.

'Come on, Bill,' Father called. 'You're behind in your

drinks.'

Before joining Father, the doctor went into a huddle with Granny and the two aunts. Whispering and colloguing. As he moved away, he said aloud:

'Give him plenty of fruit. Apples. Oranges. Pears. Bananas. And . . . ah . . . the odd bar of chocolate.'

'Nut chocolate,' he added.

All the things I loved. There could be but one reason for being so flahoolach. The case must be hopeless. Incurable. Beyond all medical aid. What Granny had read out of the book came back to me. A slow wasting away, with tremors maybe worse than hers, until a paralysed finish in a wheel-chair. Or maybe worse. For how often had I been warned that poison kills?

Quaking with fright, I sat up straight.

'Doctor Clark.'

He took a long slug out of his glass.

'Yes, James?'

'Lead. Is it very strong? I mean, do people . . . do people die from eating it?'

'If it has been . . . ah . . . ingested in sufficient quantity, a man can die –'

'*A man can die but once: we owe God a death.*'

Father was on his feet, flourishing his arms.

'Eh?' the doctor looked startled.

Face flushed and breathing heavily, Father held up his hand for silence.

'*If I must die, I will encounter darkness as a bride, and hug it in my arms.*'

Though he mouthed the words slowly and carefully, his speech was slurred.

'Great stuff, what? He's at his best on the rigor mortis, the Stratford gent. Listen to this.' He wiped his moist lips with the back of his hand. Cradled his chin in his fist. '*Ay, but to die, and go we know not where: to lie in cold obstruction and to rot.*'

'Hush up, Michael,' said Granny. 'Don't you know the child gets nightmares?'

Aunt Sarah sniffed.

'It's the drink talking.'

'Is there no way to stop dying?' I squeaked.

Flinging his arms wide, Father declaimed, *'Golden lads and girls all must, as chimney sweepers come to dust.'*

The doctor, dozing over his drink, raised his head. You could hear the champing of his jaws a mile away.

'The bright day is done and we are for the dark,' he muttered.

'Good for you, Bill.' Father was jubilant. 'I knew you'd a shot left in the locker.' He reached for the bottle. 'Here,' he said, splashing the whiskey into the doctor's glass. 'Have another sup.'

There they sat, gobbling down their drinks, not caring if I lived or died. And all the time the rotten old lead eating its way through my tortured guts. It was too much.

'Surely,' I wailed, 'there must be some cure if you happen to swallow lead?'

Jaw hanging slackly, the doctor peered stupidly at me. Pressed his hand to his forehead. Shook his head slowly, groping for words. Intoned in a high mumbling voice.

'Oh, that this too too solid flesh would melt, thaw and resolve itself into a dew.'

'Begod, you're excelling yourself tonight, Bill,' Father shouted. 'Putting me to the pin of my collar, that's what you're –' He broke off. Shook a warning forefinger. 'Hold on a minute. You've got something.' Softly he repeated the doctor's words. *'Oh, that this too too solid flesh would melt.'* He slapped his thigh delightedly. 'Do you know what it is, old son, you've hit on the cure. We'll have to melt the lead. Nothing else for it.'

'Wha?' the doctor's face was screwed up into a frown.

'Melt. The. Lead,' Father repeated slowly. 'Apply heat, d'you get me?' He lifted the poker. Waggled it. 'This gentleman would do the trick. If it was reddened a bit. And judiciously applied.' He jabbed the raised poker upwards. Winked. 'Now do you follow? *Melt, thaw and resolve itself into a dew.'*

186

The doctor's lips moved, puzzling over the words. His long mournful face broke into a grin. He threw back his head.

'Haw! Haw! Haw! That's a good one all right. *Melting into a dew.*'

And the two of them into the laughter. Rocking in their seats. Puffing and spluttering. Thumping their thighs. Spilling their drinks in all directions.

The tears stinging my eyes, I jumped to my feet and faced the pair of them.

'I hate you!' I screamed. 'I hate you! I hate you!'

Granny came stumbling across to me, wringing her hands.

'It's all right, Jim. Don't be frightened. They're only joking.'

Too well I knew they were joking. Making a mock of me, that's what they were doing. Laughing their big silly heads off at my misery. Sitting around, guzzling down their whiskey while the poison was taking root. Not caring what happened to me. And now it was too late. The injustice of it all enraged me.

I pushed Granny away. Shaking my clenched fists, I glared at them. Driven frantic by their silly, sappy grins.

'I'll die,' I shouted. 'That's what I'll do. I'll die. Maybe then you'll be sorry.'

Gulping back my sobs, I rushed from the room and slammed the door. I hesitated, listening to the clamour inside. They were all talking at once, but above them all I heard Father's voice, raised in a hoarse and peevish growl.

'Give over, Mother, will you. Between yourself and the rest of the clutch, you have the young brat thoroughly spoiled.'

This was the last straw.

Flinging open the door, I stood there in the sudden silence, racking my brains for something to say. Something that would cut to the bone. I gazed round at them. Aunt Sarah, a wrinkled little witch. Auntie May, a big bag of flesh. Granny, with her poor trembling limbs and chattering teeth. The doctor, a bald and blethering old cod. And Father, staring at me stupidly with bleary unfocused eyes, the whiskey sweat glistening on his blotchy cheeks, the poker still

187

clutched in his upraised hand.

Bubbling in my throat were the words that must be said.

'You're the same as the rest of them in this house.' I pointed an accusing finger at him. 'You're old. Do you hear me. Old.'

The tears of hurt and disappointment spurted from my eyes.

'I tell you, you're old. Old as the hills. And there's . . . there's . . . there's a shocking poor way on you.'

Pastorale

God knows, no one would want to belittle a neighbouring
farmer and his family. The more so when there's been a chair
for you at their kitchen fire every night for a score or more
years. But not to put a tooth in it and to make due allowance
for bitter tongues, the Bennetts are known throughout the
length and breadth of the parish as notorious bloody land
grabbers. They've gobbled up every small holding in the
townland that went on the market for years past. Even where
it was a forced sale. A halt was put to their gallop a while
back when James – the old man – took to the bed. Still, by
that time they had gathered together a few hundred acres of
the best land hereabouts. With a world of cattle and sheep to
keep it stocked up.

But if they are big farmers itself, they are bloody wee in
their ways. They may grant you the heat of the fire, but you'll
not be left long enough sitting idle to scorch the knees of
your pants. From the time you cross the threshold till you say
goodnight, it's a constant litany.

'There's turf wanted. Take the big creel. It'll save the
double journey.'

'Put another few sods on the fire, will you.'

'The heifer's roaring. Better go out to the byre and make
sure she's all right.'

'Bring in a couple of buckets of water.'

'The morrow's Sunday. The shoes could do with a lick of
polish.'

The rest of the time you're hunched up beside the bellows
wheel keeping the fire going or shifting the kettle up and

189

down on the arm of the crane or poking around with the tongs gathering up the scattered embers.

So it's easy to tell there's something wrong when for once you're let take your seat by the fire without being called to order. Susie, the mother, is not around herself. Only the two young fellows.

'A brave class of a night, lads.'

A civil enough remark, you'd think. But for all the heed paid to it, you might have been talking to two dummies.

'Good growthy weather, wouldn't you say?'

Not a mute out of either of them.

'That sup of rain this morning'll do no harm.'

No reply.

The thick ignorant whelps. Sitting there crouched over the fire. Without a word to throw to a dog.

'Is your father improving any?'

John, the eldest buck, turns his head, a stupid look on his face.

'Henh?' says he.

'What form is the old fellow in the day?'

'The Boss-man is it?' says he. 'He got a bad turn around tea-time. Didn't he, Martin?'

'Aye.'

Not very forthcoming, you'd be at liberty to say.

'He's had the priest and the doctor. He's in a poor way. Isn't he, Martin?'

'Aye.'

'His breathing's a class of choked. It's a fret to listen to it.'

No word of a lie in that statement. You could hear the wheezing through the closed door of the bedroom upstairs.

'He'll not last the night. Isn't that what the doctor said, Martin?'

The young chap gives him a look that would sour your stomach.

'Damned well you know what the doctor said. Weren't you there at the time?'

'I was only asking a civil question.'

'Weren't you right beside me when I was talking to the

190

doctor?'

'I was only asking –'

'You ask too many bucking questions, if you ask me. And you know the answers to them all before you start.'

And Martin into him with the castigating and the casting up. Allowing for John being a class of an idiot and Martin himself maybe having enough on his plate, it's still a bit bloody thick. There's a time and a place for everything. It's a disgrace to be chawing the fat with your poor father dying above in the room.

'You blabber too much,' says Martin.

'Only for you're a big-mouthed slob,' says he, 'there'd have been no need for either priest or doctor.'

'How do you mean?'

'What need was there to tell the Boss about the malicious antics of the neighbours?'

'Malicious antics?'

'Aye. Leaking out to him that Gormley is running up an extension to the haggard. You must have known that would put him frothing at the mouth.'

In the name of God, what's this? The River field again. For years past, the source of contention and doggery. It is a scraggy strip of land that wouldn't graze a goat, but it mears on the Bennett property, blocking them off from watering their stock in the river. Old James has been trying these many years to buy it from the owner, Peter Gormley, a half-baked sheep farmer who has as much regard for the Bennett family as he has for sheep dip. The River field lies on the far side of the road from the Gormley farmstead, so he describes it as the Out Farm. It is littered with rusting, second-hand farm machinery that Gormley trucks in as a side line. There is an old timber shed on it used for storing what is described in the local paper as:

SPECIAL OFFERS, FOR ONE WEEK ONLY

A man in his right mind wouldn't take a gift of the whole rickmatick – shed, machinery and land. But Gormley won't

191

sell. At any price. Claims the shed has become a class of a bloody emporium. With farmers coming from all arts and parts to buy top grade farm equipment. And Bennett grinding his teeth with rage every time he sees a harrow or a binder or a potato digger towed into the River field. To say nothing but the truth, for the last while back the poor man can think of nothing else but 'Gormley's haggard'. No wonder, in his present state of health, he gets a bad turn when he hears your-man is running up an addition to it.

'There's no use in you trying to make excuses.' Martin is still giving out the pay. 'You put your two big ignorant feet in it, as usual.'

'Aw jay, Martin, have a heart. You're always larding into me.'

'Haven't I every right to? The Lord knows what manner of misfortune you're after bringing about with your tattling tongue. There could be a poor enough way on us if the Boss doesn't pull out of his turn.'

Now what's all this about? You'd think to listen to him that they haven't a shilling to their name. Instead of being the wealthiest ranchers in the whole barony. Begod, some people don't know when they're well off.

John is digging the wax out of one ear, his forefinger working like the plunger of a churn.

'Och, things can't be as bad as that,' says he.

'We could well be walking the road,' says Martin, 'without a roof over our heads if the ould fellow hasn't put his affairs in order.'

'Henh?'

Finger still jammed in his ear, John gapes at the brother. Properly flummoxed. And no wonder. A statement the like of yon, would put the hair standing on your head. Walking the roads, no less. The arse out of their breeches. And sleeping at the back of a ditch with the winds of the world for company. Fat chance of that happening to greedy corbies the like of the Bennetts. Unless –? Hold on now!

'Have you no savvy, man?' says Martin. 'Don't you know that if the Boss hasn't made a will, that bloody brother of ours will fall in for his share of the property? We'll be ruined paying him out his portion.'

'Francis, is it?' John is frowning at the wax on his finger nail. 'Sure, he's abroad in Tasmania, the last we heard of him.'

'Wherever he is, it won't be long till he finds out that he can get something for nothing.'

Ho-ho! So that's it! Old James hasn't settled his affairs. Loth, like many another, to quit the jockey seat. Well, it looks as if it's too late now. If the old fellow snuffs it, Francis can claim his share of the kitty – house, lands, stock and the nest egg that's surely in the bank. You can hardly fault Martin for being worried. After all, when Francis was hunted out of the country twenty years ago, the Bennetts were small farmers like the rest of us. And now that they're wealthy ranchers, the black sheep of the family can levy a toll on all those years of sweat and skulduggery.

Martin is on his feet, prowling about the kitchen, every so often stopping at the foot of the stairs to cock an ear towards the room above.

'Bad enough,' says he, 'if we have to cripple ourselves for life paying him out his share, as long as he stays away from us. In Australia or Tasmania or wherever the hell he's supposed to be. But,' says he, with a look of horror on his face, the like of what you'd see on a Redemptorist when he's describing the fate of the damned, 'what will we do if he takes it into his head to come home and squat here, drinking the piece out till he has us ruined and disgraced with his blackguardly behaviour?'

It's a queer thing about young bucks the like of Martin. They're all the time beefing off to other people. Laying down the law as though they are the only ones who know the answers. But if you listen closely, you find they are really talking to themselves. Especially if they are worried or excited. It would seem as if they build up such a head of steam that they must let it off. No matter who is listening. So here is Martin giving out the pay like a hoor at a christening.

'That Francie fellow,' says he, 'was a proper affliction. No

193

wonder the Boss gave him the run. If he had been let fly his kite for much longer, the whole bloody farm would have come under the hammer. He was nothing but a drunken bum.'

You could say a lot more than that about Francie without repeating yourself. He would drink the cross off an ass. For the price of a pint, he'd perform any manner of villainy, let it be grand larceny itself. And when he was drunk – which was every night of the week – he was a notorious ruffian. Singing and shouting, arguing the point, spilling drinks, breaking glasses, puking up his guts, before he wrecked the jakes. He would latch on to you at the bar counter. Never let up till he had you milked dry. Then you'd be lucky if he didn't mill you with a bottle for refusing to buy him a drink. A barbarous bloody savage, that's what he was. And yet he could get any woman he wanted. Whatever they saw in him.

'Sure you're maybe worrying your head about nothing,' says John. 'The Boss-man would never overlook a thing like making a will.'

'Well, you're wrong there. He has no will made. I'm positive of that.'

'Isn't it a wonder now you never tackled him about it long since?'

'Tackled him about it?' Martin, neck outstretched, hisses like an angry goose. 'Haven't I been harping at him since he took to the bed six months ago. But it's no use. He keeps on saying that he can't put his affairs in order till he has the River field got. He can think of nothing else but that bloody field. And the wretched haggard. He has himself convinced that Gormley put up yon ould shed just to annoy him. Between the pair of them, I'm bloody near demented.'

And God knows, the sight of him striding up and down, waving his arms and spitting out maledictions against his poor dying father, would put you wondering. After all, the Bennetts were a queer broody class of a connection. You would never know where you were with them. There was Uncle Dan, a godless heathen if ever there was one, always giving off about relics and statues and religion in general, who had a framed picture of the Sacred Heart, almost as big as himself, tied round his bare chest with a hay rope. And Rosie, the aunt, a withered up old maid, who used to go out to the fields every morning at daybreak and roll herself stark naked in the dew so as to keep her skin young. And the grandfather, who would wear you down with talk of temperance, the while he was lapping up the booze in the security of his bedroom until at the latter end, overcome by the horrors of drink, he would parade the village in the small hours of the morning clad in nothing but his shirt and pledge-pin, a lighted candle in each hand and him roaring: 'Sprinkle me for fear of God!' Not to speak of the present company, for John was never considered to be more than a half-wit. If the truth be told, there was a want in the whole seed, breed and generation of them.

'So help me Jaysus, I'd be better off –' Martin is just getting properly into his stride when Susie comes out of the bedroom, the finger to her lips.

'Ssh!' says she. 'He's just dozed off.'

She's at the foot of the stairs before she says:

'Oh *you're* here!'

There's barely time to mutter: 'Sorry to hear poor James was taken bad,' before she starts giving off.

'My God!' she says. 'What's come over you? Sitting there with the fire dying out before your eyes. No! No! Gather up the embers first. Get a few sods of turf. Small dry ones. Put them at the back where they'll light quicker. Not that way! On their ends. Now give a spin to the bellows wheel. Take it easy! Don't you see you're scattering sparks?'

She's a professional cribber, the Susie one. Satisfied with nothing. If the old fellow above in the room were to croak, she would be grumbling about how inconsiderate it was of him to die and him knowing full well how expensive it would be, what with feeding the mourners and stuffing them with drink and cigarettes and keeping fires going day and night in every room and folk trampling about everywhere, ruining the floors with their dirty boots and the cost of a funeral with hearse, mourning cars and a coffin, more than likely of unseasoned timber that would buckle and warp before it's rightly underground and what in God's holy name will a High Mass run to, with priests to no end loafing around inside the altar rails making no effort to earn their money and grave diggers that get better paid than County Council workers for digging a bit of a hole in the ground and then filling it up again.

'How is he, Ma?' says John, who, dim-witted as he is, has still more savvy than to get up off his arse and help with the fire.

'I've seen him worse,' says she. 'He'll maybe pull out of it.' She draws up a chair to the fire and squats down straddle-legged, toasting her thighs.

'The doctor says he won't last till morning,' says Martin. And you would know by the whine in his voice what class of a worry is on him.

'Och, I suppose if it's laid down,' says she, 'it'll come to pass.'

She starts swaying back and forth, massaging her legs with the flat of her hands. Says she:

'Father Bourke was talking to me after he gave your poor father the last rites. "Don't worry, Mrs Bennett," says he. "I never saw a man better prepared for death. Completely resigned," says he. "It was a most edifying sight. There is no doubt in my mind," says he, "that God will forgive him his trespasses as James himself," says he, "has forgiven those of his neighbours." And what's more –'

Before she can say any more, Martin reins her back on her haunches.

'What about Gormley?' says he.

'Gormley?' says she.

'Aye. If there's trespasses to be forgiven, wouldn't it be as well, before it's too late, for himself and the Boss to make the peace?'

Could you beat that for sheer effrontery? Proposing a death-bed reconciliation so that he can lay hands on the loot. He has the neck of a giraffe, that young fellow.

Susie gapes at him, goggle-eyed.

196

'Are you gone out of your mind,' says she. 'Allow that ruffian into the house to rant and rave at your poor father's bedside? Dragging up old scandals that are best forgotten? Sure there's no sense to the man. Nothing will convince him but that our Francie was responsible for –'

'Ma!' says Martin. You'd think he's checking a dog that's after lifting a leg against the dresser.

And no wonder. Susie's chapfallen expression tells its own story. She has let the cat out of the bag. A disreputable tomcat by the name of Francie. Very liable to commit scandal when on the prowl. And in this parish, scandal means only the one thing – poling a woman. So very likely that's why Francie decamped. And wait now! A short while after the flitting didn't Gormley's daughter, Helen, get herself, what her father described as 'a grand job' in England? A notorious kittling-ground for colleens in disgrace. Bejeezus, that's it! She sneaked off to that immoral country to have her ba. And . . . Hold on! Hold on! Wasn't that the same year that Robert, Helen's brother, left the Seminary in his last term. Just before he was due for ordination. They were bloody strict in those days. One rattle from the closet where your family skeleton was stored and you were out the window. Nothing for it but to creep home in the guise of a spoiled priest, giving out to all and sundry that you had the misfortune to lose your vocation. After all, if it became known that you were turfed out of the College because your sister was a manifest trollop, your family could never hold up their heads in the village again.

So Robert is shipped off to the States where if he opens his mouth too wide over a few pints, it'll not give rise to local gossip. And everybody sympathises with his poor father in his sad bereavement, for spoiled priests are a rare enough commodity in this part of the country.

Can you beat it? Over all these years Mister Slippy-tit has been codding the natives with his bragging and boasting that no one can point the finger of scorn at one of the Gormleys. But the cost of keeping his halo intact has been high. There he is, clocking in a big barn of a house, with nothing but the walls for company. Small blame to him if he hates the guts of the Bennett family and holds them to ransom for a patch of ground and a rickety shed.

Susie has recovered herself and is holding forth once more as though nothing has happened.

'He was a good man, your father,' says she. 'None better. In the front seat at Mass every Sunday. Year in, year out. Always attended to his Easter duty. Headed the list in every church collection. Father Burke claims there wasn't a pick of malice in his bones. It's a great comfort to hear the like of that from a priest.'

Over by the fireplace, John wags his poll in agreement.

'Aye, indeed,' says he. 'A great comfort.'

Martin is gritting his teeth like he's chewing granite. But before he can get a word in edgeways, the uproar breaks out in the room above. It is a cross between a howl and a moan. The sort of a bellow a person lets out of him when he is struggling out of a nightmare.

Susie throws up her hands in holy horror.

'Mother of God!' she says. 'He's done for!'

There's a rush for the stairs with everyone stumbling and tripping over each other and muttering pious ejaculations and getting wedged in the bedroom door.

Now you'll always discover in upstarts the like of the Bennetts that no matter how much land or coin they muster together, never can they shake off the mean streak that was their driving force from the beginning. Stingy they were reared and they'll give up the ghost in the same condition. Still you'd think they'd throw a strip of lino on the bare boards of a sick room or have something better than an army blanket on the bed or stretch a curtain itself across the window.

The old fellow is propped up on the pillow, hands clawing at the blanket, eyes squeezed shut. His jaw is hanging and there's a shocking wheeze to his breathing. You can see by the look of him he's a done duck. So it's down on your knees and into the prayers for the dying, with Susie reading out the litany at the rate of no man's business from a battered old prayer book. It's maybe as well the poor bugger perishing in the bed is panting too loud to hear the words, for it would be cold comfort to him to hear his wife rattling off the blood and thunder invocations, with their talk of damnation and eternal night, punishment with darkness, chastisement with flames and condemnation to torments. She is going full blast when his breathing eases a little and he opens his eyes. As he glowers at her, she keeps babbling on, one eye on the book, the other on the bed.

'Deliver, O Lord,' she says, 'the soul of Thy servant from all danger of hell, from all pain and tribulation.'

'What's all this commotion about?' says he, in a hoarse whisper.

They scramble to their feet. Not a cheep out of one of them. Their hands hanging the one length with embarrassment.

'You'll not get shut of me before my time,' says he.

He's badly out in that statement, but a cranky little weasel he always was and you can hardly expect him to change at the latter end of his days.

Martin clears his throat and starts rummaging in the inner pocket of his jacket.

'What else could we do?' says he. 'And you getting another attack just after you were anointed.'

The old fellow is puffing through his pursed lips like a goods train labouring on a hill.

'There's men,' says he, 'got the last rites . . . years ago . . . and they're still . . . walking the roads.'

'What did the doctor tell you?' says he.

Martin pays no heed. He is studying the rumpled paper he has pulled from his pocket.

'What did the doctor say?' says the old fellow.

Martin looks up. Casual like.

'He said you're dying,' says he.

Christ, that's sinking the boot in to the uppers with a vengeance. Jeffreys, the hanging judge, could hardly have made a better job of passing sentence at the Bloody Assizes.

'My Jesus, mercy!' says Susie. And you wouldn't know whether it was pity or piety was moving her.

199

'Amen,' says John.

'Dying?' says the old fellow.

'Aye.' Martin spreads the paper out on the blanket and takes a pen from his pocket. 'Wouldn't this be a good time to settle your affairs?'

'Well, you'd have to hand it to that young thick. He never takes his eye off the ball. Not till it's in the back of the net. He must have been carrying that paper around with him for months. Only waiting for the chance to get it signed. And what better time than when the party concerned is stretched on the bed with nothing between himself and the Day of Judgment but the last few gasps. What harm if it is your own old fellow. He's a Bennett like yourself and there'll be no hard feelings.

Old James is staring down at the paper spread out on the blanket. The breathing is coming hard on him again and there's a class of a whistle to it that you'd find in a horse with the heaves.

'The doctor,' says he, wheezing out the words. 'Was he . . . positive?'

'He was,' says Martin. 'He said 'tis beyond dispute.' He is crouched over the bed, tapping the paper with his pen.

'You sign your name down here,' says he.

The old fellow goes into a fit of coughing and spluttering.

'Beyond . . . dispute,' says he. 'That's . . . a good one.'

The next thing his head is back on the pillow and he's quaking and quivering and jerking till the bed is clattering under him like a rattley-box. The eyes are squinting out of his head. He's slobbering at the mouth. His jaws are gaping open with the teeth showing to the roots. And there are queer clucking noises coming out of the back of his throat that you'd hear nowhere barring a fowl house. To say nothing but the truth, the sight and sound of him would scare the living daylights out of you.

Susie is wringing her hands.

'He's done for this time,' says she. 'It's the last agony.'

'He's gone into convulsions,' says she.

'Convulsions, begor,' says John, the eyebrows up in his

200

hair.

'Convulsions, me arse!' says Martin. 'He's making a mock of us all.'

And sure enough, the old fellow is cackling away to himself. Laughing his head off as though he hadn't a care in the world.

Martin is fit to be tied. There's a scowl on his face that would scare rats and he's muttering away under his breath. You can be full sure it's not the praying he's at, but laying maledictions on his silly old fool of a father for making a buck idiot of himself on his deathbed when he'd be better employed regulating his testamentary obligations.

The old man has cackled himself to a standstill. He is stretched out on the bed, groaning and gasping, his chest going like a bellows. If the sweat pouring out of him is any indication, he is well and truly invoiced.

'Martin,' says he, and you'd hardly hear him, the voice is so weak. 'Come here, son.'

Martin is like a man that's after getting a glimpse of the Promised Land. You can see the glory of this vision shining out of his greedy little eyes. Land and cattle and coin to be had for the scribbling of a couple of words. He wastes no time moving in for the kill.

'Now,' says he, proddling the old man's fingers with the pen. 'Down here you sign.'

Not so much as a 'by your leave' or 'after you, MacNaughton'. It's a case of disgorge the loot and away you go to Kingdom Come.

But James has no notion of signing wills or the like. He pushes the pen aside.

'Martin,' says he. 'What do you think yourself? Will I last till morning?' says he.

Martin is still stooped over the bed, trying to get the unwilling fingers to grasp the pen.

'Not a hope,' says he, without looking up.

The old fellow gathers himself together, lips working, eyebrows drawn down in concentration. You can see by the queer gleam in his eye that he has something important to say. Something that'll not let him die easy till he's got it off his chest. Perhaps he's worried about what'll happen to Susie after he's gone. Or it could be the question about where he wants to be buried. Or maybe 'tis some old debt that's still outstanding.

He levers himself up in the bed, knocking pen and paper flying.

'Listen, son,' says he. 'This would be the blessed night to burn down Gormley's haggard.'

In Adversity Be Ye Steadfast

You don't work as a farm labourer for twenty-five solid years, day in, day out, fair weather and foul, without getting to know the peculiarities of your employer. And Andrew McFetridge is a queer duck surely. The neighbours claim he's a dour, thin-lipped Presbyterian, greedy for money and too mean to spend a fluke on the jollifications they themselves indulge in. But that's not the whole of the story. He's certainly a hard-driving boss who'll work the guts out of you from dawn till dusk. Still, he won't ask you to do a job he wouldn't tackle himself. And the pay is good. No, all's wrong with the man is that he has a bee in his bonnet about religion.

Now religion is a funny bloody thing. It is a bit like the drink – most people can take it or leave it alone: the odd one becomes an addict. And you can safely describe Andrew as a religious addict. It is his belief – a fundamental article of his faith – that any kind of relaxation is sinful and merits the wrath of God. He neither drinks nor smokes. Never in all his sixty years has he set foot in dance hall or cinema. In his farmhouse you'll find no such works of the devil as a radio or a television set. Not even an old-fashioned gramophone. And there's neither chick nor child about the place, although he's married this many a year.

As you'd expect, this way of life does not encourage neighbourly traffic. So the evening when there comes a loud knock at McFetridge's back door, there is a stir out of no one in the kitchen. Andrew, who is sitting at the big open hearth-fire, easing off his wellingtons, stays motionless, one boot held up like a question mark. Over by the dresser, the wife, Jane, stands glowering, a finger to her lips.

There is no second knock. Instead the latch clicks and a man's head is poked round the door.

'Evening folks. Hope we're not intruding.'

You'd know at once by the soapy voice and the big black Bible tucked under his oxter that he's one of these travelling preachers. A Holy Roller. Or a Dunker. Or maybe even a Mormon. Without as much as a 'by your leave' he comes sailing into the kitchen, followed by his mate, a much smaller man, carrying a class of a leather case.

'Is this where Andrew McFetridge lives?' says the tall man.

Andrew deposits his wellington boot on the floor.

'Aye,' says he.

'My name is Bryson,' the preacher says. 'And this,' he points, 'is a fellow worker in the vineyard of the Lord, Brother Clarke.'

Jane is quick off the mark. She clears away the unused dishes, already laid on the bare kitchen table.

'We were just sitting down for a mouthful of tea,' she says. 'You'll maybe join us.'

Without waiting for an answer, she gets out the damask tablecloth and the tea set and the swanky cutlery and the silver teapot – wedding presents kept under lock and key – and she starts setting the table in the new.

'We were told in the village that you were an upright God-fearing Christian, Brother McFetridge,' says Bryson.

Jane by now is fluttering around, pulling out chairs from the table.

'Will you not sit down?' says she.

'Thank you, Sister,' he says. 'We just stopped by to see if you would join us in invoking the blessing of the Lord Jesus on both your labours and on ours. A short family prayer session.' He gives a pious sort of a giggle. 'A cup of tea when we are finished would be most welcome.'

Andrew frowns. You can see he is embarrassed.

'We'd be glad to join you in prayer,' he says. 'Only –'

Bryson eyes the dishes on the table and the kettle singing

on the hob.

'We could call back later if we are disturbing you,' says he.

'Oh, no,' says Andrew. "Deed you're not disturbing us in any way. It's just that,' he jerks his skull as if he were heading a ball, 'James here isn't one of us.'

'Didn't the good Lord say, *'In my Father's house are many mansions'*? There is shelter for every man, be he Baptist, Presbyterian, Methodist, Anglican –'

'He's a Roman Catholic,' says Andrew, as though he's just after donning the black cap.

'No matter,' says Bryson. 'We are all brethren in Christ, gathered here together to seek the blessings that only heartful prayer can obtain.'

'Hallelujah!' says Clarke, the first time he opens his trap.

Andrew clears his throat.

'Well, James,' says he. 'Would you like to join us?'

Would a duck swim? Sure a man would have to be a born idiot to forego a chance like this. Don't people say that at these prayer meetings they roll about the floor grinding their teeth? Or go into a fit of the shakes? Or even tear their clothes off? And forby all that, going home now would mean missing up on the tea.

'Och, sure there could be no great harm in saying a mouthful of prayers.'

'Very well,' says Andrew. 'Close over the door, Jane.'

As the ould one goes to the door, the cat comes in from the yard, saunters across the kitchen floor and settles down at the fireside. A big brute of a white Persian with its hair trailing the ground, it scowls at the assembled company as though accusing them of trying to hold a religious service in its absence.

Bryson starts leafing through the Bible.

'Now, folks,' he says, 'I am sure there is no need to remind you that if you are seeking help or guidance or consolation, you have only to go to the Book of Psalms. David has the answers to everything. So we will begin with a reading from Psalm 23.'

The chairs are pulled back and the company gets to their

knees around the kitchen table. For a few seconds the preacher stares up at the ceiling like you'd see a missioner doing in the pulpit, until the coughing and the rustling and the shuffling have died down. At length he starts reading from the Bible, *'The Lord is my shepherd: I shall not want.'*

A class of an agricultural discourse, no less! The care and rearing of black-faced sheep. Specially laid on for mountainy slobs.

'He maketh me to lie down in green pastures: He leadeth me beside the still waters.'

Green pastures, how are you! And still waters! Little the big fat gulpin knows about herding sheep on the side of a mountain. With grass as scarce as gold dust and waterlogged bog-holes waiting to swallow up the unwary. Not to speak of snow and storm and the depredations of hunting dogs at the dead of night. Oh, 'tis far from the Sperrin Mountains this man of God was reared.

He goes on reading about restoring souls and walking through Death Valley and a lot of other tripe, and then he comes out with, *'Thou preparest a table for me in the presence of mine enemies.'*

Believe it or not, those are the preacher's exact words. Not satisfied with persuading a poor bugger to take part in a sectarian gathering, he starts rubbing in the fact that the table you're kneeling beside is laid for the tea and that damn the bite you'll get till they're finished with their bloody ould abracadabra. And on top of everything, reminding you that your enemies are gathered about you, smacking their lips over your plight. Oh, there's no doubt about it, there's little change in this country over the last few hundred years. But what can you do except soldier on and hope that the acrobatics will start before you're destroyed with the hunger.

You'd think he's reading your thoughts, for the next thing he comes out with is, *'I will dwell in the house of the Lord for ever.'*

And it looks bloody like it, for he closes the Bible and starts a long harangue about the value of prayer. Making contact with the Lord Jesus, he calls it. You would think he's a radio ham the way he talks of switching on the infinite power of the Creator, getting the right wavelength for salvation, tuning in to the Only Begotten Son and babbling away about frequencies and modulations and faulty elements and now and then – cute corbie that he is – getting back again to the sheep farming with the odd reference to slaughtered lambs and wandering sheep and a daft remark about 'the mountains skipping like rams, and little hills like lambs'. You'd wonder that anyone – let alone a clergyman – could come out with such a load of crap.

Andrew is kneeling up very straight, head askew, face ploughed up into a ferocious frown as though he's having trouble sorting out the meaning of the preacher's words. And no wonder. A mountainy farmer, so thick that he won't give house-room to a wireless set, is hardly likely to make sense out of high frequency prayer. Much less hills lepping around like lambs.

The ould dolly is crouched over a chair, nursing her chin on her clasped hands and gazing into space. Every so often her empty stomach sets up a growling protest that would rouse your sympathy if you weren't feeling worse yourself.

But Brother Bryson must be preaching on a full stomach for he keeps gabbling on, regardless of grumbling guts and scowling faces and dying fire.

At last the sermon ends. But does that conclude the proceedings? No such bloody luck.

'And now, friends,' says the preacher, 'we will invoke the pity and clemency of our heavenly Father. And what better way to preface our supplication than the first few verses of Psalm 102?'

He throws back his head, the eyes rolling in their sockets, and addresses the rafters, '*Hear my prayer, O Lord, and let my cry come unto thee. Hide not thy face from me in the day when I am in trouble: incline thine ear to me: in the day when I call answer me speedily.*'

He has the whole thing off by heart, rattling it out like a nursery rhyme, only taking an occasional skelly at the open book.

'My heart is smitten, and withered like grass: so that I forget to eat my bread.'

D'you hear that? He has a brass neck on him! Making out that he has hammered at you with his exhortations till the spit has dried in your mouth and the hunger gone off you.

'By reason of the voice of my groaning my bones cleave to my skin.'

Well, you can say that again. The sight of the food on the table and you kneeling so close is enough to rise turmoil in anyone's guts. Though no doubt the preacher would claim it is the Word of God that is driving the burps out of you.

On and on he goes, blethering about pelicans and owls and house-sparrows: stones and dust and grass: indignation, wrath and drunken weeping; you could make neither sense nor meaning out of it. 'Twould put you to sleep instead of giving you the Holy Roller shakes. Indeed, looking round the company you can see that they are all beginning to show signs of wear and tear. Jane is yawning her head off. Andrew's eyes are closed, his head hanging, his body swaying backwards and forwards. He's flogged out after a hard day's work. And ready for nothing but the bed. Even the cat, sitting up proud as a bloody pasha, is squinting at the dying fire with drowsy, slitted eyes.

And now Brother Bryson is in full cry. He has closed the Bible and is waving it aloft, extolling its wisdom and prescience, its reliability, as the answer to all the troubles of the world – fear, loneliness, anxiety, discouragement, sorrow and weariness, its indispensability to the Good Life and the ultimate crown of salvation, its significance as the corner-stone of the Christian faith. He drones on, with Brother Clarke chiming in with an occasional Amen or Hallelujah and the old lady's yawns becoming more audible and the cat settling down for a comfortable snooze and Andrew snoring gently as he teeters back and forth, until –

Suddenly his body sags and he slumps forward, his head fetching up against the table with a crunch that would put the heart across you. The preacher breaks off in the middle of a sentence. Dead silence for a couple of seconds.

208

Then, like a drunken man gathering himself together, Andrew pushes himself back from the table and squats down on his haunches. There is a dazed look on his face and a lump on his forehead the size of a duck-egg.

Jane jumps to her feet.

'Andrew,' she cries, rushing over to him. 'Are you badly hurt?'

'That's a nasty bump you got, Brother McFetridge,' says Bryson.

'Still it didn't draw blood,' Clarke says.

Andrew looks at them dully. He draws a hand across his forehead.

'Och, 'tis a thing of nothing.' The bruise is now as big as an orange.

'He could have split his skull,' says Clarke.

'Will you not sit down?' says Bryson, pulling up a chair.

'Should I put a poultice on it?' Jane says. 'Or would it be as well to get a doctor?'

Andrew eyes them irritably.

'What's all the fuss about? Doctors and poultices and sit-down prayer meetings? Over a bit of a clout on the head.' He squares his shoulders and draws himself up, clasping his hands together again. You have to hand it to Andrew. No half measures about him. If there's praying to be done, it must be done regimental fashion.

'Maybe there's a bone broken,' says Jane. 'Or some damage to the –'

'Get down on your knees, woman, and let the Reverend get on with his discourse.'

'But you wouldn't mind a poultice? It's only to keep down the swelling.'

'Nonsense. I'm as right as the rain.'

Fighting words, all right. But the voice is a kinda squeaky. And he has gone very pale in the face.

Jane thrusts her hands out in a gesture of despair.

'He'll pay no heed to me,' she says.

Bryson leaves his Bible down on the table beside a plate of oat-cakes that would put you slobbering with the hunger. He turns to Andrew.

'Brother McFetridge,' he says earnestly. 'Our little prayer session is concluded.'

Andrew gapes at him stupidly.

'Concluded?' he says.

'Yes. We can omit the usual closing hymn.'

But Andrew is not taking surrender terms from anyone. Clerical or lay.

'Indeed you will not. Not on my account you won't.'

The preacher glances across at the old dolly for guidance but she shrugs her shoulders helplessly.

'Very well,' he says. He clasps his hands and gets in touch with the rafters again.

'Abide with us, dear Lord,' says he, 'for it is towards evening and the day is far spent.'

He has the neck of a giraffe. If it hadn't been for himself and his butty, the tea would be long since over and the company well on its way to dreamland.

'Brother Clarke,' he says. 'The closing hymn.'

Your-man grabs up the leather case, places it on the dresser and opens it up. A blast of music fills the room, rumbling, thundering, booming. It must be some sort of recording machine.

Andrew and Jane are listening open-mouthed and out of the tail of an eye you can see the cat standing stiff-legged, its back arched in terror. And why not? For the poor brute, no more than its master and mistress, has no conception of the wonders of amplified music.

The next bloody thing, pandemonium breaks out. A male voice choir, assisted by the two preachers, are bellowing at the top of their voices, 'Abide with me: fast falls the eventide.'

Above the clamour can be heard the screeching of the cat as, roused to panic, it claws its way up the bricks of the fireplace. Lucky enough, the fire is nearly dead so it comes to no harm. But as it disappears up the chimney, Jane comes to life and starts screaming:

'Oh, the cat! The poor cat! It'll be roasted alive.'

Andrew is leaning against the table, his hand to his

forehead. Bryson, who has been conducting the unseen choir, stands with his hands raised in a papal benediction. Clarke is clutching his mouth as though a note has stuck in his gullet and he's in danger of puking. The machine is still belting out the hymn.

> *'When other helpers fail, and comforts flee,*
> *Help of the helpless, O abide with me.'*

Somewhere up the flue of the chimney the cat is howling, the sound muffled but quite audible above the uproar. Jane darts across to the fireplace and, in the lull between verses, calls up:

'Pussy! Poor old pussy! Come down, will you. Come down.'

Her voice is nearly drowned out with the choir starting up again.

'Swiftly to its close ebbs out life's little day.'

You can hardly blame the bloody cat for staying where it is with all these strange voices bawling out in unison that it's gone closing time to drink up your drinks don't you know it's after hours the premises must be closed and have you no homes to go to.

The old girl is worried to hell about what's after happening to her pet and she starts wringing her hands and shouting blue murder.

'Will somebody do something. Do something, will you. Don't just stand there gaping. Do something.'

The two preachers rush over to join her and the three of them crouch around the hearth, shouting up the chimney:

'Pussy! Pussy! Pussy! Come down, Pussy. Puss! Puss! The naughty puss. Come down, pussykins. You can't stay there all night.'

Damn the bit heed the cat pays to their exhortations. No more than it does to the mechanised hallions now roaring, *'Through cloud and sunshine, Lord, abide with me.'*

If the muffled yowling is any indication, the poor brute is up near the chimney pot by this time, with every intention of abiding there till the coast is clear.

This possibility dawns on Jane, for she straightens up and turns to Bryson.

'The roof,' she says. 'There's nothing for it but the roof.'

'How do you mean,' says he. 'The roof?'

'You'll have to get up on the roof. It's the only way to reach the poor thing.'

You can see that Brother Bryson has no stomach for this caper. He starts back-pedalling at once.

'Maybe we should try just once more,' he says. 'To see if it will come down.' And then, as an afterthought, 'What name do you call it?'

'Eh?' says Jane.

'What name does it answer to?'

'Pussy, of course. Or sometimes, Puss.'

'Has it no proper name? Like Felix? Or Blanche?'

Jane is getting impatient.

'You don't give Christian names to cats. Come on,' says she, starting for the door. 'I'll show you where the ladder is.'

The choir is still going full blast when she comes back into the kitchen but she pays no attention. She makes straight for the fireplace, where she starts calling up the chimney.

'Are you there, Pussy? Oh, good! We'll have the poor old puss cat out of there and safe and sound in a few minutes. There's two good men gone up on the roof to take you down.' She swings round. 'Isn't that right, Andrew?'

Andrew, hands grasping his knees, is sitting up very straight on a chair. But his face has gone a class of grey and you can hear the clatter of his teeth above the sound of the recording machine.

'What's wrong?' says Jane, dashing over to him.

'I'm cold,' says he. 'Bitter cold.'

She runs a hand across his forehead.

'He's done for,' she wails. 'Och, God help us all, he's done for.'

After all these years she should know her husband better. Sure there's only one way you can hurt a tough old cormorant like him and that is through his pocket-book.

'Stop your whinging, woman,' he says, 'and throw a sod or two of turf on the fire.'

So away with Jane to the creel at the hearth-side where she gathers up an armful of turf and starts building up the fire again, her ears cocked to the chattering teeth of the boss and paying no heed to the crying cat or the noise of the preachers on the roof or the choir bawling, '*I fear no foe with thee at hand to bless.*'

But the bloody fire won't light and Andrew is getting impatient.

'What's keeping you?' he says. 'Can you not get the fire going?'

You can see the old birdie is rattled. She glares around, looking for kindling. Spots a bottle on the dresser. Grabs it up and darts back to the fireplace. The screw-top seems to be jammed and as she is struggling to release it a voice is heard from the chimney. It is Brother Clarke.

'I can't reach far enough,' says he. 'You'd better try.'

You can hear them shuffling about on the roof. Changing places carefully. And then Bryson's voice. Very clear. As though he has his big head poked into the chimney pot.

'I see the little fellow. There should be no trouble getting him out.'

Just then Andrew lets a groan out of him. Not a groan of pain, but of irritation. He has come to the realization, not for the first time, that you must do everything yourself. That a woman can never be trusted to handle anything. He tries to ease himself off the chair.

'Here,' he says. 'Give me that bottle.'

But Jane has been roused to a flurry of action. The top of the bottle is off. She is splashing the contents wildly over the dying fire.

It must be petrol she is using, for suddenly there is a WHOOOOSH, and a sheet of flame rushes up the chimney. After that it is pure bloody Bedlam. From the old dolly a scream. From the rooftop a roar of pain, ending in what sounds awful like a well-known expletive. From the cat in the chimney a muffled howl, mounting to a screech as it loses its grip and tumbles down the flue, to land, tail ablaze, in the hearth.

For a split second it crouches there, blazing tail threshing back and forth. Then, like a shot off a shovel, it starts careering around the room. You know how the squib they call the Jumping Jenny behaves when you light it – leaping madly around and banging against walls and furniture. Well, that's the way the cat is performing, only now and then it starts whirling around with the sparks flying off it as though it is giving an imitation of a Catherine Wheel. The long hairs of the Persian breed make ideal bonfire fuel, so by the time it dashes out the open door into the yard, screeching blue murder, the poor brute is ablaze from stem to stern.

The company is too stunned to make a move or say a word. But overhead you can hear Clarke's awestricken voice:

'Hey, look at the cat! It's on fire!'

Between grunts and moans, Bryson can be heard casting doubts on its ancestry and expressing an unchristian disregard for its ultimate fate. These sentiments seem to rouse Jane from her stupor, for she starts rushing to the door.

'My God!' she says. 'The poor creature!'

She is soon pulled to a halt.

'The tablecloth, woman!'

It is Andrew. He has struggled to his feet and is pointing with outstretched hand. He appears excited. And who would blame him. In its fiery exit, the cat must have brushed against the tablecloth. Now the draft from the open door is just starting to set alight the smouldering material. It is confined to a single fold of the cloth and anyone with half an once of wit could quench it with a clap of the hand. But Jane, the poor slob, yanks the cloth and its precious burden off the table and, in her excitement, stamps and grinds and tramples it into submission on the floor.

You would nearly find it in your heart to feel sorry for Andrew. There he stands, a look of horror on his face as the full extent of the catastrophe dawns on him. A pedigree tea-set, cutlery of the best, a damask tablecloth and a valuable silver teapot, the only surviving relics of the past, maybe never before put to use, now lying smashed and damaged and scattered on the kitchen floor. Not to mention that he is going weak in the knees and the cold sweat is rising on him and the lump on his head is still swelling from the bang he got only now it has started throbbing like an old-fashioned threshing machine and he is so hungry that he'd eat his way through the two ends of a dunghill and he is dog tired after a hard day's work and if everyone would only go home he would clear off to bed and he wishes to goodness that the choir would lower their voices a little for it is driving him completely crackers. Mouth open, he is about to make his protest when the commotion starts up overhead. The two preachers are banging on the roof-tiles and bellowing at the top of their voices:

'Fire! Fire! Fire!'

Andrew stumbles to the kitchen door and you can hear his gasp as he realises that his hay barn is ablaze. The flames are roaring up sky-high and you can hear the hiss and crackle as the fire spreads through the tightly packed hay. Above the sound of the fire, and like a class of an accompaniment, the choir is chanting,

'Hold Thou Thy cross before my closing eyes,
Shine through the gloom and point me to the skies.'

You would think they were deliberately making a mock of poor Andrew's reaction to this final catastrophe. For in the glare from the fire you can see him leaning against the door-post with his eyes closed as though he doesn't want to see what is happening. It is a cruel sight, to say nothing but the truth. Jane is over at the pump in the middle of the yard, her arm going like a fiddler's elbow as she drives the pump handle up and down. The two preachers have collected buckets and are running backwards and forwards, shouting encouragement to each other as they try to throw water on the flames. With the heat, they cannot get near enough for the water to reach the fire. But even if it did, it would have as much effect as the squirt of a tobacco spit.

The fire has a right hold now over the whole hay barn and in its light you can see the bruise on Andrew's forehead

215

pulsing and his lips murmuring. You'd gamble the last tosser in your pocket that what he is muttering about is the undesirability of house-cats, the crass stupidity of wives, the doubtful value of travelling preachers to the Evangelical cause, and the folly of carrying thrift to the point of refusing to insure your hay barn against fire. You would be very wrong. For if you incline your ear close, you will hear him repeating fervently in time with the choir,

'In life, in death, O Lord, abide with me.'

A Quiet Respectable Couple

The McDarras were strangers to the mountain. Their cottage, a one-up-and-two-down structure, perched high on the slopes of Meenalack, was always freshly thatched and whitewashed. The windows sparkled in the sun. At the porch the flagstone was scrubbed to glowing point. In the front of the house, the stretch of street was scrupulously weeded and cindered. Between solid concrete pillars the gate to the mountain path swung proudly, putting to shame the sagging bedsteads, timber baulks and sheets of galvanized iron used by the rest of us in place of gates.

But their half-door was the only one in Meenalack that was never used. Day and night their door stayed closed, for the McDarras sought friendship from no one. They were civil enough people to meet abroad. In the porch of the chapel or walking the mountain after sheep, they would bid the time of day to all and sundry. Beyond that – nothing more.

From the word go, that is the way things were. Maybe it was because they did not know our ways but came from the Lagan Valley falling into the farm when an old uncle of theirs died twelve years back.

Overnight they materialized. The first we knew of their coming was when we saw the smoke rising from the chimney of the once empty house. Folk drifted over to bid them welcome though they found it odd to knock at the door. Odder still to stand at the threshold.

It could not be said that the visitors were rebuffed. The two McDarras, stationed at either side of the open door, talked to them as friendly as you please. Cattle, sheep, the state of the crops, the weather; all were discussed at length but no one was allowed to put a foot over the doorstep.

Though none of us took kindly to this treatment, it was allowed that a man's home was his castle. And the fact that the couple were childless – a fruitful source of oddity – was acknowledged a possible reason for their unsociable behaviour. In time we got used to the closed door and the McDarras came to be accepted into the community.

They were the queer pair of fowl all right. For a start, they never went about together. It wasn't so much that she stayed cooped up in the house when he was abroad on the mountain or below in the Glen Tavern. Or that McDarra would start repairing the door of the byre or maybe clean out a clogged spouting or give a lick of paint to the window frames while the wife was gone on an errand to the village. No, that was the common practice of all of us. It was just that they never went to the Chapel together. McDarra would go to late Mass: the wife to early. They would take odd Sundays about, to attend Benediction or the Stations of the Cross. As for funerals, Mrs McDarra never stirred a foot, leaving her husband to follow the coffin to the graveyard. A practice we somehow thought unchristian.

And yet if someone were ill or in trouble, the McDarras were the first on the scene. Prepared to cook a meal or stay up all night or leave a pound note under a mug on the dresser. Let a neighbour have a sick cow or lack help to win turf and before very long McDarra would be seen, striding up the lane, jacket dangling from one shoulder, teeth bared as he whistled through them.

He had never learned the mountainy man's way of walking, head and shoulders thrust forward against the slope of the hill. Instead he marched along, chest out, chin up, his heels thudding on the ground. Cropped hair, bronzed face, jaw built for a chin-strap, no wonder people maintained he had been a soldier in his day. All the more shock then when you discovered that the blue eyes, instead of fixing you with a drill sergeant's glare, slithered away from your gaze, one minute staring over your shoulder, the next flicking from side to side with the whites showing. Often he would break off in mid-sentence and swing around to stare back the way he had come.

Mrs McDarra was even odder in her way of going. A tall woman, she would turn her shoulder to you when she was talking, and stand straddle-legged, folded arms dandling her elders, eyes scouring the country side, whilst she spoke to you out of the corner of her mouth. You would swear she was all the time calling the roll of the McDarra sheep, scattered over the slopes of the mountain.

The neighbours, sitting at night around a blazing turf fire, were never without ammunition for gossip.

'Did you hear the snores of McDarra at the Mass this morning?'

'You'd need to be deaf not to! Sure the Elevation bell was drowned out from first to last.'

'Aye, it was an odious uproar. It's a wonder the priest didn't give out about it.'

'The way Father Carr kept glaring at him, you could say it was touch and go.'

'McDarra's the queer duck, all right.'

'Och, the poor man's maybe not getting a proper night's sleep. That's all's the matter with him.'

'And what would be keeping him awake, d'you think?'

A chair creaks. A throat is cleared.

'Did you notice Mrs McDarra at first Mass?'

'Aye, that was very queer. What took her up to the organ loft, would you say now? Doesn't she always stay in the body of the church?'

'It was to get sitting fornenst the side window, of course. You can see right across to Meenalack from there.'

'Whatever was to be seen, she used neither beads nor prayer book throughout the entirety of the Mass.'

'And then rushing out helter-skelter before the Last Gospel.'

'The Curate will have something to say about it next Sunday.'

'What hurry was on her anyway?'

219

'You might well ask.'

Over the hearth, the bubbling kettle is shifted up to the arm of the crane.

'D'you know what it is, it's odder they're getting, the pair of them. Aye moving around with their heads cocked back as though there was someone after them.'

'Take care but that's what it is. Maybe they're afeared of something.'

'How d'you mean?'

'Och, it's hard to say. Going through life a body makes bad friends once in a while.'

'Very true. And a grievance gets no less when it's brooded on for a wheen of years.'

'Aye, folk have long memories when they think they've been wronged.'

'It's a shame for you talking that way. The McDarras have been good neighbours since they came here. No one can say a word against them. And no matter where they were afore they came here, there'd be no differ.'

'You could well be right. But there's little known about them afore they turned up in Meenalack.'

The tongs jingle as fresh sods of turf are ringed round the heaped up pile of smouldering embers. Chairs are shifted into new positions. Pipes relit. Cigarettes passed round.

'The ould uncle now. Did he make a will, would you say? A proper affair, drawn up in regimental order?'

'Michael John is it? Sure the poor man could hardly write his name.'

'He could get an attorney, couldn't he?'

'Aye, if he got one for nothing.'

'Very true. The bould Michael – God be good to him – was a tight one. Every shilling he earned was a prisoner.'

'He must have had a world of money.'

'Well cared for, you can be sure.'

'They say below in the village that he had the Post Office polluted.'

'In and out of the Bank he was too. I saw him with my own two eyes.'

'He could very well have a nest egg in both.'

'Nonsense, man. Michael John would trust neither Bank nor Post Office. Whatever store he had would be nearer at hand. Spogged in the rafters maybe. Where he'd keep an eye on it.'

'Aye, 'deed.'

'More than likely.'

A foot taps impatiently on the flagged floor.

'To listen to the lot of you giving off, you'd think the poor man was a rancher instead of a small farmer scratching out a living on the side of the mountain. Lucky for him if he'd save enough to pay rent and rates.'

'There's that in it too.'

'You're right there. Who ever heard of a mountainy man leaving a fortune after him?'

'That'll do now! The like of Michael John – peace rest him – would thrive on an acre of granite. Let alone a sheep run that covers a whole townland.'

A gust of wind rattles the door latch and sends the turf smoke whooshing out into the kitchen. Squalls of rain claw at the window.

'A bad ould night.'

'There'll come no change yet a while.'

'No. The crickets were screeching all evening.'

Chairs are pulled nearer the hearth.

'Hadn't Michael John another nephew living abroad in Scotland? Working up North. In the tunnels. A wild class of a fellow, they used to say.'

'That would be Peadar.'

'A bad rascal. He would turn his hand to any manner of villainy.'

''Twas said he was smuggling across the border before ever he took off for Scotland.'

'Hadn't he the name of keeping a disorderly house in the city of Glasgow?'

'You'd get people to say he was peddling drugs or the like.'

'Isn't it well known he was running a knocking shop for the tunnel men? Moving from camp to camp with a squad of shameless harpies. Intent on stripping the last shilling from horn-mad poor hallions who hadn't glimpsed hide nor hair of a woman for months on end.'

'That'll do now!'

'No bad chat.'

'Filthy tittle-tattle, that's all it is.'

'Tittle-tattle, how are you! Didn't he get eighteen months for robbery with violence. Broke into a warehouse in the Gorbals. Assaulted the night watchman. "Daring crime" was what the paper called it. The magistrate said he was a dangerous criminal.'

There is a rustle as the glowing coals of turf settle themselves into a more comfortable position. From the dresser the tick of the alarum clock deepens in tone. A pipe-bowl is tapped out sharply on the heel of a boot.

'Aye, it could well be.'

'Would you say so now?'

'It's been known to happen.'

''Twould account for many's the thing.'

'No smoke without fire, they say.'

'Indeed, aye.'

'In God's name, what are you all havering about? If you've anything to say against the McDarras, why don't you come out with it plain and straight?'

'Not much charity around these days.'

'If you were jurymen, there'd be short shrift given.'

A sod of turf collapses, sending out a shower of sparks. The tongs are lifted and the fragments whipped up and replaced, the last glowing coal being applied to a freshly charged pipe bowl.

'God grant you wit, woman dear.' Carefully the dying ember is laid on the smouldering heap. 'No one's blackguarding the McDarras. It's just that we all know they're afeared of something. And more nor likely what they're afread of is –' from the heart of the fire a tobacco spit sizzles as it strikes, '– that the nephew in Scotland – a dangerous whelp, if ever there was one – might take a notion of paying them a visit. There'd be the queer turmoil that day, you can be assured.

That young ruffian, if he found he was thwarted, would make a pot-roast of the McDarras in their own home. Oh, it'll be a poor day for all of us if he ever returns.'

The mountainy children – and for that matter, all of us – came to dread the advent of McDarra's nephew, Peadar Dubh, as he came to be called. He was the bogeyman of Meenalack. Parents would threaten troublesome brats: 'If you don't have manners, we'll send for Peadar Dubh.' A black-avised monster with glaring eyes and shaggy hands outstretched to clutch, he walked the roads after dark, lurking in the shelter of turf ricks or lonely haggards or even the gable-end of your own cottage, ready to pounce if he got the chance.

As for passing the McDarra house, it was not so bad in the daytime – in fact, curiosity usually overcame fear – but at night it was difficult to avoid breaking into flight at the menace of the closed door and the dull glow from the thickly shrouded window. Eyes fixed ahead and whistling shakily through dry lips, it was possible to walk smartly past the bohreen leading to the house. But oh, the relief to reach the first neighbour's cottage, with the light blazing through the uncurtained kitchen window and over the top of the open half-door.

Useless trying to convince yourself that there was no substance in these fears: you had but to look at the McDarras to know the truth. Here were two solid, sensible people reduced to such a state of apprehension that they acted like stoat-ridden rabbits, cowering in apathy before approaching doom.

And so they waited. Waited in quiet respectable hard-working isolation, entrenched behind shrouded window and bolted door. Waited with eyes dodging and ducking and jouking around in their sockets, forever on the alert for the pursuer. Waited for close on twelve years. Waited until the night Mrs McDarra tapped hesitantly at the door of her nearest neighbour, Packy O'Donnell. It was nearly twelve o'clock but there was still a few of us lingering over the dying fire. Packy went to the door.

'Well, Ma'am?'

'Sorry to bother you, Mr O'Donnell.' She must have run all the way from the house, stumbling and floundering in the dark. Yet her manner was as distant as usual: her voice as harsh and measured.

'No bother in the world, Ma'am. Come in to the heat.'

'Oh, I couldn't really. Not at this time of night.'

'Sure, this is early. We never go to bed while there's a spark left in the fire.'

Two steps over the threshold she took. No more.

She stood as she always stood – legs apart, arms akimbo, eyes roving the room taking in everything. A fine looking big woman. A solid rock, you'd say, of common sense. But the fingers gripping her arms were white at the knuckle and her mouth kept opening and closing like a freshly caught fish.

'Nothing the matter, I hope?' said Packy.

'It's John. He never . . . he didn't . . . he's still –'

Across the fire we looked at each other, the same thought in each one's head.

'Aye?' Packy's voice was gentle. Encouraging.

'He's never back from the mountain. Left the house this morning after breakfast. Worried about the sheep, he was. There's been strange dogs around this while back. Hunting the sheep. After breakfast he went. And never back since.' Once started, she seemed unable to stop. 'There was a lamb killed yesterday. Two the day before. You wouldn't know where it would end. Real worried he was. And no wonder, God knows.'

'He took the shep with him, of course?'

'Bran, is it? No, he left the dog at home.'

'Now you'd wonder at that, wouldn't you?'

'He was afeared it might join in with the other dogs if it came on them worrying sheep. But he took the gun with him. Just in case.'

Just in case. You could almost hear the hiss as we all puckered up our lips and sucked in breath. *In case he met someone? Or was waylaid?* Long awaited comes at last. An old saying. And a true one.

Packy wheeled around.

'We'd better get going, lads. It's been left late enough as it is.' And turning to Mrs McDarra: 'In the name of God, woman, what possessed you to wait till this unmerciful hour before raising the alarm?'

She gulped.

'I thought all the time . . . that the next minute . . . I'd see him coming over the brow of the hill . . . or hear his step in the yard . . . and anyway I couldn't leave the house . . . not till he'd be back.'

'Well begod, Ma'am, it's as well to do a thing first as last. You had to leave the house to shift for itself at the latter end.'

Her hand flew to her mouth.

'Oh, dear!' she exclaimed.

Whirling about, she rushed out into the night, with Packy shouting after her:

'Fit you better to worry about your poor husband and him lost above in the mountain –' He stopped to draw breath. Or to let his anger gather. Then at full screech: '– instead of fretting over the fortune they say you've stowed away in the rafters.'

In the kitchen there was a murmur of disapproval.

'Packy spoke out of turn there, I'd say.'

'The poor creature is troubled enough as it is.'

'No need of dragging in the ould uncle and his money.'

'To hell with casting up.'

When Packy came back in from the yard with a coil of rope and an army blanket, the chittering died away.

''Twas time someone spoke up,' he said. 'They should have been challenged long since, the pair of them. Slinking around for years past with the sockets of their eyes worn smooth from skellying about them every step they took. It would be the price of them if Michael John's nephew turned up to haunt them.'

Hesitantly someone asked:

'Would you say now that there's any truth . . . any backing for that old story about Peadar . . . about him coming back . . . to claim his share of the fortune?'

225

'It could be right. And it could be wrong.'

'But what d'you think yourself, Packy?'

'Well, anybody watching the antics of the McDarra woman just now would know they had surely something to hide.' He went to the dresser and took down a torch. 'I better take this as well.'

'Could the McDarras have had any word about Peadar? About him coming back, I mean? Would he ever be prowling around somewhere at the moment?'

'It could very well be.'

'And if he were to come across McDarra somewhere on the mountain?'

'It would be die dog or ate the hatchet.' He moved to the door. 'Come on, boys.'

Meenalack does not appear on the school atlas. It is just a peak, and not nearly the highest one, in the Blue Stack mountains. But if it is not tall, it has the bulk. It stretches out in a sprawl of glens and foothills, bog-holes and lonely lakes, that covers a dozen townlands and the better part of three parishes. A regiment of illicit distillers and their gear could operate on its slopes without a grazing sheep lifting its head, as many a Civic Guard patrol discovered when the unfortunate poor gawms set out to uncover reported poteen making. In daylight it would have been possible to spread out and comb the mountain thoroughly. On a moonless night, with only a torch light for guidance, it was necessary to stick together in the hope that luck or inspiration would lead us to McDarra's whereabouts.

As we climbed, sticking to sheep pads and winding rutted tracks, Packy kept swinging the beam of the torch from side to side. Feeble though it was, it served to prevent us tripping over whin bushes or falling into bog-holes. Every few hundred yards we stopped, stood around back to back and shouted:

'McDarra! Hi there, McDarra!'

For a few minutes we stayed listening to the sounds of the night – the squeak and rustle of vermin, the coughing of sheep, the banshee wail of curlew. Then:

'No sign of him.'

'Better keep moving.'

'Lough Beg might be a good place to try.'

'Aye, he was about there last week.'

Once there came the sound of barking, far away to the west.

'Did you hear yon?'

'Would you say they'd be hunting sheep?'

'Mabbe that's where McDarra is?'

''Twould be worth trying anyway.'

Packy hawked deep in his throat. Spat noisily. Wiped his dripping chin with the back of his hand.

'Foxes!' he said. 'Fucking foxes!'

Sometimes the beam of the swinging torch would be trapped by the sheen of a dark mountain pool or by the yellow flame of a whin bush. Rocks loomed up, barring the way – crouching brutes of rock stubbed with moss, or towering monsters ready to topple on shielding arms. Eyes, disembodied and impassive, stared back out of the darkness – outposts of those that lurked beyond the small circle of light.

'Give you the bloody creeps,' said Packy, 'glaring at you like that.'

As he waved the torch at them, the sheep lowered their heads and backed away.

'Though God knows you'd be glad enough of their company if you were lying out alone on the side of the mountain with a ruffian the like of Peadar Dubh stalking you.'

'Sure hasn't McDarra got the gun with him?'

'Gun, is it? Wouldn't that antiquated ould blunderbuss explode in his face if he fired a shot?'

'True for you, Packy.'

'A proper bloody clem.'

About half way up to Lough Beg, the sound of barking came again. Very faint.

'The foxes are making a night of it, eh Packy?'

'Somebody's turkeys are in sore danger.'

227

Packy had stopped. Head to one side.

'Foxes, me arse! That's a dog.'

Listening, we stood. Grouped in a tight cluster.

Again the sound came. From far back down the mountain side. In the direction from which we had come.

It was not the frenzied yapping of a dog that scents a bitch in heat. Nor yet the monotonous barking that comes from loneliness or boredom.

'Sounds as if it's after something, the way it's roaring.'

'Coming this way too, I'd say.'

'It's hard to tell.'

'Dry up, the lot of you!'

Silently we waited, as the barking drew gradually nearer. Suddenly Packy put his cupped hands to his mouth and shouted:

'Bran! Bran!'

He was answered by a volley of excited yelping.

'Can you beat that?'

'Leave it to the bould Packy.'

'The bloody dog must have broken loose.'

'Aye, the door of yon outhouse of theirs doesnay look too secure.'

'Mebbe the Missus let him out so he could help us track down McDarra.'

'Is it doting you are? And her alone in the house? Dreading a visit from Peadar Dubh?' Once more Packy cupped his hands. 'Bran! Bran!' Already the answering barks were much nearer. 'She should have known by this time that Bran's not cut out for a watch dog.'

When the small black and tan sheep dog broke into the circle of light, it launched itself at Packy, yelping wildly.

'Down, sir!' He brushed it aside roughly. Swing around, he directed the beam of the torch up the steep slopes of the mountain. 'Seek him, Bran!' he ordered. 'Seek him!'

Obediently the dog trotted ahead to the limit of the light. Faced about, head aslant, tongue lolling.

'Get after him, Bran!' Packy shouted, waving the torch peremptorily. 'Seek him out, you silly bugger!'

228

The dog made off into the blackness of the night, wagging its tail. Thereafter it circled ahead, barking continuously. Urging us to hasten our steps. Periodically it would come trotting back, to lap thirstily at the circle of light before loping off once more into the darkness, refreshed and encouraged.

It was on one of these occasions that the dog halted abruptly with upflung head, ears cocked, tail swaying gently. As though at a word of command, we all pulled up. Heads craned forward. Listening.

There was nothing to be heard but the far away lilt of running water and the wheeze of Packy's laboured breathing.

For perhaps half a minute we stood there, rooted into an attitude of expectancy. Then the dog barked, Packy shouted: 'That's him!' and we were scrambling after the pair of them, intent on keeping up with the rapidly diminishing beam of light. We bumped into rocks: struggled through bracken: stumbled and fell and staggered up cursing.

'Fuck this for a caper!'

'Better keep after him or we'll lose the bastard.'

'He's going like a bloody greyhound.'

'So well he might, with the bucking torch to guide him.'

'What's got into the little hoor anyway?'

'He must have heard something.'

'More than I did.'

'Damn the sound there was at all.'

'Watch where you're going, for Jasus' sake!'

'Christ, man, d'you think I done it on purpose?'

We caught up with Packy near the White Mare's Tail, a waterfall that cascaded down the steep west face of the mountain into Lough Beg. He was stooped over a flat rock on which he had placed the torch. By its light he was tying a running noose in the coil of rope. Without looking up, he jerked his head towards where Bran crouched at the edge of the cliff.

'Your-man's down there.'

He tugged hard at the knot. First against one hand. Then the other. Satisfied, he flung the coiled rope over his shoulder. Walked to the cliff edge. Played the beam of the torch down its face.

'See,' he said.

McDarra was lying on a narrow ledge about twenty foot down. He was stretched flat on his back with his left leg twisted under him in a grotesque and abnormal fashion. His face was badly battered and caked with dried blood. His eyes were closed.

'In the name of God, how did he get down there?'

'And what was he doing up here, in the first place? Where you wouldn't graze a flea?'

'Wouldn't he have to be stone-blind or stupid with drink to saunter over a verge as well marked as this?'

'Could he have been running like mad from somebody and lost his footing?'

'Mebbe he was flung down there the way you'd toss a lifeless sheep. Eh?'

Packy dropped the coil of rope on the ground.

'How the hell would I know?'

'Did you hear him crying or what? The time yourself and the dog made off?'

'Aye. He must have been conscious then.'

'Would you say he's badly hurt?'

'Broken leg. Mebbe a fractured skull. God knows what forby.' Packy turned the beam of light on to the coil of rope. 'Come on, some of you. We've got to get this poor devil up.'

It took us the most of two hours hoisting him up to the cliff top, moaning and muttering continually, and grunting every time his body came into contact with the rock face. Never once did he open his eyes.

There was little we could do for him except rig up a splint for his broken leg. Only when we started to carry him down the mountain side in the army blanket, did someone say:

'Where's the gun?'

We struggled to a halt.

'Bejesus, that's a question worth the asking.'

'God, aye.'

'There was nothing to be seen up at the Mare's Tail.'

'Nor down on the ledge where he was lying.'

'It could have been snatched from him before he was thrown over.'

'Bloody apt!'

'Mebbe he hadn't the gun with him at all.'

Hunkering down beside him, Packy quickly rummaged through the unconscious man's pockets. When he straightened up, it was to display, in the palm of his outstretched hand, two cartridges. Number five shot.

'He had the gun with him all right,' he said.

McDarra stirred. Uttered a prolonged cry, half sigh, half moan. Packy swung the torch light on the closed eyes and working lips.

'It's more nor likely lying at the foot of the Mare's Tail. Where it fell when McDarra lost his grip on it.'

'Could very well be.'

'Aye, surely.'

In Packy's half closed fist, the two cartridges rattled out their own version of the night's happenings. We stood around, gazing at the blanketed figure, avoiding each other's eyes. At length someone sniffed.

'A murderous ruffian the like of Peadar roving the hills with a loaded shot-gun!'

'It's criminal, that's what it is.'

'Where are the bloody Guards?'

'You may well ask.'

Packy flicked the torch on and off.

'Better get going,' he said. 'The battery's running out.'

In the dim light from the dying torch and burdened with the awkward sagging load, it was difficult to scramble down the uneven slope. As the circle of light contracted, so did our scattered grouping until we were huddled together, leagued against the threatening onslaught of darkness. No one spoke. Any sudden noise halted the bearers and put every head aslant. Within sight of the McDarra cottage, Packy called a halt.

'Better see how he looks,' he said.

As we eased our burden to the ground, McDarra stirred

and groaned.

'Wh-wh-what is it?' he muttered.

Packy stooped down.

'You're all right, John. No need to worry.'

'What's the matter? Wh-wh-wh-where –' He gazed wildly up at us, his head rolling from side to side.

'You had a bit of an accident. A few perches more and you'll be home with the Missus.'

'It's a thing of nothing.' McDarra flung off the blanket and struggled to raise himself. 'I can manage . . . my lone . . . the rest of the –' Whimpering with anguish, he slumped back, his face beaded with sweat.

'Take it easy, now.' Packy's flapping hands admonished gently. 'You've a broken leg, you know.'

'I'll be all right in a minute,' McDarra muttered.

'Faith, you'll not then. Come on, men, get moving.'

During the short journey to the cottage, McDarra never let up. He kept urging: 'Let me down, will yous?' 'I'm all right now, I tell you.' 'There's no need at all of this carry-on.' 'I've nothing the matter with me, d'you hear?'

To crown all, the dog – excited by its master's cries – began leaping around, barking madly. No wonder Mrs McDarra had the door opened before we reached the yard gate.

She stood there, etched in the warm glow of the light, peering out into the darkness.

'Bran!' she called.

The dog rushed at her, whining softly.

'Is that you, John?' she called again.

'It's all right, Ma'am.' Packy was wagging the torch with one hand and hooshing down McDarra with the other. 'He's with us. He's had a bit of a toss.'

She gasped.

'Dear God!'

She started forward. Hesitated. Stood her ground.

'He's not badly hurt?'

'Put me down, I say!' hissed McDarra. 'Amn't I at my own door?'

'He has a broken leg, Ma'am. And a few nasty bruises.'
Packy brushed past her. Pointed to an old settle bed in the
corner of the kitchen. 'Leave him down there, lads.'

Mrs McDarra's distracted gaze swung round the crowded
kitchen.

'But that bed's not used any more,' she said.

'It's beside the fire,' said Packy. 'And warmth is what the
poor fellow wants. He's perished to the core.'

'We couldn't find the gun,' he added.

'The gun?' She frowned. 'Oh, the gun! What harm if it's
lost.'

Only when he was stretched out on the bed, shrouded in
the grey army blanket, did Mrs McDarra see for the first time
the white face, blood-caked and glistening with sweat, the
pain-puckered lips, the dull and harassed eyes.

'Sweet Mother of Jesus, what happened to you, John?' she
cried.

'He'd be as well to see the doctor,' said Packy.

'Doctor?'

'Aye. Some of the lads can dodge into the village and
leave word for him to call out.'

'You'll do no such-ana thing.' McDarra had hoisted
himself up on his elbows and was glaring round at the
astonished company. 'Didn't I tell you that there's nothing
wrong with me that a wheen of days in the bed wouldn't
cure.'

'But, John dear –'

'No arguing. These decent men were kind enough to help
me home. Don't be keeping them out of their beds any
longer.'

'But you'll have to –'

'That'll do now! A good night's sleep and I'll be right as
the mail the morrow.'

'Shouldn't they have a little something to drink before
they go?'

'Don't you know fine well there's not a drop of drink in
the house?'

Closing his eyes, he lay back in the bed.

We were shifting about, one arm as long as the other, each of us waiting for someone to make the first move, when we heard the sound from upstairs. It was a creaking sound – the slow creak of feet shuffling cautiously along warped and shrunken floorboards.

No one spoke. We stared up at the rafters, Packy with his Adam's apple dipping as he swallowed hard, Mrs McDarra shuttling her gaze between ceiling and husband. McDarra himself lay motionless, eyes squeezed shut.

The shuffling steps moved across towards the stair-head and commenced to descend. Instead of the crisp sound of leather on wood, there was the soft stealthy pad of an animal. You could hear a tentative paw being placed carefully on each succeeding step, the faint grating as wood gradually gave way under weight, the pregnant pause as the whole burden of the body was shifted warily to the forward foot.

Overhead a moth wheeled around the naked light bulb, battering itself against the scorching glass, its clumsy brown body haloed by a haze of whirling wings. At the door, the dog scraped the timber half-heartedly. Seeking silence. Packy's right hand was raised to shoulder level as though calling for silence.

Down the stairwell came the stealthy padding. Deliberate. Purposeful. Half-way down, a stair creaked and the padding ceased. You could sense pricked ears: tautened muscles: a body frozen into stasis.

Breathless, we waited. Bran had ceased scratching at the door. The moth no longer circled the light bulb but clung like a dead leaf to the twisted flex. A dense smothering silence filled the house. Mrs McDarra gazed in horror at the stairwell, her rapidly moving lips scurrying out prayers and invocations.

When the slow descent was once more resumed, she turned a look of agonized appeal towards her husband. McDarra, grim face upturned to the ceiling, eyes still tight shut, never stirred.

Packy moved towards the foot of the stairs but stopped in his tracks as the squat bare-footed figure lurched down the last step and came into view.

He was dressed like a schoolboy in short pants and jersey. The pants, obviously cut down from the cast-off serge trousers of a grown-up, hung in two stiff cylinders to below the knee, where the scrawny hairless shanks of youth sprouted from huge flattened feet with splayed toes that were wrinkled with the dry folded flesh of age. The skimpy sleeves of the jersey disclosed the same opposing traits – rickety wrists ending in broad hands with gnarled and stubby fingers. The eyes too – deep blue eyes of a singular clarity that you would find only in babies and animals – belied the beetling brows, the receding forehead, the protruding lower lip with its dangling tongue. He was pot-bellied, swarthy skinned and had oily black hair cut in a fringe across his forehead.

At the bottom of the stairs he hesitated, licking his upper lip with drooling tongue. Cautiously he took a pace forward, gaze fixed ahead, eyes blank and expressionless.

'Larry!' Mrs McDarra called softly.

'Mahm! Mahm!' he mouthed. It was the shrill cry of a seagull sighting a moving plough.

He plunged forward, arms outstretched, barging straight into Packy's motionless figure.

'Hey, what d'you think you're doing?' Packy gripped the stubby fingers probing his whiskered cheeks and balding scalp.

The squat figure struggled free and backed away.

'Mahm! Mahm! Mahm!'

Arms whirling, he staggered round the kitchen, bouncing from one flinching body to another, screeching with rage like a frightened gull.

'Good Jesus!' someone near the door muttered in an awed voice.

'Mahm! Mahm!' a flailing arm sent a mug crashing from the dresser. Knuckles slammed sickeningly against cement.

'Watch out!'

'Get hold of him somebody.'

'He'll do harm.'

'Take it easy, boy,' said Packy.

'Larry! Larry! Mammy's here.'

She rushed across the room. Gathered the flailing figure into her arms.

'It's all right, pet. No one will touch you.'

Her harsh voice had sunk to a gentle croon; her flinty gaze softened. Even the thin straight-lipped mouth seemed to have relaxed. She stroked the matted hair and the loose folds of skin on the tear-stained cheeks.

'You must be a good boy, darling. Daddy's sick and mustn't be plagued.' Her troubled gaze sought the grim figure on the bed.

McDarra's eyes were open. He glared at her.

'You can't blame me. I warned you, didn't I? Time and again I warned you. But it was no use. Right go wrong, you had to have your way. Never allowing for the upshot. Or who would get hurt. Oh, it was the foolish day I ever gave in to you.'

She paid no heed to his reproaches. Clutched tight by fierce ungentle hands: beslobbered by coarse and blubbery lips: her own salted by mingled tears; she gazed ahead. Unseeing. Uncaring. Enraptured.